# The Risk Of Falling

USA TODAY BESTSELLING AUTHOR

## NIKKI ASH

I'll always choose you.

## The Risk of Falling Playlist

"Bad Habits" Ed Sheeran
"Leave Before You Love Me" Marshmello &
Jonas Brothers
"I don't Mind" Usher featuring Juicy J
"Strip that Down" Liam Payne featuring Quavo
"You can Get it All" Bow Wow
"Ballerina" Belly
"Dangerous" Kardinal Offishall featuring Akon
"I'm in Luv (wit a stripper)" T-Pain
"Come Get Her" Rae Sremmurd
"Hypnotized" Plies featuring Akon
"Bust it, Baby, Pt. 2 Plies featuring Ne-Yo
"Thinking Out Loud" Ed Sheeran
"You are the Reason" Calum Scott
"Obsessed" Mariah Carey
"I Wanna Love You" Akon featuring Snoop Dogg

*Don't let the risk of falling keep you from flying.*
*-Unknown*

# One

## SIENNA

"ELIZA BARDOT, WE NEED TO GO NOW!" I YELL FROM THE doorway, checking my phone, *again*. When I don't hear anything back, I shout in annoyance, "I'm going to be late for my shift. We need—"

"I'm right here." My sister huffs. "No need to use my government name. I was trying to find something to eat. I'm starved and today was pizza day at school." She mock gags. "There's nothing in the fridge," she whines, her sad eyes meeting mine. Guilt wraps around my heart and chokes it because she's right—the fridge is empty. It's been rough the past couple of months, ever since I lost my job. The place I was working at shut down, but thankfully, I've found another one that pays much better. I just need to get caught up and then we'll be okay again.

"I know," I tell her, softening my voice, since none of this is her fault. "But if we're late, I'm going to get fired, and then we won't have any money to eat. I'll get Ricco to make you something in the kitchen once we get to the club."

She grabs her backpack so she can do her homework while I perform, and we take off in my old beater of a car. It's not worth the insurance I'm required to pay on it, but it's a necessity since we live on the west side of Tesoro, in Booker Park, and I work on the east side, where the buses don't run.

"You're late!" Lincoln—my boss and the owner of Wanderlust—yells as I fly down the hallway past his office.

"I'm sorry," I shout back, not bothering to say it won't happen again. In the world I live in, it's better not to make promises I can't keep.

When I open the door to the dressing room, I'm hit with various smells, from flowery perfume to hair spray, to the burning of hair, as more than two dozen scantily clad women bustle around half-naked, getting ready for tonight.

"Sienna, you're on in five," Marina says, handing me my outfit for my performance.

"Can you do me a huge favor and order Ellie something to eat from the kitchen?" I pull out a twenty and try to hand it to her, but she waves me off.

"Go change. I'll get her fed."

"Thank you." I kiss her wrinkled cheek, grateful to have people in our life who care. Marina has been working in the entertainment industry since before I was even born. It's been years since she's been on stage, but she loves her job as house mom, and during the day, she teaches pole dance classes. She never had any children of her own, but she treats all of us like we're hers, including my little sister.

After changing into my outfit, I double check my makeup, and then go in search of Ellie.

She's where she always is—on the couch with her books spread out across the table in front of her.

"I gotta get on stage. Behave," I tell her, leaning down and giving her a kiss on the top of her head.

I pull back in time to see her dramatically roll her eyes. "I always behave, *Mom*." She glances up at me, her innocent green eyes meeting my blue, and my heart surges with love and protectiveness for my fourteen-year-old sister, wishing she were born into a different world, to a different mom, one who was capable of loving her. Then she wouldn't have to hang out at a gentleman's club all night while her older sister strips and gives strange men private shows and dances.

"I know you do," I tell her, trying not to choke up at the fact that my sister deserves better than this life, better than the hand she's been dealt. Despite the odds against her—geography and circumstance—my sister *is* well behaved. She gets straight A's, spends her free time at the dance studio, and never gets into any trouble. Most would use their crappy upbringing as an excuse to lash out and seek attention, but instead, it only makes Ellie that much more determined to succeed.

"Closer" by Nine Inch Nails starts, and I saunter onto the stage, mentally preparing for what I have to do. The second my hands land on the pole, I'm transported out of the club and into Lola's Dance Studio, where Ellie and I have studied dance our entire lives.

Instead of being dressed in black leather and lace with fuck me stilettos, I imagine I'm wearing a pretty pink leotard with a fluffy tutu and pointe shoes, my hair up in a tight bun.

Instead of dancing for men who are imagining all the ways they would fuck me if I let them, I pretend I'm at a dance recital or auditioning for a spot in a ballet company, performing for an audience who values my moves and grace.

It's been years since I've performed for a real audience, not since I quit dancing so I could get a job to pay the bills, Ellie's dance classes, and later, my college classes. Still, every time I get on stage, I'm taken back to the days when I was able to use dance as my escape—before the harsh reality of life shattered my dreams, knocking me to the ground and forcing me to crawl across the sharp shards left behind.

As I dance seductively, shedding each article of clothing until I'm completely naked, I'm taken away from here. Away from the ogling men, away from the smell of sex that permeates the air—far, far away.

And then the song ends, the lights go down, and I'm back in the present. At Wanderlust, I perform on a stage for money, three nights a week, just so my sister and I can barely skate by. While I pay the bills for the shitty apartment we're stuck in, our prostitute mom goes off fucking countless men in order to support her out-of-control drug addiction, as well as her pimp-slash-boyfriend's gambling problem—all in the name of love.

I quickly collect my clothes, then head backstage to put on a robe. Unlike most strip clubs, Wanderlust doesn't allow men to throw cash at the dancers. This is an exclusive members-only club for the obscenely wealthy. It has three levels: The bottom floor—underground—is a private sex club called Elite, where men and women can partake in various sexual acts while utilizing the club's carnal amenities. The ground floor is a high-class strip club and bar, which is where I work, and the top floor will be a restaurant called Impulse that's currently under construction.

We're paid a set amount per performance—each dancer performing two times per night—and then for every private show, we're paid a percentage of what is charged. Men can tip the dancers—which they do, *a lot*—and at the end of the night, it's split amongst the women working that shift. We can also provide *extras* in the private rooms, and a few of the dancers also choose to work the floor at Elite, providing a full range of services to that particular clientele. Between the dancing, the private shows, and the other options, many of the women who work here easily make in the high four figures per night.

After checking on my sister, who's practically inhaling

her dinner, I change into my floor outfit—tiny, black leather booty shorts with a matching halter top that zips down the middle and dips low, showing off my naturally full-size D breasts. I pair the outfit with knee-high black leather combat boots and then make my way onto the floor.

Like every Friday night, as I walk around my assigned tables, I'm propositioned to partake in extras—to which I sweetly decline. Most of the regulars already know it's not going to happen, but a few newbies ask, unaware that aside from private dances and shows, I don't do any extras. It means less money, but I refuse to put a price on my self-worth.

When a group of businessmen walk in and the hostess says they've requested a private performance, I change, *again*, and then head back to the room they're holding their meeting in. Until I started working in this industry, I had no idea how common it is for men to hold business meetings in a gentleman's club. Oftentimes, they barely even notice me dancing. I'm more of a pretty backdrop that makes them feel powerful—I don't get it, but the truth is, I don't really understand men in general, and what little I do know, makes me wish I were attracted to women—it's a shame I'm not enticed by the female body in that way.

Marina once told me the annual membership fee here starts at seven figures. I can't even imagine having that kind of money to blow. But then again, the men who come here are worth millions, sometimes billions, so for them that fee is nothing more than a drop in the bucket.

The private show goes smoothly, and before I know it, I'm back on stage for my second performance of the night. Different outfit, song, and routine, but it's all the same—after a while, it all blurs together.

I'm about three-fourths through my routine when something—a spark, a zap of some sort—shoots through me, sending a shiver up my spine. It knocks me out of my escape and sends me flying back into the present. My gaze collides with a man, and for the first time in... I don't even know how long—if ever—my moves falter. I can't see the color of his eyes from here, but the heat of his stare sears into me.

I want to look away—to avoid making eye contact—but I can't. It's as if he's holding me in place, his eyes locked with mine, demanding my undivided attention.

I continue my routine, knowing every move by heart, but I can't stop watching him, fully aware that his eyes never leave me. It's almost as if he and I are in a private room, and I'm dancing just for him. As I remove my bra and then bend, my legs spreading to tease the crowd before I take my panties off, I take in the man who's captured my attention.

He's standing by the bar, dressed in a typical power suit, sans tie, and even though he's completely clothed, I can tell he's built by the span of his broad shoulders and the way his shirt stretches across his chest. His jacket is unbuttoned and open, and his pants mold to his muscular thighs. His eyes are dark and piercing. He has a roman nose—slightly bent with a prominent curve—and his angular jaw is peppered with next-day stubble.

I imagine straddling him as I dance to "Rocket" by Beyonce, grinding against his groin. My fingers stroking the scruff on his face while his hands glide down my sides and land on the globes of my ass, massaging circles into my—

The lights come down, and I'm snapped out of my— *Holy shit*, was I just fantasizing about a member? I shake myself out of it as I scoop up my clothes—not even remembering when I got naked—and hastily make my exit.

I don't think about men, especially the members, and I *never* make eye contact. When I'm on that stage, when I'm giving them a lap dance, they don't exist. It's just me and the music. Yet, that man existed.

When I go to the dressing room to change back into my floor attire, I check on Ellie, who's asleep on the couch since it's after midnight, and then I ask Violet if I have any private room reservations.

"One," she says, glancing at her tablet. "Room four."

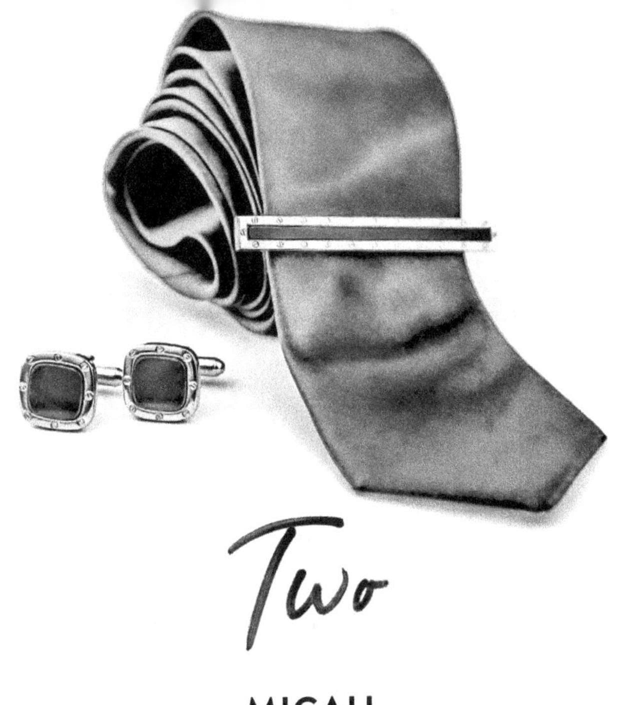

# *Two*

## MICAH

"Who was that?"

"Who was what?" My brother glances around like he didn't just witness the most delectable, mesmerizing, fucking hypnotizing woman dancing on the stage. I guess when you're in the business he's in, you become desensitized to the women, to the dancing…

"The woman who was just on stage," I say, nodding in the direction she was a second ago, before the damn lights blacked out and she disappeared.

"A dancer," he says, being purposely obtuse.

"No shit," I growl, not in the mood for his crap. "I've never seen her here before."

"That's because you rarely come around and she's new. Was working at Pussycats until it closed down. A bunch of women came here wanting jobs. Most were trash, but as you can see, she's not." He smirks. Not because he's into her. My brother doesn't fuck where he eats. No, he's smirking because he knows what I know—I wasn't the only man getting hard from watching her on stage. She's not just sexy, she's fucking gorgeous…and real.

Most women in this industry are fake. Fake tits, fake face, fake tan, fake personality. I'm not knocking them. You do what you have to do to survive, to get ahead in this world, and a lot of men like that shit. But I prefer real. And that woman on stage was…All. Fucking. Real.

Those perfect tits with rose-dusted nipples. My mouth was practically watering at the thought of wrapping my lips around them. Sucking the hardened tips into my mouth.

*Fuck.*

And those luscious curves. The way she danced, swaying her hips to the beat, like she was one with the music. When she dropped to the floor and spread her legs, all I could think about was her riding my cock to that same rhythm. I've seen dozens of women naked, but not a single one has ever had that effect on me.

"I want her in a private room."

Lincoln chuckles and shakes his head. "She's not like that."

"What the fuck do you mean she's not like that? They're all like that." I've never been with any of the women here, but that doesn't mean I don't know what goes on. Lincoln might be the one who runs Wanderlust and Elite, but we co-own everything that's part of Alexander Enterprises.

"Not her," he says. "She only dances, does private shows, and will give the occasional lap dance, but that's it."

"You can't be fucking serious. Does she know how much money she could be making?" A woman like her could easily bring in five figures a night. Hell, I'd pay six if it meant she'd spread those creamy thighs and let me in.

"Trust me, I've tried," he says. "The guys are obsessed with her since she started here, some have offered to pay double...*triple* the going rate to get a room with her at Elite, but she won't do it."

My thoughts go back to the way our eyes connected, as if we were the only ones in the room. The way I could feel the heat between us—even from afar. She might not be willing to give just anyone her body, but I'm not *just* anyone.

"We'll see about that," I say, standing and grabbing my drink. I swallow it in one go and set it down.

"Where are you going?" Lincoln asks.

"To book a private party for two."

Only when I walk over to Violet, I realize I never got the dancer's name. After Violet helps me out—and I learn her name is Sienna—I head back to room four and get comfortable. There are two hours left of Sienna's shift, and I've booked her for the entire time.

The music starts, and I couldn't tell you what song it is, only that it's upbeat and pulsates against the four walls of the room. The woman sings about wanting someone to give her more, and all I can think about is how much *more* I want to give this dancer, a woman I'm desperate to get to know.

A second later, Sienna appears on stage, dressed in a shimmery silver number and tall as fuck matching heels. When she gets to the center, she pulls the material off, exposing tight silver shorts and a sparkly bra. Her full breasts are spilling out of the cups and her flat stomach is on display. As my gaze descends, I notice her thighs are toned, and as she saunters over to the pole, I can see the muscular definition in her calves. I don't notice any piercings or tattoos on her skin. She's flawless, and fuck, if that doesn't make me want to leave my mark on her.

Her hands grip the pole and when she turns around, slowly bending over, my cock swells in my pants as I get a good look at her luscious ass that's on display, imagining her bending over and letting me take a bite out of her plump ass cheek.

I watch, completely enthralled, as she works the pole over. The strip club is Lincoln's area of expertise, but I've been in enough of them to know what good dancing looks like, and this woman knows what she's doing. She's sexy without appearing trashy. Seductive without it screaming desperate. She gets lost in the music, lost in her moves.

When the song transitions to the next, she smoothly removes her bra and moves from the pole to the front of the stage. She's graceful like a ballerina, reminding me of the time my mom forced us to go see Swan Lake at the Metropolitan Opera House. It was boring as hell, and

I'm pretty sure Lincoln and I both passed out halfway through it. But watching her reminds me of the way those dancers moved their bodies, with passion and rhythm. It doesn't matter that she's dancing in front of a stripper pole to some song laced with sexual innuendos or that she's topless. Her every move is threaded with elegance and grace.

I know the moment she finally *looks* at me because her eyes lock with mine, widening fractionally with recognition. The same spark from earlier ignites in her gaze, and it's clear that the chemistry I felt earlier wasn't one sided. But as quickly as it comes, she snuffs it out, her expression turning distant and cold.

Since I paid for a lap dance, she glides down the stairs that connect the stage to the floor and stops in front of me. Some women are willing to get completely naked for lap dances since they make more money, but Violet told me Sienna only does topless, and she doesn't allow touching. So, I sit back, drop my leg that was perched on my knee to the ground, and place my hands onto the arms of the chair, making it clear I'm ready and know the score.

She takes that as her cue and, turning around so her back is to me, swivels her hips seductively, shaking her ass from side to side. It takes everything in me not to grip her hips and pull her down to me, but I wouldn't disrespect her like that. The women here deserve to feel safe. But that doesn't stop me from trying to memorize every inch of her while she dances.

When she turns around, my eyes go to hers, searching for that heat, determined to light us aflame. Only she's not looking at me—she's looking through me—once again lost in her own world. She might be dancing for me, but really, she's dancing for herself.

She dances in front of me for several seconds and then circles around my chair, stopping behind me. She leans in and slides her hands down my shoulders, along my chest and torso, stroking me seductively as she presses closer, her bare tits rubbing into my back. Her hands brush against either side of my groin, and if she were to move her hands a couple inches toward the middle, she'd feel just how turned on I am by her.

When her hair tickles the side of my face, I turn my head and inhale her scent. I don't know what it is... something floral I'm guessing, but it fits her perfectly. Sweet yet delicate. And then she backs up, taking her scent and hands with her. My fingers itch to grab her and pull her back toward me, but I sit still, letting her run the show.

She sashays toward me, then drops to her knees and rolls onto her back, spreading her legs up and out. The shorts she's wearing are so tiny, I get a glimpse of her cunt. It's not enough to satiate my appetite—it never will be until I'm tasting her essence on my tongue. But it's enough to cause my cock to thicken in my pants, damn near turning it to stone.

She parts her legs a bit farther then brings them back together, sitting up in front of me. And then she crawls...

*motherfucking* crawls toward me, her tits hanging like the most beautiful, mouthwatering raindrops.

I assume she's going to climb into my lap, but instead, she dips her head and rolls forward, her legs coming up into a split before they wrap around my waist. With fluid ease, she uses my knees to pull herself up to where she's suddenly straddling me. It happens so quickly and smoothly, I have no time to mentally prepare for her body wrapping around mine. She reaches back with one hand and the other lands on my chest to steady herself.

And then she starts to move. Rolling her hips, grinding her warm cunt against me. I get a good look at her face. It's soft and feminine like the rest of her. Her eyes are bright blue like the color of a cloudless day. The light amidst a darkened world. Her makeup is natural, and her lips are shiny from the shimmery gloss she's wearing.

When she brings her other hand around to the front, I notice how they're small and delicate. Her nails are real and painted a light pink. Everything about her screams innocent, like she should be dancing at the Opera House instead of a strip club.

Her eyes meet mine momentarily before she backs off me and twirls around, giving me another view of that pert ass. Without thinking, I reach out to grab her hip, not wanting her to walk away, and in return, she swivels around and shakes her head, silently reminding me not to touch.

I sigh in frustration but remove my hand, and as a reward, she climbs back onto my lap, moving her body to the beat of the music. When she rises slightly, increasing the tempo of her movements, her luscious tits come into my line of vision. Her pink nipples are hard, and my mouth waters, begging me to suck them. I want nothing more than to taste her, touch her, feel her, and get fucking lost in her.

"What will it take?" I ask, leaning in slightly until our mouths are only inches apart.

She doesn't answer at first, so I assume she didn't hear me. I'm about to repeat myself when her eyes connect with mine, as she finally responds questionably, "What will what take?"

I draw in a sharp breath, the chemistry between us so hot, so intense, it's almost hard to breathe. I lean in closer, so close, I can feel her warm breath on my lips. "For you to give me *more*."

Still straddling my thighs, she slows her movements, the music continuing to play in the background. Her tongue glides slowly across the seam of her plump lips, and I home in on the way they glisten, desperate to lick them myself.

"There's nothing," she says, snapping me from my thoughts.

"What?"

"There's *nothing* you can offer me to give you *more*," she says, climbing off my lap. She turns her back on me and saunters onto the stage, scooping up her bra and putting it on as she walks away. "Enjoy your night," she calls out over her shoulder, just before she disappears from my line of vision and the music abruptly comes to a halt. As I sit in my seat, with my cock still hard, I can't help but wonder who the hell this woman is and what it will take to make her mine.

One thing I've learned in this life is that everyone has a price. You just have to find out what it is and be able and willing to pay it. And since I'm a rich man, I'm more than capable of paying whatever the fuck her price is.

# Three

## SIENNA

It isn't until I'm out of the private room and back in the safety of the dressing room that I'm able to breathe again. I don't know what it is about that man that gets my blood flowing and my lady parts tingling, but that can't happen. I have a plan, goals that I've made to get my sister and me out of this hell hole of a life, and I'm only a year away from making it happen. I'm not about to let some ridiculously sexy man derail me. I can't afford distractions. Hell, I can't afford to even *think* about him. I don't know who he is, but hopefully, he now knows I can't be bought and will seek pleasure elsewhere because he won't be getting it from me, that's for damn sure—I witnessed firsthand my mom putting men before herself, and I refuse to follow in her footsteps.

Since I still have a little over an hour left of my shift, I change my outfit and help out on the floor until the club closes. I give two lap dances, which I'm grateful for, since I'm sure that asshole who wanted *more* will be pissed I wouldn't cave to his request and will likely take it out on my tip.

When the place is empty, I change back into my street clothes—a hoodie and sweats—and remove my makeup, not wanting to risk drawing attention to anyone in our neighborhood.

Once I'm ready to go, I say good night to the other women and wake up Ellie. As she staggers down the hall, half-asleep and mumbling about her bed, Lincoln comes out of his office and hands me an envelope.

"Thanks," I say with a laugh. "I was so busy trying to get miss sleepyhead over here out the door, I forgot to collect my tips." The manager on duty is the one who counts and gives us our tips, and usually that's Damon since he's the weekend manager. But since he recently got married and is on his honeymoon, Lincoln's been here more than usual—at least compared to how little I saw him when I first started a little over a month ago.

"Hey, Lincoln," Ellie says sweetly, a stark contrast to her grouchy demeanor only a few seconds ago. "How's the restaurant coming along?" I roll my eyes at her obvious crush on him. I told her once it's not happening, that he's a good decade older than her and she should focus her energy on the boys her age, but she just scoffed and said those boys were immature and she'd never date them.

"Hey Ellie," Lincoln says with a smile, ruffling her hair playfully. "It's coming along nicely. Working on the menu. How's school? You get that essay written?"

They discuss her writing assignment while Lincoln walks us to my car. Ellie loves dance and ballet, and she works hard to get good grades because her dream is to get into one of the top schools for the arts in the country, but she does struggle academically. And since I'm a math person, English is *not* my strong suit. Last week, she was struggling with an essay she had to write, and he spent hours helping her, which led to her newfound crush.

"I know you're all independent and shit," Lincoln says once Ellie is in the passenger seat. "And this is a good area. But please have one of the security guys walk you out when I'm not here. If something happened to either of you, I'd be forced to kill whoever touched you, and I would *not* do well in prison. I'm too pretty for that place." He smirks, ending his statement with a joke, but that doesn't stop my heart from warming at the sentiment, unaccustomed to someone caring without a hidden agenda.

"Will do. And… thanks again for letting Ellie hang out while I work."

"Sienna," Lincoln says with a laugh. "You thank me every time you see me. It's not a big deal. She's a great kid, and you're a damn good employee."

"Well, still…thank you," I say again, unable to help myself as he opens the door and I slide in. "See you tomorrow night."

We get home and Ellie heads straight to bed. I shower

and then sort my tips to figure out how much more I'll need to get caught up on the bills.

Only when I count the cash, my heart damn near stops. This can't be right. There's no way I made this much in tips. I think back to tonight. I did a private performance for that business meeting and a couple of lap dances. And then after my second performance I had… No. No way. There's no way he tipped that much after I told him no.

I grab my phone and send a text to Lincoln, telling him I think he messed up on my tips. All the girls have his number in case of an emergency. I assume since it's late, he won't see it and respond until tomorrow, but almost immediately, a text from him comes in:

LINCOLN

**Too little or too much?**

I type back:

SIERRA

**Too much… way too much.**

Not that I'm complaining, but we're talking thousands too much. And if he turns around and says he messed up and I need to pay it back, I'll be screwed if I have to return money that has already been spent.

LINCOLN

**It's the right amount. Apparently, you made a big impression on someone tonight. Get some sleep.**

SIERRA

**Thanks. You, too.**

I set my phone down and stare at the money. I want to refuse it, tell that guy that he can't buy me. That I'm not for sale. But at the same time, did he buy me if I refused him? I danced for him like I do for many guys. I didn't suck him or fuck him. I didn't give him my body in exchange for money. I gave him my time, just like I always do.

And this money will go a long way. It will mean paying for Ellie's dance classes for the next month in full and paying the rent without a late penalty. I can even pay the electric and water bill and have some money left over for next month. I already feel the pressure lifting off my chest. My head is finally above water, and I'm able to suck in oxygen without my lungs filling with liquid. For the first time in months, it feels as though I'm not drowning. Now I just need to stay afloat.

I should probably return the money to prove a point to him, but I don't even know who *he* is or if I'll ever see him again. Besides, I do have my pride. I also have a sister I need to take care of, and if he wants to hand over that much money thinking it will entice me into giving him *more*, he's in for a rude awakening. Because I'm not up for sale.

# *Four*

## SIENNA

"Time to get up, sleepy head!" I draw open the curtains and Ellie groans, pulling her covers over her head. It's early, seven in the morning, but thanks to that mystery man and his ridiculous tip, we're in the green for the moment, which means…

"Ellie, c'mon. I was thinking we could hit the farmers market and then make your favorite: Minestrone with meatballs. And afterward, we could go by Lola's to pick up that new leo you've been wanting."

This gets her attention. "Are you serious?" She gasps. "Meatball soup and a new leo?" Her brow furrows. "Is something wrong?" She flies up into a sitting position. "Are you dying?" Her eyes bug out. "Am I dying?"

"What?" I bark out a laugh. "No, nobody is dying,

crazy."

"Then why the heck are we spending money we don't have?"

My chest tightens at her question. A fourteen-year-old shouldn't ever have to worry about money. She should be naturally selfish and lost in her own teenage world. But thanks to the shitty hand we were dealt, we were forced to grow up a lot quicker than other kids.

"Because for today, we're okay," I tell her honestly. "So, get your butt up and go get ready so we can head out." I know she's accepted my answer when a genuine smile spreads across her face and she jumps out of bed.

It's a beautiful morning, and we find tons of fruits and veggies at the farmers market. Ellie falls in love with a pretty summer dress, and I splurge, buying it for her. She's so shocked and happy, she throws her arms around me and tells me she loves me and how I'm the best sister ever.

At Lola's, she tries on the leo, and it fits perfectly, so I purchase it and pay for the next month of her classes.

"I'll see you girls on Monday," Grace says, handing Ellie her bag. Grace is Lola's daughter and the owner of the dance studio, who inherited the studio after her mom passed away two years ago.

Ellie takes a dance class three days a week, and I teach the beginner class two evenings a week in exchange for a discount toward Ellie's classes. Since I have school during the day, I make sure to plan my classes around Ellie's school and dance schedule, which allows me to be home with her.

Once we're home, we spend the next couple hours making her favorite soup. She always insists we make enough for leftovers, and today she's asked if we can bring Lincoln some to thank him for helping her with her essay.

We've just sat down to eat when the front door unlocks and then swings open, and our mom comes stumbling into the apartment.

"What the fuck is that smell?" she hisses. "It's stinking up the house."

Ellie visibly flinches. "It's soup, Mom," she says. "Are… are you hungry?"

"Not for that nasty shit," Mom spits, knocking over the lamp when her arm flails out and hits it. It crashes against the tile floor causing shards of ceramic to fly everywhere.

"Just fucking great," she slurs, clearly high…or drunk…or probably both. She rarely comes home anymore, choosing to crash at her boyfriend-slash-pimp's place, but when she does grace us with her presence, she's usually loaded.

"I need to go to bed. I'm fucking exhausted," she says. "It's been a long night. Phil is being an asshole again." Clearly, she has no real perception of time, and the thought that Phil is ever not an asshole, causes me to roll my eyes. I go back to eating, but then I stop when she adds, "The landlord raised the rent. You'll need to come up with an extra five hundred a month if you want to stay."

"What?" I gasp. "He can't raise it that much."

"He raised it two hundred. The other three hundred is for me allowing you to stay here." She smirks.

"I'm not giving you five hundred more a month for this shithole," I bark, pissed at the games she plays. Every time she and Phil fight, Mom comes home starting shit.

"You have any other options?" she asks, leaning against the wall since she's probably too fucked up to stand on her own. "Didn't think so."

She turns around and disappears, while Ellie sits there quietly, frowning down at her soup. I make the mistake of assuming she's out of earshot when I say to Ellie, "It's okay… One day soon, we're getting out of here."

"Oh really?" Mom snarks. "And where the fuck do you think you're going?" She storms back into the room and knocks my bowl of soup onto the floor. "You think you're so much better than me since you got that fancy fucking job at that fancy fucking strip club? If you don't like it here, move the fuck out!" She gets in my face, her rancid breath forcing me to hold mine. "Better yet… How about I kick you out?"

And here we go again… When my dad left, she would say she couldn't look at me because I looked too much like him. I have his blue eyes and brown hair and pale complexion. I reminded her too much of him and all that she lost. But the more depressed she became, the more she used alcohol and narcotics to escape, and that led to her blaming me. I didn't behave myself enough. I required too much attention. I was a mistake, and he wasn't ready to be a dad. He didn't leave her—he left me. Somehow she's convinced herself that I'm the reason for her life falling apart, and because of that, she despises me.

"Mom, no! Please," Ellie cries.

"*Yes*." Mom cackles. "We'll see how fancy you are living on the streets."

The truth is, with the amount I pay toward the bills and rent here, I could find a small place for me and Ellie and we'd be okay. Especially since our mom doesn't help with anything. With a year still left of college, it'd be rough like it is now, but we'd be safe and away from her.

But I can't do that because—

"And before you get any ideas," Mom says. "Eliza isn't going anywhere with you."

—the only reason I stay is because my sister is a minor, so our mom is her legal guardian. And since I'm a full-time college student and work as a stripper to pay my way through school, as well as the bills, no judge would ever grant me guardianship.

If I try to prove *she's* unfit, I run the risk of the state taking Ellie away from me, and I just can't take that chance. Instead, I stay here and put up with my mom's shit, so I can take care of my sister.

Next year, though, when I graduate, that's all going to change. I'm going to get myself a socially acceptable job and move us into a decent apartment. Since Ellie will be sixteen when I graduate, I can petition the court for guardianship, and they'll let her decide where she wants to live. Then our piece-of-shit mom can rot here all by herself.

Thankfully, Mom stumbles back to her room and slams the door behind her, ending her threats. She does this often, and tomorrow when she wakes up, she won't even remember this conversation. But that doesn't stop Ellie from looking at me with a pained expression etched into her features.

"I'm not going anywhere," I assure her. If it came down to it, I'd take her with me. Even if that means going on the run. I'd never leave her in this hellhole, *ever*.

I glance at the time and see it's getting late. "We need to leave soon."

***

"I'm going to need to borrow your sister," Lincoln says when we walk into the backdoor of Wanderlust.

"For what?" I ask skeptically, at the same time Ellie says, "Sure!"

Lincoln chuckles. "The chef I'm looking to hire is upstairs making an array of dishes for me to sample. I'd love a second opinion."

"I'm starved," Ellie lies, and I internally groan but don't say anything, not wanting to embarrass her.

"Okay, but I need her real quick. Can she meet you in a few minutes?"

"Sure," Lincoln says. "See you in a few," he says to Ellie.

"Oh, wait!" Ellie says, remembering the container in her hands. "This is for you. A thank you for helping me with my essay. It's homemade soup."

He takes it from her and lifts the lid, taking a whiff. "Smells good. You make this yourself?"

"Yep," she tells him with pride in her tone. "All you have to do is heat it up. It's delicious."

"Thanks," he says. "Meet me in my office when you're ready to go upstairs."

When we get in the dressing room, I pull Ellie to the side, making sure no one can hear what I have to say. "He's too old for you. You know that, right?" I've told her this before, but I feel like she's not listening.

Ellie's brows furrow. "Age is just a number."

*Oh, Lord…*

"Unless it's a number under eighteen. Then it's statutory rape."

Like the teenager she is, she rolls her eyes. "I'll be fifteen soon. Eighteen is only three years away."

I shake my head, making a mental note to have a chat with Lincoln. He's a good guy, and I'd like to believe he wouldn't cross that line, but I've come across enough sleazy men in my life—courtesy of our piece-of-shit mother—that I've stopped trusting in men altogether. So, while I'd like to believe that good, decent men do exist, when it comes to my little sister, I won't be taking any chances.

My thoughts go back to the night I walked into the house after my shift at Oswald's, the local twenty-four-hour diner I worked at throughout high school and my first year of college…

*As I walk up to the front door of our apartment, I sigh in exhaustion. It's almost three in the morning and my shift sucked. I pull my keys out of my purse, ready to unlock the door, when I notice it isn't closed all the way.*

*A chill races up my spine. When I left at seven, Ellie was sitting at the desk in our room working on her homework. At nine, she texted me that she was going to bed. I hate leaving her alone, but since I'm in school full-time during the day, I have no choice but to work in the evenings. She's eleven years old, so technically she's okay to stay home by herself, but just because she can, doesn't mean she should.*

*I swing the door open, not bothering to be stealth. If our mom came home and left it open, she's probably passed out and won't wake up anyway. And if something's happened…*

*I swallow thickly, unable to finish my thought, and rush through the door and into the apartment. The sound of my sister screaming will forever haunt me.*

*I run down the hall and pull the man who's on top of Ellie off of her. Grabbing the closest item to me—a ceramic lamp—I smash it across his face, and he flies backward with a groan.*

*I expect him to go down like I've seen in the movies, but instead, he barks, "You fucking bitch!" and comes after me.*

*I fight him off the best I can, but he's stronger and bigger, so I don't stand a chance. He climbs on top of me and slaps me across the face—and just like in the movies, stars fill my vision.*

*He rips my shirt off my body, and even though I'm helpless to stop him from raping me, I fight back with all my strength, refusing to be a victim.*

*I'm so focused on him, I don't realize my sister has run*

*out of the room and called the cops. I'm almost completely naked, my legs spread, when the man who's about to enter me is suddenly ripped away.*

*"Police!" the man barks. "You're under arrest."*

Had I been a few minutes later, my sister would've been raped by a drugged out, piece-of- shit scumbag our mom brought home who was expecting to get laid. After she passed out from the drugs she took, he decided to go in search of someone else to get him off.

He was arrested and charged, and I thought maybe it would be our mom's wakeup call to get sober, since she was the reason both her daughters were almost raped. But instead, she simply disappeared for several months, showing up one day, high as a kite, as if nothing had happened.

After that night, I refused to leave my sister at home alone. So, I quit my job at the diner and got a job at Pussycats, where the manager agreed to let my sister hang out in the dressing room while I danced. It was all thanks to my high school best friend, Ingrid, who already worked at Pussycats and intervened on my behalf.

After Pussycats got shut down, several of the dancers went to Wanderlust in search of a job. Only a few got hired—me included—and thankfully, Lincoln agreed to let Ellie hang out in the back room while she ate and did her homework.

"Sienna, you're up first tonight," Marina says, bringing me back to the present.

Dressed in an emerald number and white thigh high

stiletto boots, I saunter onto the stage, ready to begin my first performance of the night.

Everything is going fine, my moves are on point. Until I feel eyes on me. I make the mistake of looking out into the crowd. And that's when I see him. The mystery man from last night. Watching my every move.

# Five

## MICAH

As Sienna dances once again on stage, teasing the men who are watching her, she looks as beautiful as she did last night. Her body grinds and sways in rhythm to the music, putting on a performance that will have the majority of the men in this club hard for her.

I overhear the guy next to me talk about how he's going to book a private show, and I chuckle, knowing it isn't going to happen. Because I've already booked her for the entire evening. Lincoln was pissed when he was told by the hostess what I'd done, saying I'm fucking with his business since Sienna is so popular. But Lincoln's not only my brother, he's also my best friend, so he knows better than anyone that when I'm determined, there's no trying to get in my way.

I get it from our father. While Lincoln works hard, he tends to play harder. Me, on the other hand… I'm more work, less play.

Which is why when he brought up the idea of a gentleman's club, I knew he was the perfect person to head it up. One of the most important things about running a successful business is knowing what one's strengths are and using them to the fullest.

Lincoln is the fun playboy. He manages the talent and other employees and oversees the day-to-day operation of all our clubs and hotels.

I'm the serious one. Which means, I handle the broader business side of shit.

Our father was a bit of both—at least until he met our mother and settled down—and then later handed over the reins to us when he had a stroke and our mother forced him to slow down.

The Alexanders own the majority of Tesoro and have been running this town for the past several decades. Most of the hotels and clubs belong to us. We own the marina where all import and export is handled. Not a single shipment gets in or out without our approval. Not a single business is opened without our consent. We have enough people in our pockets that we're a force to be reckoned with. The family every person in this town both respects and fears, and nobody dares to tell us no—until Sienna, that is.

Lincoln swears that's what has me coming back tonight. The chase. The determination to win, to get my way and have Sienna tell me yes. And maybe that's part of it. Up until now, when I want to get my dick wet, I snap my fingers and any number of women come begging.

Except her.

But what she doesn't know is that I don't give up that easily. And I'm not going to stop until I have her right where I want her—on her knees begging *me* to fuck her.

The song ends and Sienna scoops up her outfit then disappears behind the curtain, and I take that as my cue to head to the room where she'll be giving me a private performance.

I sit in the same chair I sat in last night, and she performs a similar routine to the one she performed for me before. Her outfit, music, and moves are different, but the outcome is the same—her gorgeous topless body dancing to the rhythm of the song.

When her eyes once again lock with mine, they widen in shock, then turn into thin slits, trying to convey her annoyance with my persistence.

But like the perfect performer she is, she doesn't break out of her routine. She saunters off the stage like she did last night and gives me a lap dance.

Only when she's grinding on me tonight, I lean in, our faces close, and visibly inhale her intoxicating scent, trying desperately to resist the urge to touch her.

"What are you doing?" she breathes, coming to a halt on my lap. "You can't—"

"—touch you? I know. But I can smell you…" Our eyes meet, and her breath catches. "I bet your cunt tastes the way you smell." I make it a point to lick my lips, drawing her attention to them. "Sweet with just a hint of spiciness. Intoxicating…" I lean in so close, our breaths are mingling. "Addicting…" Her lips part in a sensual sigh and her thighs, which are wrapped around my waist, tighten, telling me my words are affecting her.

But of course, nothing worth having ever comes easy, so I'm not surprised when instead of giving in, she says, "Off limits," and then climbs off my lap.

I watch as she stalks off—collecting her clothes along the way—and then disappears behind the curtain, leaving me wondering how many more times it will take before she finally gives in. This was only the second time, and I've already got her squirming in want. Another couple times and I have no doubt I'll have her on all fours, screaming my name while I pound into that perfect cunt from behind.

Before taking off, I stop by Lincoln's office, but he's not there, so I send him a text, asking where he is.

LINCOLN

**Taste testing the menu for the restaurant. Hungry? <insert picture of an array of food>**

MICAH

**I'm good, but thanks. I need to get some work done.**

I'm about to take off when my phone rings.

"Micah, it's Pete," one of my contacts at the Tesoro police department says when I answer. "I have some information you might find valuable." In other words, he's expecting payment for whatever he's about to say. And I'll pay him because keeping the cops' pockets padded means keeping them on my side.

"Go ahead," I say, dropping into Lincoln's seat.

"Eduardo Gutierrez was found dead. Apparent heart attack," Pete says. "He was brought to Schneider, where an autopsy was performed off the record."

This gets my attention. The Gutierrezes are one of the most notorious crime families on the East Coast. While we own the majority of Tesoro, the Gutierrezes run the underworld, making their living off drugs, prostitution, and trafficking. We don't condone any of that shit, but because the Gutierrezes are a family you don't want to piss off, and our families go way back, we turn our cheek at the shit they do and, in return, they don't fuck with us.

"Schneider's reported foul play," Pete says.

"Any suspects?"

"I'm not sure, but word on the street is that his son is back."

There's a knock on the door, and my attention steers from Pete to the brown-haired, blue-eyed goddess walking in.

"What the hell are you doing in here?" she accuses.

"Thanks for the info," I say to Pete. "Keep me updated." I hang up without waiting for his response and give Sienna my full attention.

"Where's Lincoln?" she asks, glancing around the room with wide eyes.

"Tasting food upstairs." I lean back in my brother's chair, clasping my hands behind my head. "But whatever you need, I'm sure I can help you…" I blatantly eye-fuck the hell out of her, causing her to glare my way. So damn sassy. I bet she'll be a hellcat in bed.

"Unless you're my *boss,* that's not possible."

I smirk, loving that she has no idea who I am—something that's rare. "Well, technically I do own this place." I shrug nonchalantly, lowering my arms and leaning over the desk.

"What?" she gasps. "What are you talking about? Lincoln…"

"Is my brother," I say, steepling my fingers. "And this club is owned by Alexander Enterprises, and since I'm Micah Alexander, part owner and CEO of Alexander Enterprises, that means I own this club and am *technically* your boss. So, what is it I can help you with?"

Several emotions flit through her features as she stares at me: shock, horror, a bit of curiosity. But when her eyes turn into thin slits and her lips purse together, I know she's settled on pissed.

"*Well,*" she says, her hand going to her hip as she juts her chin out. "I came in here to tell my *boss* about the psychopath member who keeps returning, requests private shows, and then proceeds to harass me. But since you're my boss—" she glares daggers my way, and if looks alone could kill, I would be a dead man "—that will be a waste of time." She tilts her head to the side and smirks. "Speaking of which…" She steps closer, a gleam in her eye. "If you're my boss, wouldn't that mean you've been hitting on your employee?" She takes another step toward me and leans against the desk casually, crossing her arms over her chest like she's got this all figured out. "I'm pretty sure there's something in the employee handbook that says sexual harassment is not allowed. I could sue you."

I chuckle, turned on by her zero-fucks-given attitude. She either has no idea who I am—and by that I mean the weight my name holds and what I'm capable of—or she doesn't give a shit.

"What the hell are you laughing at?" she barks.

"Nothing." I shake my head.

"Tell me," she demands, and I'm pretty sure I catch her stomping a foot.

"You remind me of a Hellcat," I say honestly. "Gorgeous and sexy on the outside, with sleek lines and perfect, smooth curves. From afar, you assume that's all it is—beauty—but there's more to it than meets the eye—"

"I remind you of a cat?" she says, cutting me off. "And eww, you think they're sexy?"

She scrunches her nose up in disgust, and I bark out a laugh. "Not a cat. A Hellcat. It's a car."

"A car?" Her brows kiss her forehead.

"A Hellcat is one of the most insanely beautiful cars they make. It's full of raw power. Fierce and unstoppable. But you wouldn't know what it's capable of unless you get in and take it for a drive."

She swallows thickly. "And I remind you of this *car?* From the barely three interactions we've had."

"You do. I'm good at reading people. On the outside, you're beautiful, but underneath, I can see that raw fierceness trying to claw its way out. You're strong, but you don't want anyone to know because you're trying to blend in. Only you have no idea that you could never be a chameleon."

"Whatever." She scoffs, not wanting to accept the compliment. "I need to get back out there. I'm assuming you've booked a private show for after my performance?"

"I wasn't planning to," I deadpan, not wanting to admit that she totally had me pegged. "But since you brought it up, I'd hate to let you down." I smirk, clearly toying with her, and she rolls her eyes, turning her back on me and stomping out the door like the sexy, fiery Hellcat she is.

A few seconds later, Lincoln walks in, glancing behind him. "Is there a reason Sienna just stormed past me down the hall?" He looks at me and quirks a brow. "And why the hell are you sitting at my desk, bro? Get up."

"She's totally falling for me," I say, standing. "It's going to take a little more coaxing, but we'll be on the same page soon. I can feel it." I smile wide and waggle my brows, and Lincoln groans.

"I'm pretty sure sexually harassing my employee isn't the way to win her over. As a matter of fact, I'm almost positive the only way this is going to end is with a lawsuit."

I bark out a laugh for the second time tonight. "Funny… that's exactly what she said." I glance down at my watch. It's almost time for Sienna's second performance of the night, and since I'm still here, I might as well stay and watch. "I'd love to continue this, little bro," I say, patting his shoulder as I walk past him. "But I have a show to catch." And a woman to make mine.

# Six

## SIENNA

He's in the audience. That cocky, infuriating, sexy psycho stalker is in the audience once again watching me. After I learned he was Lincoln's brother, I asked Marina about him since she knows everything about everyone—not because I'm interested, but because if I want a fighting chance at beating him at whatever game he's playing, I need to know who I'm up against.

Unfortunately, what I learned was not good. Not only is he a sexy damn psycho, but he's Micah Alexander: the notorious, wealthy businessman whose family runs this town. I don't know why I never put two and two together, but now that I know who Lincoln's related to, it all makes sense.

According to Marina, Lincoln is the fun, playboy

brother who everyone gets along with, making him the perfect front man to run a gentleman's club. His affable personality also translates well when it comes to handling all of the clubs, restaurants, and hotels that Alexander Enterprises owns and operates. Micah, however, has a personality that everyone seems to fear. He runs the business side of things with an iron fist and has the reputation of being a savage dressed in Armani. Nobody dares to fuck with him because he'll take you out in a heartbeat after first making an example of you.

When I told her about him showing up for my performances and booking private shows, her eyes went wide, and she said she's never known him to show any one woman special attention. Of course her suggestion was to milk him for all he's worth—she doesn't get why I refuse to sell my body for money—and once he's gotten his fill of me and my pockets are plenty padded, he'll move on.

But since that's not an option, I need to handle this differently. But the question is, how?

Micah clearly views my refusal as a challenge, so the only way to make him go away is for him to think he's won. But that would mean giving in and letting him fuck me, and that's *not* happening.

So, how the hell do I get him to go away without giving in to what he wants…? And then it hits me: What is the one thing men like Micah are afraid of? Commitment. And just like that, an idea forms in my head.

As I look out at the audience, locking eyes with the gorgeous, brown-eyed psycho, I can't help but smirk.

Micah Alexander is playing a game he's convinced he'll win, but what he doesn't realize is that the rules have just changed, and I'm the only one holding the rule book. He'll catch on soon enough, but by then, it'll be *game fucking over*.

After I finish performing, I'm told by Violet that I'm booked, which doesn't surprise me since I knew it was coming. Micah is nothing if not predictable. Before heading to the room to get ready for the private show with my psycho stalker, I make sure to grab my sexiest outfit. It's a fitted, blood red, leather bodice that's cut low and wide, barely held together by three buttons in the middle of my breasts. Completing the outfit is a matching pair of tiny cheeky panties that reveal more than they actually cover. Once Micah learns the new rules, hopefully, he'll want to quit playing this game of his and move on to someone else.

Like the previous shows, he watches while I perform my routine, but tonight, I make it a point to dance extra sensual, swaying my hips a little harder, wanting it to hurt all the more when he realizes he's lost. When I move to the chair where he's sitting, I climb into his lap. His eyes never leave mine as I grind against his groin, teasing and toying with his body and emotions. Working him up higher and higher, so the fall that will soon come will be that much more devastating.

"Fuck, Hellcat," he murmurs, using the nickname he's apparently dubbed me with. "What's going on with you? Have you changed your mind?" His fingers twitch, wanting to touch but knowing he can't.

"Actually, I *have* been thinking," I purr, gliding my hands over the tops of his shoulders and down his hard chest, scratching my nails down his torso through the material of his shirt. His entire body shivers in response, and I smirk on the inside, knowing I've got the upper hand.

"Yeah?" he chokes out. "And what have you been thinking?"

"About how you want *more* from me." He swallows thickly and nods as my ass continues to rub along the bulge in his pants. "But there's something you should know before we take things any further," I say, licking my lips tauntingly.

"Tell me," he groans, thinking he's got me right where he wants me. He's so confident, his hands go to my hips, squeezing the sides.

Leaning in, I run my nose along his jawline and up to the shell of his ear, then I whisper the words I know are going to blow his game to bits. "I'm a virgin, and I'm not going to have sex until I fall in love and then get married."

His body stills, and his fingers that are gripping my flesh, tighten. I wait a second to face him, making sure my features are devoid of all emotion, and then I pull back, meeting his shocked gaze.

That's right… Game over, motherfucker.

Without waiting for him to say anything—because let's be real, there's nothing left to say—I climb off his lap and saunter back up the stage, feeling good about my win.

Before I disappear behind the curtain, I chance a glance back and see he's still sitting there, staring at me in utter shock.

"Have a good night," I quip. "It was lovely getting to know you." And with a wink that I can't help, I saunter off, knowing this will be the last I hear from Micah Alexander.

I learned years ago from watching my mom that if you give a man free milk, he doesn't need to buy the cow. Well, I'm not giving a man anything for free, and if he wants me, he'll be willing to buy the whole damn farm. Not that Micah will—because truthfully, that man can probably get as much free milk as he wants... just not from me.

I spend the rest of my shift on the floor, and I'd be lying if I said I didn't occasionally search for him. I knew spilling my truths would send him running, but a part of me was kind of hoping he was different.

Not because I'm attracted to him... I'm not—okay, fine, he's hot, whatever. Or because I want to be with him... I don't—this I'm standing firm on.

It's just that for my entire life, men have proven to be all the same, and it would've been nice if just once a man showed himself to be something other than a selfish pig.

Honestly, though, it's for the best because the last thing I need is to get tangled up with a man like Micah. That's just asking for trouble. I'm already struggling to stay afloat, barely able to make it through a day at a time. But every day, I move an inch closer to my goals—graduate, get a real job, and get Ellie the hell away from our mom. Getting mixed up with Micah would send me off course, straight into a fucking hurricane, and in those raging waters, I'd surely drown.

Once closing rolls around, I head back to grab Ellie, who's awake and reading a book—the girl is seriously the cutest book nerd.

"How was the food?" I ask as we walk to my car, accompanied by Rex, one of the bouncers at the club.

"So freaking delicious," she says, exaggerating her words. "And Lincoln said since I helped him pick out the items for the menu, once it opens, we can go eat dinner there at no charge."

I glance at her beaming face and mentally groan, wishing she wasn't crushing on a man who's over a decade older than her. Which leads to a tidal wave of guilt crashing into me because she wouldn't be in this position if it weren't for me working at a strip club and having to bring my teenage sister along with me. Anger with the strength of a tsunami surges through me at the thought of our lowlife mother, a druggy who can't take care of her own daughter, leaving me to take up that responsibility in her stead.

"Did you hear me?" Ellie asks, knocking me out of my spiraling thoughts.

"Huh?" When she sighs all dramatically, I apologize. "I was lost in my head."

"I was thinking for my birthday we could go to the

movies," she says, batting her lashes. "They're doing an all-day Twilight marathon."

Her birthday is on Friday, which will mean taking off of work. Normally that would stress me out, but since Micah booked me in the private room three times this week—tipping like he has something to prove—money isn't an issue at the moment. I'm ahead bills-wise, and my sister deserves to have an amazing birthday. It's kind of last minute, but as long as I find someone to cover my shift, Lincoln shouldn't have a problem with me taking that night off.

"It's a birthday date," I tell her.

THE NEXT SEVERAL DAYS FLY BY. I'M IN MY JUNIOR YEAR and taking the core classes needed for my accounting degree, so, between going to school and studying like crazy, working at Lola's and finding time to hang out with Ellie, my days bleed together. And before I know it, it's Thursday night, and I'm back on stage at Wanderlust.

As I dance to "West Coast" by Lana Del Rey, moving my body in a sultry yet erotic way, I can't help but search for Micah. It's been five days since I last saw him, but I can't seem to shake him from my thoughts. When I walked out, he didn't say a word, didn't stop me, and that should've been enough to tell me all I needed to know— he was only after a quick fuck, and once he learned that wouldn't be happening, he let me walk away. But something in the back of my head keeps niggling at me. I've only conversed with Micah once, but he didn't seem like the type to let someone have the last word. Yet, as my eyes gloss over the various men, finding him noticeably absent, it's suddenly clear that Micah did have the last word after all.

I finish my performance and then locate Violet to find out if I have any private shows. When she lets me know that I have one, I change outfits and then head to the room. The music starts and I walk onto the stage. Until Micah, I would never look out at who was watching. The only way I could get through what I was doing—taking my clothes off for strange men—was to pretend, escape. But Micah fucked that all up because as I reach the center of the stage, my gaze goes straight to the table…to find *him* sitting there, one ankle perched over his knee, his hands resting on either side of the armrests, his heated stare searing straight through me.

Back before my dad took off, he and my mom were both dancers. So, I guess you could say that dancing is quite literally in my blood. I've been dancing ever since I learned to walk, and I could easily do my routines blindfolded. But when my gaze collides with Micah's, I stumble for the second time since I've met this man. My tall stilettos get caught on the wood, and I nearly hit the floor, only catching myself at the last second.

The song continues to play in the background, but I stop moving, my hands gripping the pole for support as if it's my lifeline. We stare at each other for several beats, and I wonder if I dreamt the conversation we had last week. Because why else would he be sitting in this room, paying for me to dance for him?

"What are you doing here?" I ask, getting straight to the point. When the corner of his mouth quirks into a cocky smirk, my blood boils. "Did you not hear what I said Saturday night? Or did you not understand?" I strut to the front of the stage and pop my hip out, my hand resting on it.

He cocks his head to the side, saying nothing, so I continue. "Let me spell it out for you. I'm a virgin. I won't be having sex with you, or anyone else, until I fall in love and marry. So, unless you plan to force me—"

He unfolds out of the chair and stalks toward me. Since the stage is only a couple feet above the floor, he jumps onto the stage with ease and steps into my personal space. "Go out with me."

"What?" I hiss in confusion because *what the fuck?* Did he seriously just ask me out?

"Go out with me," he repeats.

"Hello. I'm a—"

"—virgin," he finishes. "Yeah, I heard you loud and clear. But even virgins can go out on dates, right?"

"I'm not going to have sex with you," I tell him, releasing each word slowly so he fully comprehends.

A wolfish grin spreads across his too-damn-handsome-for-his-own-good face, and his eyes light up, looking like a delicious mixture of melted chocolate and caramel. "You will," he says, bridging the little bit of gap we had between us. "First comes love, then comes marriage… then comes me fucking you." A devilish smirk quirks at the corner of his mouth as he cages me in, pressing one hand against the wall next to my head, the other landing on the curve of my hip. "I can't convince you to fall in love with me and marry me without taking you out on a proper date, so first things first. Go out with me."

His words knock me back—figuratively and literally. On the inside, I'm struggling to catch my breath, but on the outside, I'm stone cold, my features devoid of all emotion. I refuse to let a man in. I know what they're capable of. How easy it is for them to reach in and grab your heart and yank it straight from your chest.

I was there the day my dad destroyed my mom's heart, leaving it battered and bruised and barely able to beat. Only functioning just enough to keep her alive while she wished it would just fucking stop.

And a year later, I thought maybe my mom was starting to heal…Until she found out she was pregnant, and the man she had fallen for didn't feel the same way in return. He took off, and as he drove away, he ran over what was left of her heart.

A few years after Ellie was born, she met Phil. Mom was so desperate for love and affection, for someone to take care of her, that it didn't take much for Phil to convince her to become his puppet. He fed her drugs and promised her the world, and in exchange, she gave herself over to him—and the thousands of men she's fucked because he's told her to. He's her pimp and her enabler. He feeds her addiction, and she makes him money.

When my dad took off to create a new family with another woman, my mom stopped parenting. But that doesn't mean she stopped teaching. And the biggest lesson I've learned from her is to be careful who you give your heart to. She gave hers to three different men and all three had a hand in destroying her. Little by little, they broke her down, until there was nothing left but a decimated heart that had once beat healthy and strong. I've had a front row seat to the utter carnage, and one day that crushed and battered heart will cease to beat altogether. Maybe then, she will finally be at peace.

When Micah squeezes my hip, I'm brought back to the present—him asking me on a date and me freaking the hell out.

"One, that's not how the song goes, and two, you're insane," I say, because who the fuck goes through all this trouble to get in a woman's pants?

"Eh." He quirks his head to the side. "That's neither here nor there. I want to take you out. Go out with me. One date."

"No." I dip under his arm and walk quickly across the stage, hoping he'll let me go like he did the last time. Only before I can make it out of the room, he wraps his strong hand around my bicep and twirls me around, pushing us back against another wall.

"Why not?" he asks, his mouth so close to mine I can smell the liquor on his breath. It's spicy with a hint of sweet. And as his tongue darts out, wetting his lips, I wonder if he tastes the same way.

No! No. No. No.

"I don't date," I say matter-of-factly. "So, let it go because you're just wasting your damn time. I'm not going to agree to go on a date with you, I'm sure as hell not going to marry you, and you're never getting in my pants."

This time, when I slip away from the wall and take off toward the door, Micah doesn't stop me. I'm so rattled from our encounter, I ask Marina if I can leave early, feigning illness. She agrees, and I tell her I'll see her Saturday night.

It's not until I'm out of the club and into the fresh night air that I feel like I can finally breathe again. Ellie asks if everything's okay, but I distract her by saying that I have a surprise for her. Her birthday begins at midnight, so I run by the store and grab a cake, and then we head to the docks down by the marina. At exactly midnight, I light the candles and sing happy birthday.

"Thank you, Sienna," Ellie says once we've devoured the mini cake. "I know you're not my mom, but you've been more of a mom to me than ours has ever been." She lays her head on my shoulder, and my heart fills with both pride and pain. "I love you," she murmurs, "and I don't know what I would do without you."

I kiss the side of her temple. "You'll never find out."

And just like that, I'm reminded of my goals—graduate, get a job, get Ellie away from here. Dating is not on that list, nor will it be any time soon. Ellie is my one and only priority.

# Seven

## SIENNA

"I could seriously watch those movies over and over again," Ellie says, as we walk out of the theater.

"And I'm sure it has nothing to do with you practically drooling over that wolf's abs," I joke.

"I mean, that's definitely part of it," she says. "But, also, I love the way Edward looks at Bella. The ways he's protective and devoted to her and would do anything in his power to make sure she's loved and safe." She shrugs. "Maybe if Mom had someone like that, she wouldn't be the way she is. Things wouldn't be the way they are."

"Maybe," I agree, wishing my sister would stay little and naïve for a little longer.

Her phone buzzes in her pocket and she pulls it out—it's an older model that a friend of mine gave me. It has a crack in the corner, but it works, and I like knowing she has one in case of an emergency.

When she frowns and then pockets it, it feels as though barbwire wraps around my heart and squeezes tightly because I know what has her sad.

"Mom's probably still asleep," I say.

Ellie stops in her place and spins around to face me, her harsh eyes connecting with mine. "You know I'm not a baby anymore, right? I haven't been one in years. I know she's a whore who cares more about herself than her kids and that you pay all the bills while she snorts what little she makes up her nose. You don't have to lie to defend her anymore."

*Oh shit.* Her words are so real, so raw, that I freeze, having no clue what to say, almost positive my mouth is opening and closing like a fish out of water.

And then she softens her features and takes my hand in hers. "I know exactly who our mom is, Sienna. But more than that, I know who *you* are, what you've done to protect me, to take care of me, and I'm sorry, but that bitch doesn't deserve your loyalty."

I should probably chide her for her language, but I'm too busy wondering when the hell my baby sister grew up. I don't know whether to be proud that her attitude is all in defense of me or ashamed that, despite my best efforts to protect and hide her from the harsh truths, she knows everything.

"Lenora might've given birth to me," she adds, "but you're the only *mom* I've ever had."

Pride. I'm going with pride.

"I just downloaded season one of Gilmore Girls." I waggle my brows, hoping it will convince Ellie to watch it with me.

"No way, it's still my birthday." She side eyes me. "Gossip—"

The front door swings open, and our mom flits inside with a maniacal grin on her face.

"Oh, good, you're home!" Mom gushes. "Happy Birthday, baby!" She lifts her arms, letting several bags dangle in the air from various expensive stores. She drops them all into Ellie's lap and sits next to her, her eyes wide in excitement. "Go ahead, open them!"

Ellie glances at me in confusion but does as Mom says, opening the first bag. "Mom," she breathes, staring at the bright pink bag in horror. "Is this...?"

"A real Coach purse? Yes!" Mom bounces in her seat and claps her hands. "Every girl should own one. And I know how much you love pink."

Ellie hasn't loved pink since she was like five, but that's beside the point, because that purse had to have cost a few hundred dollars. And that's only one bag.

Ellie thanks her and opens up the next bag—an expensive pair of heels she'll never wear. Inside the next bag is another purse, the one after that has jewelry, and the one after that has a laptop.

When she opens the final gift—a brand new iPhone—Ellie shrieks in excitement, thanks Mom, and then runs off to our room to go put everything away and set up her new electronics.

"Mom," I say carefully once Ellie is gone. "How did you afford all those gifts?"

Her head whips around and she glares my way, already on the defense. "It's none of your damn business," she hisses. "You're always so fucking negative, and I'm sick of it." She stands and stalks over to me. I assume she's going to get in my face to argue, but instead, she reaches out and grabs a fistful of my hair, dragging me off the couch and toward the door.

"What the fuck!" I shout, my scalp stinging with pain. Because of the drugs, her body is frail and unfit, and it doesn't take much to shove her back, so she lets go. "Where the hell did you get that money? And don't lie to me because I'll be the one cleaning up the damn mess you've made, as usual."

"All you need to know is that I don't need shit from you anymore."

"Until you snort through whatever money you've magically come into," I scoff.

"You're such a judge-y little bitch. I've had enough of your shit. Get your things and get out, for good."

Seeing the fire in her eyes, I refrain from rolling my own. "Fine. Ellie," I call out. "Let's go." When Mom does this shit, we rent a motel for the night so she can calm down. By tomorrow morning, she'll be back to her usual non-existent, drugged-up self.

"No," Mom says. "Ellie isn't going anywhere with you."

"Yes, I am," Ellie says with a sigh, an overnight bag slung over her shoulder. We've done this so many times over the years, we keep a small bag packed at the ready. "Let's go, Sienna."

"Hey!" Mom reaches out and grabs Ellie's arm, making her squeak out in shock. "You're going to choose her over me? You're my daughter, not hers, and I can take care of you now."

"Are you serious?" Ellie asks incredulously. "Of course I'm choosing Sienna. I don't know what you did to get that money, but maybe you should use it to go to rehab. You came in here, throwing gifts at me, and for a second I forgot who you are, until you reminded me by kicking out the only real mom I've ever known."

Mom gasps as if she's been backhanded and then her eyes turn into thin slits. "Fine," she spits. "Leave... both of you! Get out and never come back. I don't need either of you. But don't come crying to me and begging for money when you're broke and homeless."

Since it's pointless to argue with her, we leave without saying another word. The drive to the motel is quiet, but instead of going to the shitty one I usually check us into, I make a left at the last second and pull up into a nicer resort we've seen a million times but could never afford to stay at.

"What are you doing?" Ellie asks.

"I've made decent money recently, and it's still your birthday. I say we splurge and spend the weekend in style."

Ellie's green eyes light up. "Really?"

"Yeah, really." I lean over and kiss her cheek. "Happy Birthday, El."

After we check-in to the cheapest room they offer—which is insanely more expensive than I thought—we ooh and aah over the gorgeous two-bedroom suite and then spend the rest of the evening at the indoor heated pool. Since the motel we planned to stay at doesn't have a pool, I decided another splurge was warranted and purchased us swimsuits from the hotel's boutique.

The next morning, we go downstairs to check out the breakfast they offer. It's probably going to be as expensive as the room, but I want Ellie to have a good weekend, despite our mom almost ruining her birthday. She deserves to have good days. And my hope is that even though there are more bad than good, maybe the good will overshadow the bad.

"I'm sorry, ma'am," the hostess says. "This restaurant is reservation only, and we're booked solid. I recommend—"

"Actually, they're my *personal* guests," a masculine voice cuts in. When I glance up, I find Micah Alexander standing there in a power suit looking as gorgeous in the daylight as he does in the dark of the club.

"Miss Bardot, you're looking beautiful this morning," he croons, blatantly eye fucking me.

"Micah," I deadpan.

"Oh, Mr. Alexander," the hostess purrs. "I'm sorry,

I didn't know. But regardless, there aren't any available tables." She pouts dramatically, and I have to hold back from snorting out a laugh.

"Very well. They can sit with me," Micah says, locking eyes with me. "That is, if you don't mind having breakfast with your future husband."

Ellie gasps, and I groan.

"I know you!" Ellie says. "You're Lincoln's brother, right?"

"I am," Micah says with a nod. "And you are…?"

"I'm Ellie," my sister says. "Sienna's sister. You called the night Lincoln was helping me write my essay in his office."

Micah grins wide, and a single dimple pops out of his left cheek—like he wasn't already gorgeous enough, God had to give him a fucking dimple. "He told me about that. It's nice to meet you. How did your essay turn out?"

"I got an A." Ellie beams.

The hostess clears her throat. "Mr. Alexander, would you like to be seated?"

"I would, and will you ladies be joining me?"

Before I can answer, Ellie says, "Yes! It's my birthday weekend, and Sienna brought me here for a special getaway."

Micah smiles warmly at her. "Happy Birthday. I'm honored you chose my hotel to celebrate your birthday."

I groan, again. Of course, Hotel Blu is his damn hotel.

We're seated at the table and a second later, Lincoln sits, glancing at Ellie and me in confusion. Then his eyes land on Micah and he chuckles.

"Sorry, we're crashing," I say to my *real* boss. "Micah invited us when we were told the restaurant was booked, and Ellie agreed."

"No worries," Lincoln says. "The breakfast here is delicious."

"Do you guys come here to eat often?" I ask, making conversation.

"We live in the penthouses on the top floor," Lincoln says, "so it's convenient."

"You live here?" Ellie gasps. "In a hotel?"

"This hotel actually has the option to purchase," Lincoln explains to her. "A lot of the guests own condos and will rent them out when they leave for the winter."

"That's so cool," Ellie says. "I wish I could live here. A pool, restaurant, and spa all at your disposal." She sighs dramatically. "I wish I were rich."

Lincoln and Micah both chuckle.

"Have you checked out the pool and spa yet?" Micah asks, his eyes landing on me.

"The pool, but not the spa," Ellie answers. "We want to get massages, but they don't have any appointments available."

I flinch and hold my breath, afraid of getting caught in my lie. The truth is, the services are too much money, and I've already splurged on the hotel and swimsuits. So, when Ellie asked, I told her nothing was available, not wanting to put a damper on our mini vacation.

"Hmm," Micah says. "I'll look into that for you. Are

you here all weekend?"

"Yep," Ellie says. "Sienna has to go to work tonight, but we're staying until tomorrow."

"If you want…" Lincoln begins, but I'm already shaking my head.

"I need to work," I say quickly. I already missed last night, and with the added expense of the hotel this weekend, I need money coming in—especially if, by some chance, our mom really meant what she said and we're out on our asses.

Lincoln nods in understanding. Thankfully, the conversation is cut short when the waitress comes over to bring us glasses of ice water and then proceeds to take our drink order.

Of course, leave it to my sister to find an even worse topic to bring up.

"So, what's this about you being my sister's future husband?" she asks, after we've all ordered various types of coffees.

Lincoln snorts out a laugh, I stop myself from banging my head on the table, and Micah grins like a Cheshire cat.

"He was joking," I say, glaring at Micah, at the same time he says, "One day we're going to get married… as soon as she agrees to go on a date with me."

Ellie finds this amusing. "You haven't even gotten her to go on a date with you and you think you're going to convince her to marry you?" She shakes her head. "Good luck with that."

Micah's grin only grows wider as he leans in, pretending

to whisper. "Any pointers?"

"Nope," she says, popping the P. "She doesn't date. Ever. If it weren't for me coming across the porn she was watching once by mistake, I'd think she was a lesbian."

I'm drinking my water when she says this, and the liquid gets stuck in my throat as I choke on her words. I start coughing violently, so Micah reaches over and pats my back. His eyes, filled with mirth, connect with mine, and he whispers so no one can hear, "You know, if you let me take you out, you won't need porn anymore."

My breath hitches and I move away from his touch. "Hey, El, how about we don't share personal info with others, yeah?"

She tucks her lips in to hide her smile, and I know she did that shit on purpose to fuck with me. "Sorry, sis."

Once our coffees arrive and we order our food, Lincoln steers the conversation down a safer road, asking Ellie how her dance practice is going for her upcoming showcase. Excited that Lincoln remembered and always ready to talk dance, she tells everyone about her performance and how she wants to one day attend a college of the arts.

"What do you do with dance?" Lincoln asks curiously.

"Some people join a company, perform professionally." She glances at me. "Sienna was so good she was invited to join a company right out of high school."

The guys turn their attention on me, and I find myself suddenly flushed. "I thought you were an accounting major," Lincoln says.

"That's because dancing professionally doesn't pay

very well," Ellie says, not knowing when to be quiet. "She needs a job that pays enough to cover the bills, since we'd be living on the streets if we left that up to our mom. She glances at me and smiles softly. "She's only working at your club so she can take care of me. She doesn't belong there, she's only doing it because of me."

And just like that, my sister is forgiven.

"I am *not* doing it because of you," I say, not at all okay with the misplaced guilt that's wrapped around her words.

"Yes, you are," she says, not caring that we're sitting with two men who are practically strangers and airing our dirty laundry out in front of them. "If it weren't for you having to take care of me, you'd be dancing right now— and not on a pole. And you wouldn't be stuck in college, majoring in something you don't even like." Her brow furrows and then she adds, "Is that why you never date? Because you're always with me?"

Oh, Jesus. This girl is killing me.

"Eliza," I hiss, my gaze swinging between her and the guys who are listening, trying to convey to her to stop. But of course, like the clueless teenager she is, she tilts her head to the side in confusion.

Thankfully, the food arrives, and she shuts up to eat. Lincoln and Micah make small talk over breakfast, and once our plates are cleared, I thank them for letting us crash. When I pull out some cash to give to Micah, not wanting to owe him anything, he shakes his head.

"Not happening, Hellcat."

"Hellcat?" Ellie asks, not missing a damn beat.

"It's an inside joke," Micah says with a smirk.

Of course his non answer has Ellie intrigued. "You guys have inside jokes? How well do you know each other?"

"Eliza Bardot, enough," I growl under my breath, making Micah and Lincoln laugh.

"What?" she asks. "The guy introduced himself as your future husband, has a pet name for you, and I don't even know how the two of you met."

"We met at the club," I explain. "He's *not* my future husband. I don't even like him, and that stupid name is his way of aggravating me."

Ellie grins like she was birthed straight from the devil. "Sounds like he likes you. Maybe you should go out with him."

"And now it's time to go," I say, standing. "Gentleman, it's been great. Thank you again for breakfast."

# Eight

## SIENNA

"WHAT THE HELL WAS THAT ABOUT?" I HISS, PRESSING THE button for our floor when we enter the elevator.

"What?" she asks, sounding and looking like she genuinely doesn't get it. "I know you like Lincoln, who is still too old for you, by the way…" I give her a pointed glare. "But our money situation and why I'm working where I am isn't anyone's business. And my God, you told them I watch porn! And don't get me started on the way you were trying to play matchmaker. That was embarrassing."

Her face falls, her features showing a mixture of remorse and regret. "I… I didn't even think," she says. "I'm sorry. I was joking and talking, and I didn't mean to embarrass you. We always play around."

"Yeah, we do. But they're my bosses. That's different."

"He clearly likes you," Ellie points out. "Micah couldn't take his eyes off of you the entire time."

"Well, the feeling isn't mutual," I say, as we step off the elevator.

"You don't think he's cute?"

"Of course he is."

"And he's sweet. He invited us to breakfast."

"Yep," I say noncommittally, unlocking and opening the door to our room.

"You should go out with him."

"I don't have time to date, El."

"Because of me," she says. "Because you're too busy taking care of me. Which I get, but also, I'm fifteen now. It's okay to have your own life, too."

"Not because of you," I repeat. "Because—"

I stop in my tracks, my words freezing, when I see a dozen beautiful white and pink roses in a vase on the counter that weren't there before.

"Oh! So pretty!" Ellie bounces over and snatches up the card. "It has your name on it," she says.

I roll my eyes and open the envelope, pulling the card out and reading it…

Sienna, it was a wonderful surprise getting to have breakfast with you. I look forward to seeing you tonight. - Micah

Jesus, how the hell did he get this delivered so quickly? He must've done it when he was briefly on his phone.

"Oh! Another envelope. This one is addressed to me."

Ellie rips it open and reads the card out loud…

"Thank you for staying at Hotel Blu. Enclosed you will find two complimentary day passes to the hotel's spa to celebrate your birthday. - Micah."

Ellie's eyes go wide. "He totally likes you." I open my mouth to argue but she continues before I can get a word in. "And he's nothing like the nasty assholes mom hangs out with. He's a good guy. Both he and Lincoln are. You seriously need to go out with him." She fans her face with the card. "But right now, we have a spa day to get to!"

"I GUESS I SHOULD SAY THANK YOU." I'M STRADDLING Micah's legs, my arms are wrapped around his neck, and my fingers are idly playing with his hair while a song is playing in the background. I'm supposed to be giving him a lap dance in this private room, but since he's holding me in place, his strong hands gripping the curves of my hips, it's more like we're sitting in an extremely intimate position. Especially since I'm topless and wearing only a tiny pair of panties that barely cover my lady parts.

"For what?" Micah breathes, his heated gaze searing into me.

"For the spa day. My entire body is relaxed and smooth and pretty."

Micah groans. "Any chance you'll let me feel the smooth and pretty parts?"

"Nope," I say. "And speaking of which…" I reach down and peel his hands off me. "No touching."

He rolls his eyes but obeys, lifting his arms behind his head. When he stretches back to relax, he shifts slightly, giving me a good feel of the hardness between his legs as it slides against my center.

A soft gasp escapes before I can prevent it, and Micah catches it, the corner of his lips curling into a knowing smirk.

"There's a cure for that built-up sexual tension," he murmurs. "Go out with me."

"Did you not hear my sister? I don't date."

"Why?"

Well, if that isn't a loaded question—one I have no desire to answer. I give him a half-truth instead. "Relationships require the time and attention I don't have."

He quirks a brow, waiting for the rest of the explanation, but since that's all I'm giving him, I start to move my body again to finish the lap dance. It's the least I can do since—if history is accurate—he'll be tipping very well afterward.

Surprisingly, Micah isn't in the audience for my second performance, nor does he book me for another private show. Before he started buying all of my time, I used to be booked solid, so I'm surprised when Violet tells me I have none booked for the evening. But the shock dies down when I get my tips for the night and see that Micah gave me enough for two performances. I should be annoyed that he basically bought himself a private dance even though he couldn't be here, but if he wants to waste his money to prevent me from dancing in another man's lap, I'm not going to look a gift horse in the mouth.

It's late when Ellie and I get back to the hotel room, so we both pass out right after we shower.

I'm not sure what time it is when I wake up, but when I open my eyes, the first thing I notice is that Ellie's awake and sitting in the chair by my bed, fidgeting like crazy and glancing at me like she's done something wrong.

"What's up?" I ask, rolling onto my side.

"I did something."

"Okay."

"I ran into Micah last night." Oh, jeez. This can't be good. "And I saw him go into Lincoln's office."

"Ellie, just say whatever the hell you did so I can fix it."

"That's just it. I don't want you to fix it. I wrote him a note, saying you wanted to go out with him and signed your name. Then I had Trixie give it to him on his way out."

"Ellie!" I bark, sitting up. "What the hell? Now I'm going to have to tell him what you did when he asks me out *again* and I say *no* again."

She swallows thickly, and I groan out loud. "What else did you do?"

"I wrote on the note that you're available today."

"Oh my God!"

"Just hear me out," she says, her eyes pleading. "I know

part of the reason you never go out or date is because you won't leave me alone at our house... not since..." She trails off, unable to say the words—*not since we were both almost raped in our own home.* "But we're not there. We're here, in a safe hotel, where nobody can get to me. And I'm old enough to hang out by myself. I have homework to do, and I can order in room service. I won't go anywhere or—" Her words are cut off by a knock on the door, and her eyes go wide.

"Is that him?" I hiss.

She nods. "Yeah. I might've told him to pick you up at ten o'clock. You're usually up early, but you woke up late, and I overslept and..."

"Jesus." I scamper out of bed. "Go answer the door while I put on some clothes!"

She runs out of the room, closing the door behind her, and I dash into the bathroom to see how crazy I look. Not too bad since I showered and removed my makeup last night. I quickly wash my face and slip on a bra so I'm somewhat presentable when I let Micah know my sister is playing games and we're not actually going on a date.

But when I walk out into the main room and find him standing there dressed in a gray Henley and jeans, holding a bouquet of flowers, the words get stuck in my throat... because holy hell, how is it possible the man looks even more delicious dressed down than he does in his power suits?

And then he smiles—not the cocky, confident smirks I get at the club, but a genuine, almost boyish grin—and butterflies that have no business being anywhere near me flutter in my chest. And even though I have every reason not to go out with this man, suddenly I want to be a normal twenty-four-year-old being picked up for a date by a gorgeous man who's interested in me, consequences be damned.

"Not that I care what you wear out, but you don't exactly look like you're ready for our date," he says, cutting through my brain fog.

I glance down and groan. I'm wearing the t-shirt I wore to bed with tiny cotton boy shorts. I might've thought to put on a bra, but I forgot I'm not wearing any pants.

"Ummm..."

"We overslept," Ellie says. "If you can just give her a few minutes, she'll go get ready, and then you guys can be on your way."

Micah stares at me for a long moment, and I can see his features change when he comes to the realization that he's been had by the fifteen-year-old.

"You didn't write that note, did you?" His voice is uncharacteristically vulnerable, and the words drift into my chest and wrap around my heart, squeezing it tightly.

When I shake my head, he chuckles.

"What do you think?" he asks Ellie, who's standing to the side, gnawing on her bottom lip because she knows she's fucked up. "Should I give her an out or convince her to take pity on me and go out with me anyway?"

Ellie's eyes light up. "Pity date, for sure. I think once

she's out, she'll have a good time."

Micah nods in agreement. "All right, pity date it is," he says. "Sienna…" He steps over to me, hitting me with the most pitiful puppy dog eyes I've ever seen. "It will absolutely devastate me if you don't go on this date with me. So, will you please take pity on me and go?"

I stare at him, knowing if I say yes, it's going to change everything. It goes against my rules, my plan. And I know that if I give in to him, if I let him suck me in, there's no going back. He's the type of man who gets what he wants and doesn't settle for anything less than everything. He doesn't just want a date with me. He wants to own me, possess me—my heart, my body, and everything in between. And there's a chance he's going to take it all, every part of me, and then destroy me, leaving me only a fraction of myself—just like my mother.

And for the first time, I understand why my mom allowed herself to get hurt by so many men. Why she continued to give herself over to them even though each one took a turn at destroying her.

Because despite knowing all that can go wrong, when a man looks at you the way Micah is looking at me right now, all common sense flies out the window, and you find yourself saying, "Yes, I'll go out with you."

# Nine

## MICAH

"You know what you did was wrong, right?" I say to Ellie once Sienna has disappeared into her room to get ready for our date.

"It was worth it," Ellie says, zero remorse in her words. "Sienna deserves to go out and have fun. She's always working and studying and dealing with our shitty mom. If I didn't do something, she'd be alone forever."

I chuckle at her dramatics. She's still young, but I appreciate the push.

"So what are your plans to make my sister fall in love with you?" she asks, not mincing her words.

"Brunch and a movie. If you want to join—"

"No way." She shakes her head in disgust. "I'm not playing third wheel on your date. Although—" a spark suddenly alights in her eyes "—if you want to get Lincoln to join, I'd be down for a double date." She waggles her brows suggestively, and I bark out a laugh.

"Not happening. When you're hungry, call for room service, and they'll put it on my tab."

"Thanks," she says with a smile. Then she steps toward me, her features turning serious. "Sienna's the way she is because our life has been a bit messed up. Our mom really is a piece of shit, and we've seen things we shouldn't see. So, if you're wanting to go out with her for the wrong reasons, let her go. She's been through enough."

I stare at this kid, who's wise beyond her years, and I know it's because what she's saying is true. They've been through some serious shit, and they've had to grow up fast. To a certain extent I get it because my dad brought us into the business at a young age, so I've seen some crazy shit myself.  But by the way Ellie is looking at me, I have a feeling the things they've been through goes so much deeper.

I'm about to tell her she doesn't have to worry, that I have no intention of hurting her sister, when Sienna reappears, dressed in a pair of dark ripped jeans and a turquoise off-the-shoulder sweater with sandals on her feet. Her hair is up in a high ponytail, and her face is makeup free, except for a bit of gloss making her plump lips shiny.

"This is as good as it's going to get," she says with a shrug. "Didn't bring any dress up clothes, so I hope you didn't plan anything too extravagant."

"You look beautiful," I tell her, handing her the flowers I've been holding this entire time. "And don't worry—" I lean in and whisper so her sister can't hear "—you can be completely naked if you'd like for what I have planned." I shoot her a wink and she glares, making me laugh.

She's going to make me work for everything—every date, every smile, every laugh, every word—but that's okay because I'm wearing her down. I can feel it. Look at how far I've already come. In a short span of time, I went from paying for a lap dance to taking her out on a date. Soon, she'll be legally changing her last name to Alexander.

"You ready?" she asks, knocking me out of my thoughts.

"Yeah." I glance at her sister. "You sure you don't want to join?"

"Nope, I'm good. I'll just be here binging on Netflix and eating everything on the menu." She glances at her sister. "On Micah's tab, of course. He insisted."

Sienna gives her a faux glare. "Behave."

"Always, *Mom*," she says, taking the flowers from Sienna. "Now you two have fun, but don't do anything I wouldn't do. And if you do, remember 'No Glove, No—'"

Sienna reaches out and covers her mouth. "Nope, you do not need to finish that statement." She releases her hand and says to me, "Let's go before I change my mind."

Ellie's cackling can be heard as we close the door behind us and head to the elevator. Since Lincoln and I live in the penthouses, our places are only accessible from the main elevator, so we have to take one down and then get on the other to go back up with my key card.

"Umm, what are we doing?" Sienna asks, glancing up at the numbers in confusion.

"Going up to my place," I say, as the elevator doors open and we step off onto my floor.

Her head whips around and she hits me with a hard glare. "Seriously? Can you get any more cliché? What part of I'm not going to have sex with you did you not understand?" she hisses.

The elevator door slides open, and I step out, but she doesn't follow. Instead, she stands there with her arms crossed over her chest, her nose pointed upward in a stubborn gesture.

"I'm not going in there with you. I knew this was a bad idea, but of course—"

Her words are cut off when I stalk back into the elevator and push her gently against the wall, having enough of her shit.

"Who hurt you?" I ask. "Who caused you to be so guarded? Is it just men you don't trust or people in general?" Her blue eyes widen, and she shakes her head, refusing to say a word.

"Jesus." I slam my palm against the wall, caging her in so our bodies are so close I can feel her warmth radiating off her, smell her feminine scent. Our eyes lock, and I watch as her features morph from fear to longing, to anger, to resigned. And I'm still staring at her when I see the light switch go off and her emotions shut down completely.

"I don't stand a chance, do I?" I whisper, reaching up with my other hand and trailing my knuckles down her cheek. "You don't even *know* me, yet you're so quick to make accusations and assumptions."

She swallows thickly, and her lids flutter closed for several seconds before she opens them back up, pain radiating in her eyes. "Can you blame me? Given the circumstances under which we met?"

"So, based on our unconventional start, you've already pushed me into the box with whoever hurt you and threw away the key. It doesn't really matter what I do, I'll never be able to claw my way out."

Her responding silence is deafening, yet I can hear the truth loud and clear. For the first time ever, I'm at such a loss. I've always gone after what I wanted, and as long as I was willing to put in the work, I would achieve what I was after.

Until Sienna.

Despite her trepidation, there's a part of her that wants me. At the very least, she's attracted to me. I can see it in her eyes when she's straddling my lap at the club, when she's dancing and looks out at the audience in search of me. But she's scared because she's been hurt. And for the first time in my life, I don't know how to fix it.

It would be a helluva lot easier to walk away, find a willing woman to spread her legs. I've been with dozens of women over the years. Women who would let me fuck them any way I want without question, who desire my company, who would marry me in a heartbeat.

Yet I can't get this stubborn, jaded, beautiful woman out of my head. It's become more than a sexual conquest. I want to get to know her. Hear her thoughts. Learn everything there is to know about her. With other women, I could never see anything beyond one night. But when I look at Sienna, I see late nights out together and lazy mornings spent in bed. I see family dinners. Weekend getaways. For the first time, I can see so much more... and it's with her.

So even though she's staring at me like she *expects* me to hurt and disappoint her, I'm not going to give up. I've helped make our family millions of dollars trusting my gut. Not every deal is black and white. Some require taking risks, making decisions nobody can understand but me. Oftentimes the numbers aren't there, but I can feel it in my soul that I'm making the right choice. And that's how I feel about Sienna.

"I didn't bring you up here to fuck you," I say, making sure my voice is calm. "Lincoln told me how protective you are of your sister, that you bring her to the club with you because you don't want to leave her alone, so I ordered brunch up to my room and thought afterward we could watch a movie in the theater. That way, we wouldn't have to leave the hotel in case she needs you at any time."

I can tell the moment my words sink in because her eyes turn soft and her body goes slack. "I...I didn't know," she mutters, her gaze dropping to the ground.

"You didn't ask," I say, pinching the tip of her chin

and lifting it so she's forced to look at me. "The first night I saw you on stage I was immediately drawn to you. I've visited my brother a dozen times and not a single woman ever caught my attention like you did. I think about you all the damn time. But it's more than sexual. I want to get to know you… all of you. I want to know what you're thinking about when your brows furrow like this." I run my finger between her brows and along her nose. "What's going through that pretty head of yours when your nose scrunches up." I continue my descent to her pouty lips. "When your lips purse together, I wonder what's wrong and if there's anything I can do to make it better."

"I'm not that interesting," she murmurs.

"I beg to differ." I back up slightly and extend my hand. "I'm giving you a choice. If you take my hand, we can go to my place and spend some time together, getting to know one another. Or…you say the word and I take you back to your room and I'll leave you alone."

She stares at my hand for several seconds, and I think she's not going to take it, but then she shocks the hell out of me when she reaches out and places her hand in mine.

"This doesn't mean I trust you," she says, her voice hard. "And I'm definitely not going to sleep with you. But I felt it too… the chemistry, so I'm willing to see where this goes. But you should know that my priorities are my sister and my future. Everything else comes after, and you… you come last. I'm not trying to be mean, but it's just the way it has to be."

I can't help but smile at her admission. I should

probably be offended, but instead, it only makes me want her that much more. She's clearly not had it easy, yet she's determined to stand on her own two feet and won't let anyone keep her down.

"Got it." I thread my fingers through hers and pull her out of the elevator and into the hall. "Now let's go eat. I'm starved, and since I can't have you *yet*, I'll have to settle for food."

# Ten

## SIENNA

THIS IS A BAD IDEA. I KNOW IT. I'VE SEEN WHAT LETTING A man in can do to a woman. But still, I said okay. As Micah leads me into his home, I keep telling myself that spending the morning with him doesn't have to mean anything. I'm not going to fall in love with him over a span of several hours. I'm not going to turn into my mom. I've watched her and learned from her mistakes, and I won't be making the same ones.

I expect his penthouse to look similar to the hotel room Ellie and I are staying in, so I'm taken aback when he opens the door to a gorgeously modern open floorplan with ceilings that look to be about fourteen-feet high. There's a state-of-the-art kitchen to the left with top-of-the-line appliances, a large living room to the right, and farther in the distance, I notice a glass staircase leading up to a second floor. The entire area is surrounded by floor to ceiling glass walls and… "Is that a pool?" I gasp, heading straight to the window that faces a wraparound infinity pool.

"Yeah," Micah says with a chuckle, as I press my hands against the glass. "My brother and I share the top floor, so we each have a corner unit. There's a privacy wall outside separating our places."

Nobody has a pool in New York unless they're stinking freaking rich. It's cold for months on end, which makes an outdoor pool useless.

"We can go in it after if you want," he adds.

"Maybe," I murmur noncommittally.

He nods and walks over to the table that's located just off the kitchen. There's a huge spread laid out: croissants, muffins, bagels, a fresh fruit and cheese platter, orange juice and champagne to make mimosas, and a carafe of delicious smelling coffee.

Micah lifts one of the silver tops where there's eggs underneath, still steaming hot. Another one reveals waffles, and the last one houses the best smelling bacon and sausage.

"Hungry?" he asks, pulling my chair out for me like a gentleman.

Before I can respond, my stomach growls, and we both laugh. "You can say that."

I make myself a mimosa, then pile on some waffles, eggs, bacon, and at the last second, tack on some fruit.

Micah takes a croissant and slices it open, then puts some eggs and bacon on it, creating a makeshift breakfast sandwich. "Egg, bacon, and cheese sandwiches are my favorite," he says, grabbing a slice of cheddar from the platter, slapping it on, and then taking a hearty bite.

I can't help the laugh that escapes past my lips as I watch him chow down.

"What?" he asks, once he's swallowed down a bite and has taken a sip of his coffee.

"Nothing, you just look so…normal." When he quirks a brow, silently asking what I'm talking about, I explain. "You're always in those expensive power suits and looking every bit the businessman. Yet, here you are, dressed down and making yourself a sandwich. I guess I imagined brunch would equal fancy foods with caterers."

"We could do that too, if you want," he says nonchalantly, "but I prefer this. Out there…" He nods toward the window, exposing the beautiful city. "I have to be someone people wouldn't dare fuck with. In my home, I can simply be me. Suits are nice, but I prefer the jeans."

Wow, I never would've expected that type of response. It seems I really don't know anything about Micah aside from his obvious wealth, affluence in this town, and his unrelenting determination to date me.

"What's going through your head?" he asks, after taking another bite of food. "I can practically see the cogs turning."

"That I don't really know much about you," I admit, "but also that I'd like to get to know the *real* you, not the person that everyone else sees."

A smile spreads across his face, and that single dimple pops out, causing butterflies to attack my belly. "Good. Because I'd really like to get to know the *real* you, as well. Starting with…Romance or action?"

I go to say action, since I'm thinking he's referring to which movie we should watch, and up until now, romance was not my jam. But since I'm trying to get to know a guy and possibly enter a romantic relationship, I go with, "Romance."

He chuckles and shakes his head. "You're so full of shit."

"What?"

"What's the last romance movie you watched?"

"Umm… Twilight?"

He barks out a laugh. "With the sparkling vampires?"

"Yeah, it's Ellie's favorite," I say with a shrug.

"Let's try this again. Action or romance?"

"Action," I admit with a sigh. "But I could go for romance. Maybe it will teach me a thing or two," I mutter.

Micah laughs even harder, apparently finding my awkwardness hilarious. "And what is it you're hoping it will teach you?"

"I don't know, like how to do this." I point back and forth between us. "I've never done this before, and the only men my mom has ever brought home are the kind who pay for sexual favors." The second the words are out of my mouth, I close my eyes and cringe, regretting my word vomit.

When I open my eyes, I expect to find pity in Micah's gaze, but instead, all I see is compassion. "We'll take this slow," he says. "The truth is, I've never done this either, but I know that I want a relationship like my parents have. They're in their fifties and still very much in love."

"You've never dated before?" I ask.

"Nope. I've been enjoying being a bachelor. Contrary to what you might believe, I'm not a manwhore by any means. I just wasn't looking to settle down yet."

"And now you are?"

"Yeah," he says contemplatively, his features turning serious. "My mom always said when I found the right woman I would know, and I think I've found her."

My heart picks up speed at his words, and I take a deep breath, trying not to let myself get too worked up. Men are good with pretty words. I've heard more than my fair share of men say pretty things to my mom before she fucked them. The problem was, after they had their way with her, those pretty words turned ugly.

"That doesn't sound very slow," I murmur, making him chuckle.

"Sorry," he says with a grin. "Sometimes I have a heavy foot."

When we finish eating, he takes me on a quick tour of his place, and it's even more gorgeous than I thought—complete with several bedrooms, bathrooms, a small gym, an office, and even a theater room.

"I thought when you said we were watching a movie, you meant your hotel had a theater."

"It does as well," he says, dropping onto the comfy, double reclining, leather couch next to me. "But I had a mini one put in here for my personal use."

As I glance at the seat below me, wondering how many women he's fucked on this couch, he must sense my mood shift because he adds, "It's a great way to watch sports with friends."

"So, you've never fucked anyone in here?" I blurt out, curiously.

He turns my direction where his hazel eyes lock with mine. "I've never brought a woman here before. Living in a hotel means having access to rooms. This is my home, where I hope to one day live with my wife and kids. Hookups don't belong here."

And yet, he brought me here. My heart inflates in my chest at the notion that I'm the first woman he's brought to his home, but I quickly find a needle and pop it.

*Stop it, Sienna! He's giving you pretty words. That's what men do.*

"So… what movie are we watching?" I choke out, needing to change the subject.

He eyes me quizzically, and I can tell he wants to ask what I'm thinking, but he hands me the remote instead, and says, "Pick something while I grab us a couple of drinks and popcorn. What do you prefer to drink?"

"If you have sweet tea, I'll take that. If not, bottled water is good."

"Sweet tea is my favorite," he says with a grin. "Be right back."

I scroll through the movies and end up settling on Fast and the Furious. Since Micah's not back yet, I send a text to Ellie to check on her. She's quick to respond with,

ELLIE

**Shouldn't you be busy on your date? If you're thinking about me, he must be doing something wrong.**

I groan at her response, wishing she could go back to being ten again, when she was cute and sweet and didn't have a smart mouth. As a teenager, I didn't have time to get into trouble—I was too busy caring for my baby sister and working minimum wage jobs after school just to put some food on the table and to help pay the bills. But something tells me Ellie is going to give me a run for my money.

SIENNA

**We're about to watch a movie. He's grabbing us snacks. And I'll never be too busy to check on you.**

ELLIE

**Yeah, yeah. Love you too, sis. Now go enjoy yourself.**

When Micah returns with a huge bowl of buttery popcorn and two bottles of sweet tea, I take a bottle and the tub of popcorn from him and hand him the remote.

He presses a button on the couch that dims the lights and then clicks play. We watch the movie in silence for a good half an hour before Micah pauses it and turns toward me. "I think I messed up."

"Oh, how?" He hasn't done anything wrong as far as I can tell. He's been a complete gentleman all morning. The food was delicious, the movie is one of my favorites, and despite me accusing him of making plans for us to hang out at his place, once he explained his reasoning, his understanding of my need to keep my sister close was both thoughtful and appreciated.

"I wanted to get to know you, but it's kind of hard to do that without being able to talk. This might be the only chance I get. It was hard enough to get you to go on this date with me. I feel like I should take advantage of it."

"Okay," I say with a laugh. "What do you have in mind?"

Twenty minutes later, Micah is stepping out of his room, ready to get into the pool. He looks good in his powerful suits, sexy in jeans and a Henley, but in board shorts... Holy shit—this is by far my favorite look on him. He's solid everywhere, his chest and abs and *Jesus*, the V that dips low into his shorts, all look like they were airbrushed on. I suck my lips into my mouth, praying I'm not actually drooling, while wondering if he would think it's weird if I walked over and ran my fingers down his abs to see if they're actually real.

My eyes move to his arms. Since I've only ever seen him in long sleeve shirts, this is my first time seeing his bare arms. They're not only corded with muscle, but both forearms are covered in ink. With a suit on, he exudes power and money, but underneath, he looks like a sexy bad boy.

*Not good,* I tell myself, thinking about all the bad boys my mom has brought home. Bad boys equal trouble. They're good with pretty words… that lead to hurtful actions.

"Damn, you look gorgeous," he says, dragging his eyes down my body and knocking me out of my thoughts. Since I didn't have my suit with me, I ran down to my room and grabbed the one I bought in the boutique yesterday. Ellie was on the phone with her friend, eating a buffet of food she ordered from room service, and when I asked if she wanted to join us, she shooed me away.

"You've seen me naked several times," I scoff.

"That doesn't change the fact that you're gorgeous," he says.

The wraparound balcony is even bigger than it looks from the inside. It houses an outdoor kitchen and grill, a few lounge chairs, and a pool.

I ease my way into the pool and sigh as the cool water envelops my legs, then dive right in, plummeting under the water and not coming up until I get to the other side. When I push through the surface, I come face to face with a very wet Micah.

"Hey," he says, backing me up against the side of the pool.

"Hey," I say back.

He reaches out and tucks the wet hair that's clinging to my face behind my ear, and my breath hitches at his touch. This is exactly why I've made it a point not to date, not to be alone with a man—outside of work. It doesn't matter how smart a woman is, as soon as a man gives her that look, touches her like so, she turns into a puddle of stupid at his feet.

"Tell me something about you that no one knows," Micah says, caging me in with his strong arms.

"I don't want to be stupid," I admit without thinking.

"I think you're far from stupid. Aren't you majoring in accounting?"

"I might be book smart, but being here with you, letting you into my life, definitely makes me stupid."

"You haven't even begun to let me in," he says with a half-smile.

"Then maybe there's still hope for me yet."

"If you could do anything for the rest of your life, what would you do?"

"No way." I shake my head. "You have to answer, too. Tell me something about you no one knows."

He thinks for a second before he says, "My biological mom didn't want me, even threatened to have an abortion. My dad compensated her quite generously to carry me to term and then paid her another hefty sum to sign over her rights and disappear from my life forever.

"So, you and Lincoln aren't..."

He shakes his head. "No, everyone thinks we share the same mom. But the truth is, my dad met Lincoln's mom, Donna, when my bio mom was pregnant with me. They fell hard and fast, and she accepted me as her own after I was born." He smiles softly. "Everyone thinks she's my mom because she's always loved me the same as Lincoln, her own flesh and blood. She chose for me to be a part of her life when my own mom chose to discard me.

"Maybe that's the best kind of love," I say. "The kind where someone *chooses* to love you when they don't have to."

"As opposed to what?" he asks.

"Forced love. From my experience, when it's forced, it doesn't end well. My parents were both professional dancers who got pregnant with me by accident and were forced to marry. In the beginning, I think they tried to make it work. But dancing was more than a career to them, it was their dream. My mom had to give up that dream in order to care for me, and when my dad got injured and could no longer dance, things really started to unravel. My dad eventually left us, choosing to start another family, one he wanted. When my mom became pregnant with Ellie and her deadbeat dad skipped town, she was forced to care for two children on her own. Trapped and looking for an escape, she chose a path of drugs and prostitution and a string of men who were nothing more than a series of poor choices. Time and again, our mom has abandoned us, choosing that life over the children she is supposed to love."

"You love Ellie, and she loves you," he points out.

"True, but our love is tainted. You heard her at breakfast. She thinks she's a burden to me. That I'm giving up what I love to take care of her. What I want is for someone to *choose* to love me. To not see me as a burden or associate me with heartbreak. I want someone to look at me and think I'm the best part of their day. I want to feel a love that is pure and good and doesn't come with any strings attached. I don't know if that kind of love actually exists, but I want to believe in the fairytale."

"Yet, you refuse to date."

I chuckle at his truth. "It's not that I don't want to one day fall in love. It's just that right now, the only person I have room in my heart for is Ellie. She comes first. Our mom is a drug-addicted prostitute who gives all her money to her pimp. Ellie deserves the world, and I'm going to make sure she gets it, regardless of the odds against us."

Micah palms my cheek and tilts my face to look at him. "What if you had someone to carry the burden with you? Maybe then you'd have some more room in your heart to find your own love."

"I don't want to depend on anyone but myself," I admit. "My mom depended on my dad, and he eventually left us. Ellie's dad disappeared. Her pimp boyfriend promised to take care of her, but he preyed on her weakness instead. My mom wanted to be loved, and in the end, it's what broke her. I would be a fool if I didn't learn from her mistakes.

"Besides, I have work and school and Ellie. Once I graduate, I can get a job the state will approve of and petition the court for full custody of my sister. I need to get Ellie away from our mom, and I can't afford to risk falling in love before that happens because if it were to break me the way it broke my mom, who would Ellie have left? I can't risk it."

Micah nods in understanding, but I can see it in his face that he doesn't get it, which is precisely why I never should've agreed to go on this date with him. It doesn't matter how good looking he is, how strong the chemistry is between us. I can't afford to let him in.

"I appreciate your attempt at getting to know me," I tell him. "But I'm not in a place to be dating anyone. I think it's best if we end this date right now."

I dip under the water and swim away from him toward the steps. I'm out of the pool and grabbing a towel before he even makes it out of the water. By the time he joins me, I've gotten my towel wrapped around my body, my flip flops on my feet, and I'm heading inside to grab my clothes so I can leave.

I assume Micah is going to let me go, until I turn around and run right into his hard chest. His hands land on my hips, and he holds me tight, steadying me so I don't fall back. I glance up at him, ready to tell him I'm good, when his mouth descends on mine.

His strong yet soft lips curl around my own. He waits a beat, probably to see if I'm going to push him away, and when I don't, he takes that as his cue to deepen the kiss. Gliding his tongue across the seam of my lips, he coaxes them open and then slips his tongue inside while I stand frozen in place, experiencing my first kiss since high school.

Unlike the boy who kissed me back then—awkwardly and sloppily—Micah kisses me with slow, methodical movements. He tastes like the perfect mix of sweet and salty from our snacks earlier, and I find myself wanting to kiss him back. My tongue tangles with his, and he sucks it into his mouth as he encircles his arm around my waist. He tugs me toward him, bringing our bodies flush, my hands landing on his muscular chest. Instinctively, I run the tips of my fingers up his hot, smooth flesh, until my arms are wrapped around his neck.

But it doesn't feel like enough. Not my arms around his neck, not his mouth fucking my own, not our bodies flush against one another, or his arms holding me tight. I need more.

I blame the next move on the oxytocin fogging my brain.

Parting my legs slightly, I trap Micah's muscular thigh between my legs and then grind my center against him, using him like my own personal pole. With only a thin layer of material covering my center, his hard leg pushes against my clit, and I let out a breathy moan.

And then he breaks the kiss…leaving me a panting, breathless mess.

"You feel that?" he murmurs against my lips, holding me close so our bodies are still connected. "That chemistry…" He pulls back slightly, his hazel eyes burning with desire. "You can continue to deny how much you want me, but the way your body, your mouth, *your fucking cunt* is practically begging for my touch proves that you crave me the way I desperately crave you."

He darts his tongue out and swipes it across my

bottom lip before he bites down on it and tugs, causing an electrical current to shoot through me straight to my core.

"I bet if I stuck my fingers in you, you'd be soaked," he says, his voice deep with want. "But I'm not going to do that," he adds, backing up and breaking our connection. My body immediately goes cold, and I find myself moving toward him, wanting his warmth back.

But he shakes his head, stopping me in my place. "I feel it, how amazing it would be between us." He cups the side of my face and presses a chaste kiss to my lips. "But in the same way you want someone to *choose you*, Sienna, I want someone to *choose me*."

# Eleven

## SIENNA

"All right, ladies, we're going to finish class by working on some technique." The girls moan, and I have to stifle my laugh. When I was their age, I hated working on technique too, but dance isn't just about the fun stuff. You have to train as well.

The girls already know where this is going, so they head over to the barre. I run them through several positions, knowing each count by heart. I could teach this class in my sleep, which is probably a good thing, since my head isn't in it at all today.

It's still at Hotel Blu, at Micah's penthouse. Our date was a pleasant surprise—the brunch and movie and how he wanted to actually get to know me. When I spoke, he seemed to listen.

My thoughts go to the kiss...

The way our bodies aligned perfectly with one another, almost like we were meant to be. I bring my fingers up to my lips, remembering the way his mouth devoured mine. Afterward, he walked me back to my room, and with a chaste yet intimate kiss to the corner of my mouth, he told me he'd see me soon.

Class ends, and I tell the girls they did a wonderful job and I'll see them on Wednesday, and then I spend the next hour doing homework while Ellie finishes up her class.

"So, home?" Ellie asks once we're in my car.

"Yeah." Mom wasn't there when we went by the house earlier this morning so Ellie could get dressed for school and grab her backpack. More than likely, she's taken off again, so there's no reason to spend money unnecessarily on a hotel room when we can stay at the house for free. Since she's apparently gotten her hands on some money, chances are that Mom won't return for weeks, possibly months.

We stop at the store on the way home, and then, while Ellie is showering, I make us dinner. I'm stirring the chicken in the pan when there's a loud banging on the door followed by a masculine voice. "Open this fucking door!" Phil barks.

I set the spoon down and grab a knife, not wanting to be unprepared. I have no intention of letting him inside, but who knows what this asshole is capable of.

"Lenora's not here," I yell back at Phil, hoping he'll

give up and leave.

"Open the fucking door!" he shouts again.

"Not—" I haven't finished my sentence when the door breaks open, pieces of wood flying every which way, and I stumble back before I get slammed by it.

"Where the fuck is she?" Phil growls, pushing past me. "That bitch is fucking dead."

"She's not here," I tell him, praying Ellie doesn't come out.

Phil swings mom's door open and stalks inside. He starts pulling drawers open and tossing everything everywhere, making a mess. I keep my mouth shut, not wanting to get on his bad side. Whatever he's looking for has nothing to do with me.

After he's checked her entire bedroom and bathroom, he moves on to Ellie's and my room, tearing everything apart.

When he grabs the bathroom handle and it doesn't open, he darts his gaze over to me. "Ellie's in there."

"Open the door!" he shouts.

"Fuck you!" Ellie yells back, letting her temper get the best of her.

"Ellie, please open it before he breaks it down," I say with a calmness I don't feel.

She swings the bathroom door open, and he barges in, checking to make sure our mom isn't hiding.

"Where is it?" he asks, storming out of the bathroom.

"Where is what?" I'm sure he's referring to the money she came into, but I figure it's better to play stupid since

I really don't know where she or the money is. "She came home Friday and we got into a fight. I haven't seen her since then."

He bridges the gap between us and pushes me against the wall, his hand squeezing my face. I hold the knife tight in my hand, ready to stab him if necessary. "That bitch owes me," he says, confirming my suspicions, "and I always collect. If I find out you know where she is…"

"We don't know where she is," Ellie yells.

"El," I warn, not wanting her to put herself at risk. "I don't know where she is or what you're looking for, but as you can see, neither is here."

He releases me but doesn't move back. "You better hope she turns up," he says, his eyes locking with mine. His face is so close I can smell his rancid breath. "Your whore of a mother made a grave error, and if she doesn't fix it, I can't be held accountable for what happens next," he threatens, slamming his hand against the wall before stalking out.

As I watch him leave, several thoughts and emotions flit through my head: Anger that our mom has put us in danger—again. Fear that Phil's threat wasn't an empty one and the possible ramifications of him not tracking down my mom. Exhaustion, since I seriously wish I could lie down and take a long ass nap. And desperation—because all I want is to give Ellie a safe and stable home. Why must that be so difficult?

My phone dings in my pocket and when I pull it out, I find a text from unknown:

UNKNOWN

**Hey beautiful, how was your day?**

I know instantly that it's from Micah. When he asked for my number, I caved in a moment of weakness and gave it to him. And then, like a lust-struck teenager, I spent the next twenty-four hours checking my phone for a text from him.

UNKNOWN

**<picture of the pool overlooking the sunset and city> Wish you were here with me.**

My thoughts go back to Sunday and how it was so easy to get lost in him, in the moment. The way he looked at me and listened to me and wanted to get to know me. And when he kissed me, I felt like I was in a fairytale, getting swept off my feet by my very own Prince Charming.

"Sienna," Ellie whispers, causing me to look up from my phone to where she's standing in the hallway. Her arms are wrapped around her body in a protective gesture. She's scared. And rightfully so. Because in the world Ellie and I live in, fairytales are nothing more than make-believe stories giving false hope to people just like us.

My brain flashes back to Micah's words after he ended the kiss: *"In the same way you want someone to choose you, Sienna, I want someone to choose me."*

I've been thinking about what he said, what he wants. Even considered giving him a real chance. Ellie told me I deserved to find love and happiness, and for a moment, I allowed myself to believe I could somehow possibly have it.

But as much as the thought of choosing Micah gets my heart racing a little faster, deep down, I know I can't choose him. I just don't have any room in my life for Micah—not right now, anyway. My primary focus needs to be on Ellie and keeping her safe, which means I need to figure out where she and I will be sleeping tonight because clearly, we can't stay here.

SIENNA

I'm sorry, Micah. I made a mistake going on that date with you and giving you my number. Please don't text me again. Goodbye.

"Go pack a bag," I say to Ellie, pocketing my phone. "We're going to the motel tonight."

# Twelve

## MICAH

"To thirty-two years of marriage. May the years to follow be just as amazing." Lincoln holds up his flute filled with champagne, and we all raise ours, clinking our glasses together.

We're at The Kitchen, an upscale restaurant that's located in downtown Tesoro, celebrating our parents' anniversary.

"Thank you," Mom says, leaning over and kissing Lincoln's cheek. "Maybe one day we'll be toasting to one of your engagements…"

She side eyes me, and Lincoln snorts out a laugh. To mom, hitting thirty is apparently a signal that it's time to settle down—especially since Dad was thirty when the two of them first met. And since I'm almost thirty-three, she thinks it's way past time I exchange my bachelorhood status for a long-term, committed relationship. Lincoln's twenty-nine, so he still has a little bit of time before Mom starts to get on his case.

"Never know," Lincoln says with a smirk. "Micah's been obsessing over a dancer at Wanderlust. Maybe you'll get to plan his wedding sooner than you think. Or be a character witness when she files harassment charges against him."

Both my parents' eyes swing over to me, but before either can start in on the third degree, a masculine voice speaks first. "Good evening."

We all glance up and find none other than Eleazar Gutierrez standing at our table with a beautiful woman on his arm.

"Mr. Gutierrez," Dad says, standing to shake his hand. He's the son of Eduardo Gutierrez, the crime boss who recently died from a heart attack. "I didn't know you were back. Had I known, my boys and I would've come to your home to personally extend our condolences." Lincoln and I follow our father and stand, shaking Eleazar's hand.

"Thank you," Eleazar says. "We only just got in a few days ago." He gestures toward the woman on his arm. "This is my wife, Arielle."

"Lovely to meet you," Mom says, giving the woman a two cheek kiss out of respect.

"I didn't hear anything about a funeral," Dad says, making conversation.

"Dad didn't want one. He'll be cremated and brought

back to Mexico with me."

"How long are you in town for?" Mom asks. "We would love to have you over for dinner." The truth is, my parents would like nothing less, but while we own the majority of Tesoro, the Gutierrezes run the underworld, and their family is not one to be fucked with. We've been coexisting for decades because our families go way back, but they're sleazy and dirty, and with their prostitution and trafficking rings, they make us look like boy scouts.

"Hopefully, not too long," Arielle says with a strong Spanish accent, pouting at Eleazar.

Eleazar visibly glares at his wife then smiles at my mom. "Thank you for the invite. Can I let you know? I have a few loose ends to tie up that will need my attention. You know how it is..." He glances at Dad. "Business before pleasure."

"All too well," Dad agrees.

"It's an open invitation," Mom adds.

After a few more minutes of chatting, Eleazar and Arielle say goodbye and we sit back down. I was hoping with the interruption my mom wouldn't remember the topic of conversation, but when her eyes meet mine and she says, "Now tell me about this dancer," I know I'm not in luck.

LINCOLN

**stalker: a person who harasses or persecutes someone with unwanted and obsessive attention.**

LINCOLN

**an idea or thought that continually preoccupies or intrudes on a person's mind.**

LINCOLN

**<insert company handbook>**

"If you send me one more stupid fucking text, I'm going to shoot you." I glare up at my brother from my phone.

"Just figured I'd lay it all out for you." He smirks. "Did you click on the handbook? I highlighted the important parts."

I reach out and grab the marble coaster on his coffee table and chuck it at him. He ducks and it hits the wall behind him.

"Jesus, fuck!" he barks. "You could've taken my head off with that thing."

"Consider that your warning."

"So much anger," he mutters. "Maybe if you got laid…"

"How about you worry about your own damn—"

My words are cut off when I see a certain brunette pass by the office, heading in the direction of the back door.

I hop up to follow her out and Lincoln chuckles. "Careful, you're quickly crossing from obsessing to stalking. Might want to read those definitions I sent you."

I give him a one finger response to his asinine remark as I head out the backdoor so I can talk to Sienna about the bullshit text she sent me the other night. I could've texted her back, but I figured it would be best to discuss it in person.

When I swing the door open and glance around, I spot her piece of shit car but not her. My eyes trail the area, knowing damn well I saw her come out here, when a noise catches my attention.

The first thing I notice is two guys, dressed in all black, standing with their backs to me, facing the brick wall. Even from behind, I can tell neither work for us, which immediately has me on alert. But what has me pulling out my gun is the fact that they're not just staring at the wall, they're actually cornering someone—and the flash of silver sequins confirms that the person they're cornering is Sienna.

With my gun in one hand and my cell phone in the other, I quickly shoot a one-handed 911 text to Lincoln. He'll know from those digits that he needs to get his ass out here immediately and bring backup.

"Back the fuck up," I say in a low voice.

The guys spin around, and I instantly memorize their features—black hair, black eyes, light skin, tattoos covering both their arms.

"This ain't your business," one guy says, his accent thick.

I raise my gun and point it at him. "Do you know

whose property you're on?"

"We just need the girl," the other guy says, avoiding my question.

"The girl is on our property," Lincoln says, joining me, along with Rex and Oscar. "That makes her ours. Which means, if you're trying to take her, you're taking from us."

"I'm gonna ask you again," I say. "Do you know whose property you're on?"

"Like I said…" the first guy starts to say, but before he can finish his sentence, I stalk over to him and raise my gun to his forehead.

His friend curses under his breath while he swallows thickly, lifting his hands up in surrender.

"Hellcat," I toss out, my eyes never leaving these assholes. "Go with Oscar inside."

Sienna scrambles around us and runs inside. Once I know she's safe, I nod toward the two guys. "Check them."

Rex does as I say, removing a knife from one guy and a gun from the other. He pulls out their wallets and reads their names out loud.

"Josue Gamez," he says, referring to the guy my brother is holding a gun on. "And Manuel Ortega."

"Who do you work for?" I ask Manuel, pressing the barrel of the gun against his forehead.

When he juts out his chin defiantly, I know he's about to play hardball. And since this isn't the place for shit to get messy, it's time to take this conversation somewhere more private. I pull out my phone and text Ricardo—one of my most trusted men, who has been with me for years.

He's savage as fuck and knows how torture information out of someone. I've never not seen him be successful.

Twenty minutes later, Josue and Manuel are tied to chairs in the middle of our warehouse while, little by little, Ricardo cuts into their skin every time I ask a question and they refuse to answer.

"Who are you working for?" I ask them.

When neither answer, I nod toward Ricardo to take it up a notch. He digs his knife into the meaty part of Josue's leg, and he curses. I can tell he's getting close to his breaking point, so I nod again, and he digs deeper.

"Fuck! We're not working for anyone!" he hisses.

"Again," I say.

Ricardo digs so deep that a chunk of his flesh is exposed, causing him to scream out like a little girl, "Gutierrez!"

"Nice try, he's dead."

Ricardo lifts the knife and Josue shrieks, "Not him! His son. Eleazar."

My hackles rise. Why the fuck would Eleazar be after Sienna?

And then Josue answers my silent thought. "He's got a bounty on her head. I don't know why, but whoever delivers that chick, dead or alive, will get a million-dollar pay day."

Lincoln's eyes meet mine, silently thinking the same thing as me... *What the fuck?* I pull my gun out and shoot both of the guys in their foreheads, killing them instantly.

Generally, we try to stay away from unnecessary

violence since it's bad for business and a mess to clean up, but there's no way I'm chancing either of these assholes going after Sienna again or reporting her whereabouts to Eleazar.

"Call for a cleanup," I tell our guys, knowing they'll handle it.

"Any idea what the fuck Eleazar wants with Sienna?" Lincoln asks as we walk back to his car, since we left my vehicle at the club and drove here together. "And why doesn't he care if she's handed over dead or alive?"

"No idea, but until we figure it out, we need to get Sienna and her sister hidden. Who the hell knows how many people are searching for her?"

When someone as powerful as Gutierrez puts a hit out on someone, people come running. Not just for the money, but also for the respect. If you're the one who brings him who he wants, he'll owe you, and people take that shit seriously.

As we leave the warehouse and head back to the club, I pull out my cell to make a call. "Oscar," I say when he answers the phone. "I need you to get Sienna and her sister ready to go. I'll be there in five minutes to pick them up."

"Boss, they already left," he says.

"What the fuck do you mean they left?"

"I tried to—"

"Never mind," I bark. "I'll deal with you later."

I hang up on him and slam my fist into the glovebox. "Fuck, any chance you know where she lives?"

"I know she's from Booker Park, but I'd have to get her address from my office."

When we pull up to Wanderlust, Lincoln runs in to grab the address, while I hop into my car and start driving toward Booker Park, hitting Sienna's name on my phone to call her. The neighborhood is only about fifteen minutes away, but at the speed I'm going, I'll get there in half the time.

"Micah," Sienna breathes over the Bluetooth, the fear in her voice clenching my heart like a vise.

"Where are you?"

"Pulling up to our house." Fuck, the last place she should be going is to her house.

"Sienna, listen, you can't go—"

"Shit, my phone's going to die," she says, distracted and not paying attention to me.

"Sienna!"

"Ellie, grab the—" Her words are cutoff by the sound of a blood-curling scream that has me pressing my foot on the pedal harder.

"Sienna!"

"Oh, my God," she gasps. "He's dead."

# Thirteen

## SIENNA

THE PLACE HAS BEEN DESTROYED. CUSHIONS SLASHED. Glass shattered. The few pictures I hung on the wall to try to make it a home have been smashed.

But that's not what has my heart pounding behind my rib cage. On the floor is Phil, lying in the middle of the glass coffee table with a jagged piece of glass sticking out of his chest.

"Holy shit," Ellie murmurs. "He's dead. Does that mean mom…?"

I snap my head up and glance around. Is she dead too? Is she the one who killed him?

"Fuck," a masculine voice curses, making Ellie and me jump.

We spin around to find Micah standing in the

doorway, assessing the situation.

"Do you know him?" he asks, walking inside.

"He was our mom's boyfriend and pimp," Ellie answers first.

"All right, let's go," he says, reaching for us.

"I didn't…" I shake my head. "We didn't… We found him like this."

He nods. "We need to get you out of here."

"Wait," Ellie cries. "I need to know if Mom is here somewhere…" *dead.* She can't say the word, but I know what's going through her head.

Micah looks like he wants to argue, but when he sees the tears gliding down Ellie's face, he nods in understanding. "Don't move, either of you." He pins us both with a hard look and then takes off down the hall. A few minutes later, he reappears, shaking his head. "There's no one else here. Let's go."

"What about my stuff?" Ellie asks.

"Whatever you need can be replaced," Micah snaps, clearly losing his patience. "Whoever killed this guy will be back to clean it up. We gotta go."

He ushers Ellie and me gently out the door, then he grabs my wrist when I start to head toward my car. "You're staying with me until this gets sorted."

"What? No," I argue. "We'll get a room at the motel and—"

Micah pinches my chin and forces me to look at him. "Your independence is something I find extremely attractive about you, but now is not the time to debate the issue. I know you don't have all the facts yet, but please trust me when I tell you that you and your sister aren't safe."

I open my mouth to argue, but before I can, Ellie's hand lands on my arm, and my eyes meet her panicked, scared green eyes. "Please," she whispers, and that's all I need for my stubbornness to dissipate. Ellie comes first, and if she needs to go with Micah to feel safe, that's what we'll do. Even if the thought of going with him equally terrifies me.

The ride to Micah's penthouse is filled with him barking orders to someone on the phone while Ellie and I remain quiet. When we arrive at the hotel, instead of pulling up to the front, he drives down a small side road that leads to what looks like a private garage that can only be accessed with the clicker he has clipped to his visor.

Two men are waiting for us, and he must feel me go immediately on alert because his hand lands on my thigh, squeezing it in a calming gesture. I try not to pay attention to the fact that my body does just that—calms.

"That's Ricardo and Bruno," he says. "They're two of my men. I trust them and you can as well. This hotel is secure, and no one can access my personal elevator, but they're going to be standing guard just as an extra layer of protection.

Standing guard? Why is he making it sound like…?

Oh, my God. The men who were cornering me. Seeing Phil dead fogged my brain. I had assumed they were just rapist assholes trying to take advantage of a woman alone in a dark parking lot. But what if the two incidents are somehow connected? What if whoever killed Phil came there to kill us? What if we were the targets?

Goose bumps spread along my flesh, my blood running cold at the thought that we could've ended up like Phil if we had been home.

"How much danger are we in?" I whisper.

Micah goes to get out without answering me, but I grab ahold of his bicep and lock eyes with him. "Whoever killed Phil… Was he… Do you think… he was trying to get to us?"

Micah swallows thickly, and for a split second, I see a hint of sympathy in his features, telling me all I need to know—this is exactly what he thinks.

"We'll talk once we're inside," he says.

Once we've entered his penthouse, Micah sets the alarm, and I feel like I'm able to take my first breath in hours. I'm still freaking out, but now that we're here, I know we did the right thing by trusting Micah to keep us safe. We're dozens of floors up with a private elevator and extra security protecting us.

Ellie is safe.

Micah hands Ellie and me each a bottled water and guides us over to the living room, gesturing for us to have a seat. Ellie sits in the corner, bringing her legs up to her chest in a protective manner, and I sit next to her, reaching over and rubbing her shin, trying to reassure her that everything is going to be okay even though I have no idea if that's true.

"There's a bounty on your head," Micah says, sitting on the coffee table across from me.

"What the hell does that mean?" I ask.

"Like the show?" Ellie squeaks. "Like where people who are wanted get tracked down and whoever finds them gets a reward?"

"What?" I hiss, my gaze flitting from Ellie to Micah.

"Exactly like that," Micah confirms.

"Somebody wants us? Who? Why?" I ask, my hands starting to shake.

"I don't know about Ellie," he says, glancing at my sister. "But I have it on good authority that there is a million-dollar bounty on your head. Those guys at the club were after you for the money."

"We have to run," I breathe, ready to bolt.

"No, you have to stay right the fuck here," Micah says, his tone authoritative yet calm at the same time. "Ever heard of the Gutierrez family?"

"No," my sister and I say at the same time.

"They're one of the most powerful crime families in New York, maybe even on the East Coast. They deal in drugs, trafficking, and prostitution—"

"Our mom's a prostitute," Ellie says.

And then it hits me... "Mom came home for Ellie's birthday with bags of expensive gifts. I asked her where she got the money to pay for all of it, and she flipped out on me. Phil showed up on Monday looking for her, tore the place apart, saying she owes him. Could whoever killed him... whoever is after us... be looking for whatever she has? Oh, God, do they think we have the money? Because we don't."

"It's a possibility," Micah says. "I'm going to find out, but until this gets figured out, you're both going to stay here. With a million dollars on your head… and possibly your sister's, you can't risk leaving."

I just finished my finals this week, but… "Ellie has exams… and dance." Micah glares at me and I flinch, realizing how dumb I sound. "I'm sorry." I shake my head.

"I can get my teachers to let me take them online," Ellie says, standing. "And there will be other showcases." Her voice is strong, her head held high, but I know deep down she's bummed. She's worked hard in dance, and once again, our shitty mom has taken something from her. She should be pissed and upset, lashing out, but she won't because she's a good kid who knows the score, who learned early on that life isn't always fair.

"I'm assuming there's a room in this mini mansion for me to shower and sleep in?" she says, covering her true feelings with sass.

"El," I groan.

Micah chuckles. "Upstairs, first door on the right there is a guestroom with an en suite bathroom. I'm having one of my guys pick up some clothes for both of you. I'll have Sienna bring them up to you once they arrive. But until then, there's a robe you can use in the bathroom."

"Thanks," Ellie says. She leans in and kisses my cheek. "We'll get through this, sis," she says softly. "We always do."

I nod, trying to remain strong for her. "Of course we will," I say, pulling her into a hug.

"I've worked so hard trying to provide her with a normal life," I say to Micah once she's gone. "And yet again, Lenora did something to fuck it up. It might not be confirmed yet, but whatever is going on, I'm positive she's at the heart of it.

"Lenora is your mom?"

"Yeah. The woman is a disease, hell-bent on destroying everything and everyone around her."

Micah leans in and palms my face. His thumb swipes gently across the tears I didn't realize had fallen. "She's why you're scared," he says, moving from the table to the couch and pulling me into his arms.

"She's why I have to focus on my goals. So I can get Ellie and me far away and safe. I'm the only person in this world Ellie can count on, and it's my job to protect her." I swallow thickly, trying to tamper down the lump of emotion in my throat. I don't know what Lenora has gotten herself mixed up in this time, but I can feel it...this is different, scarier. All I know for sure is that whatever it is, it's really, really bad, and somehow she's managed to drag me, and possibly Ellie, down with her.

Micah wraps his arm around my shoulders and guides my head to his chest. I should push him away, but his strong, comforting hold has me sighing into him. "I know it's hard for you to let people in," he says, tipping my chin to look up at him, "but sometimes things are too much to handle on our own. We all need someone to lean on, to be there for us, to help us through the rough patches. I have my parents and brother...a handful of men I trust. Who do you have, Sienna? Who is there looking out for you?"

I can't help but choke out a sob at his question because the truth is... "I don't have anyone," I admit, a puddle of tears filling my lids and blurring my vision. The only person I have is Ellie, but it's my job to look out for her, not the other way around.

"That's where you're wrong," Micah says. "You have me." He dips his face and kisses my forehead. "You just have to trust me enough to let me in, and I promise I will do everything in my power to make sure you and your sister are safe and happy."

"Why?" It might seem like a stupid question, but the fact is, I met this guy at a strip club, a place men go for an easy, good time. And entangling himself with me would be anything but easy.

"I told you already," he says, tucking a few strands of hair behind my ear. "There's something about you that has me wanting more. I can't explain it, but I think about you all the time." He chuckles darkly. "My brother thinks I'm obsessed, accused me of being a stalker." He shrugs, clearly not giving a shit about that accusation, and despite what's going on outside of these walls, I find myself laughing.

"I can admit that I was sexually attracted to you from the start. Can you blame me, though? You're fucking gorgeous." My cheeks heat up at his words. "But it's more than that now. I want to get to know you. You can't deny there's chemistry between us, we felt it on our date, and I want to see where things go. I understand your priority is your sister, and that only makes you more attractive in my eyes because family is everything to me."

He grips the curves of my hips and pulls me onto his lap so I'm straddling his muscular thighs. "Let me in, Hellcat. Give me a chance to show you that you don't have to go through this life alone. It's okay to find love and be loved. It doesn't make you weak...it makes you human."

I know what he's asking shouldn't be a big deal. People offer up their hearts to love all the time. But he hasn't lived the life I have. He hasn't suffered the consequences of trusting the wrong men, and he hasn't witnessed the devastation and destruction they leave behind in the aftermath.

"I..." I begin, but Micah shakes his head and presses his fingers to my lips.

"Before you say you can't, just think about it, please. Give me a chance to show you. You're here for the foreseeable future anyway, right? Let that wall you've built come down for a little bit and know that my bigger wall is protecting you both."

He leans in and presses a soft kiss to the corner of my mouth just as his phone pings with an incoming text. "My guy's here with the clothes. Let me grab them and then I'll show you to your room so you can shower today off and get some rest."

He lifts me off his lap and I follow him to retrieve the

clothes. He types in a code, then opens the door. "Here ya go, Boss," the guy says, handing him two large bags from a store that should be closed at this time of night. "I got everything on the list, and Sara said if you need anything else to let her know."

"Thanks," Micah says, before closing the door.

He leads me up the stairs, past the door he told Ellie is her temporary room, to the one right next to hers. "You can stay here," he says, opening the door. "It has its own bathroom as well. As you might recall from the last time you were here, farther down the hall is the library and gym. My room and office are downstairs, near the theater room. Laundry room is attached to the kitchen. I'll give you and Ellie a more thorough tour tomorrow."

"You don't want me to sleep in your room?" I blurt out. I thought for sure he would try to trick me into sleeping with him. He's made his desire for me more than clear.

"I told you before," he says, framing my face with the hand that's not holding the bags. "The way you want someone to choose you, I want the same. I would never force you to do anything you're not comfortable doing, Sienna. When you sleep with me, share a bed with me, it will be because you want to, not because I tricked or forced you into it."

His words are like the heat of the sun shining down and melting away a layer of ice that formed around my heart. "Thank you," I murmur, lifting onto my tiptoes and kissing his cheek. "For not only giving me a choice, but for protecting Ellie and me." I take the bags from him. "Good night."

After showering and getting dressed in clothes that somehow are magically my size, I take Ellie's clothes over to her room.

"Thanks," she says, opening the door so I can come in. I plop on the bed while she changes in front of me, not caring if I see her naked. The girl has zero insecurities when it comes to her body.

"I'm in the room next door if you need anything."

"Any chance that's Micah's room?" she asks, playfully waggling her brows.

"It's not."

She sifts through the bag and pulls out a swimsuit. "Oh, nice. Guy's got good taste. Think he'll let me head to the pool downstairs?"

"Don't need to. He has one here."

Her eyes bug out. "You seriously need to get with this guy. Can you imagine living here? It's like a castle… he's the king and you could be his queen." She drops into the reading chair in the corner. "I bet Lincoln's mini-mansion is just as nice."

"Something you'll never find out since he's much too old for you," I remind her. "And anyway, money and materialistic possessions are not reasons to be with someone. You can't let those things define your life." I lock eyes with her. "Mom has been chasing love for all the wrong reasons, and yet, she still has nothing—not even us. Don't you want to have a different life than hers?

"Of course I do," Ellie scoffs. She averts her gaze, glancing down at her lap. "But Mom's a druggy always looking for her next fix. Phil is her dealer. He hurts her. Lincoln and Micah are different. They're safe and protective. Micah saved us tonight. I don't think he would hurt us. And besides, he likes you. I see the way he looks at you. It's different..." She sniffles and her eyes flit toward the ceiling as she tries not to cry. "Maybe if Mom would've landed someone like Micah instead of Phil things would've been different. Maybe she would be clean and happy and in love.

"Is it so bad that I want you to find love and be happy? You've put your life on hold for me, taking care of everything that mom doesn't. You deserve it. The castle, the king...You deserve it all. We both do," she whispers.

"El..." I choke out as it hits me just how quickly my sister has had to grow up. She might only be fifteen, but because of the life we've been thrust into, she's been forced to grow up faster than other kids. I thought her crush on Lincoln was nothing more than a teenage crush, but now I see it...her need to feel safe, to have a stable, loving home. As much as I try to shield her from the bad, what I'm doing is just a temporary Band-Aid being placed over an open bullet wound.

I open my arms so she can come to me, and when she does, I hold her tight. "I know it's scary right now, but we'll get through this." I don't comment on what she said about Lincoln and Micah because she's not wrong. I felt it when Micah held me earlier. The safeness, the stability, the feeling of not being so alone.

Maybe it's like Micah said: *Sometimes things are too much to handle on our own. We  all need someone to lean on, to be there for us, to help us through the rough patches.*

"Do you think she's okay?" Ellie murmurs, her face tucked into my chest.

"I don't know," I tell her honestly. "She's a fighter."

"A part of me wishes she were dead," she admits. "But another part of me just wishes she could go back to being our mom again," she adds.

"Me too," I agree. "Me too."

# Fourteen

## MICAH

"Is that bacon I smell?" Ellie asks, descending the stairs, dressed in a pair of pajamas, her hair up in a messy knot on top of her head.

"And coffee," Sienna adds, dramatically sniffing the air. Like her sister, she's still in her pajamas with her messy hair pulled on top of her head.

They're both rubbing their eyes as they stumble down the stairs, the scent of breakfast seeming to guide their movements.

Ellie plops down at the table first and snatches up a piece of bacon, while Sienna goes straight for the coffee, taking a huge sip and then sighing as she drops into another chair.

With Sienna's mix of brown and blond hair, creamy

complexion, and bright blue eyes, she doesn't look the least bit related to her sister, Ellie, who has darker brown hair, olive skin, and emerald eyes. But as I watch them sip their coffees, butter their pastries, and munch on the crispy bacon, their mannerisms are very similar even if their appearances are different. Sienna has basically raised her sister, and while Ellie has a bit more sass to her—my guess is because even though Sienna might disagree, she's done a good job of providing a loving, stable home that's allowed Ellie to spread her wings—it's obvious they're close.

"Thanks for breakfast," Ellie mumbles around her bite of food.

"Any time," I tell her, taking a sip of my coffee. "There's a phone in the kitchen. Dial two-one-four and it will take you to room service. They'll deliver whatever you'd like and charge it to my account."

"Thank you," Sienna says, her eyes finally meeting mine. With caffeine now coursing through her veins, she looks more awake.

"They charge you at your own hotel?" Ellie asks.

"That's how business works," I say with a shake of my head. "Every item must be accounted for. Otherwise, the numbers won't add up. I don't own the hotel, Alexander Enterprises does."

Ellie nods in understanding.

"So, what's on the agenda?" Sienna asks.

"I was thinking the pool then the spa," Ellie answers. "Unless we can't leave here. Then the pool and a movie in the theater room. Wait, can the masseuses come here?" Her face lights up in excitement, and I laugh as Sienna glares her way.

"It's best to lay low this weekend," I tell her. "Let me see what I can do."

"Don't you have exams to study for?" Sienna says, sounding like a mom. The thought has me imagining her one day pregnant with my baby. The two of us filling this house with lots of kids, turning it into a home. She would make a damn good mother. She's kind and loving, selfless and strong, and fiercely protective of her sister.

I should probably be concerned at my train of thought, but it doesn't shock me in the slightest. Since the moment I laid eyes on Sienna, my feelings on relationships, marriage, and commitment have done a complete one-eighty. My dad always said that meeting Donna was a game changer. That the moment he met her he knew his life would never be the same. He could be cold and ruthless when it came to business, but the second he laid eyes on her, everything in him softened. I didn't get it, not until I met Sienna.

"Finc," Ellie says, bringing me back into the moment, "but after I study, I'm hitting the pool. Weekends are meant for relaxing, and since you can't go to work all weekend, you should join me."

Sienna's eyes widen, as if just remembering what day it is. Typically, she would've been working tonight and tomorrow night. But due to their current situation, that's no longer possible. No work equates to zero money coming in.

"Whatever you're thinking, stop," I say, reaching over and squeezing her hand. "I got you. Your safety comes first."

"I know but…" She releases a harsh breath and shakes her head. "Never mind."

"No, not never mind. Talk to me."

She stares at me for a long moment, as if she's warring with herself, trying to decide if she should keep that wall up or lower it enough to let me in. I sit quietly, waiting while she decides.

Then she sighs, her shoulders drop, and her eyes meet mine as she finally starts talking. I take that as a win—she's actually opening up and letting me in.

"I need to pay for my summer classes. I paid for Ellie's dance, thinking I would use my earnings from this week and next to pay for them, but now…" She shakes her head. "I can call and see if it's not too late for me to take out a loan for this semester."

"How much is it?" I ask.

"What? No, I can't let you—"

"Baby," I murmur, gently massaging the top of her hand. "Stop shutting me out. Let me help."

She lets out a shaky breath. "Okay, but I'll pay you back. Once we sort this all out and I can go back to work, I promise I'll pay you back."

There's no way in hell I'm letting her give me a cent, but I don't tell her that. My phone rings, and when I see it's Ricardo, I answer it.

"Boss," he says. "I've got an update."

Last night I had him and Bruno watch Sienna's place to see what would happen. About twenty minutes after we left, two guys showed up and burned the place to the ground. Then they torched her car and took off. When they told me what happened, I had them follow the two guys, hoping they would eventually lead us to the person who was responsible.

"Go on," I say, keeping it simple so I don't alert the girls. I need to figure out how to tell them that their home and vehicle, along with everything else they own, is all fucking gone. But before I do that, I need to get to the bottom of the situation. The asshole last night blamed Eleazar, but before I go off making accusations, I need more proof than that.

"They went home last night, but this morning, they went straight to Gutierrez's residence."

Fuck. If that's not proof, I don't know what is.

"And there's more," he adds.

"Go on."

"I spoke to my contact who confirmed the bounty on Sienna's head."

I met Ricardo several years back when he was working the streets. I was in Booker Park dealing with a situation that had gone bad and shit got real, very quickly. Had he not had my back, I'd be buried six feet under.

"And what about the other one?" I ask, silently referring to Ellie.

The girls eat quietly, both of them shooting nervous

glances my way, and I vow to do whatever I have to do to make sure they're both safe and taken care of.

"He said Gutierrez made it clear it's only for Sienna. His guess is that since her sister is barely more than a kid, he's leaving her out of it."

"Any idea why?"

"It appears that their mom is the one who killed Eduardo." *What the fuck?* "Word on the street is that she went there to fuck him and ended up drugging him instead. Gave him a heart attack that killed him. She also stole some drugs and a bit of money. Not surprisingly, Eleazer plans to make an example out of her. If whores think they can get away with that shit, it'll mess with the order of hierarchy. Since she's nowhere to be found, he's put a hit out for her daughter. Blood for blood."

Fuck, this is worse than I thought.

"Thanks. Keep me updated."

"What's going on?" Sienna asks before I've even pocketed my phone. "And please, don't lie to me."

I wasn't going to lie to her, but I also wasn't planning to tell her anything just yet. There's so much to all of this, I don't know where the hell to begin.

So I go with the least fucked up information first, hoping it will distract her from asking more questions until I can get this all sorted.

"Your house and car were torched."

"What?" Both girls gasp.

"All of our stuff is gone?" Ellie shrieks. "What about my clothes and shoes and…"

"Our pictures," Sienna whispers. "And my car? How will I get another one?" Tears fill her eyes. "Why?"

I go with the simplest answer. "To cover up killing Phil. It's the easiest way to cover up a murder."

"We're homeless," Sienna murmurs.

"Hey," I say, dragging her chair over and pulling her into my arms. "You guys are not homeless." I glance at Ellie. "It sucks that everything is gone, but you both are alive and safe here. I know the photos can't be replaced, but the clothes and car and other shit can be."

They both nod in agreement, but I can tell they're devastated and in shock. They didn't have much to begin with, and the little bit they did have is now all gone.

"Did you find out why they're after me?" Sienna asks.

"My guy has a theory, but I'll need to confirm it."

Normally this is when Sienna would argue, but she's too shaken by the loss of her home and vehicle, so she simply nods without argument instead.

"I'm going to take a shower," Sienna mutters, standing.

"I'm still kind of tired," Ellie says.

Both girls head upstairs, and I'm left feeling helpless. Up until now, I've never been in a situation before when I wasn't completely in control.

Speaking of which...I head into my office, which is soundproof, and I call the one person who has any control over this situation.

"Gutierrez," Eleazar says, when he answers my call.

"It's Micah Alexander."

"Micah, to what do I owe this phone call?"

"I need to speak to you about an important matter. I was hoping we could meet soon."

"I'm dealing with a few things at the moment, but how about Monday? Come to my place…Nine A.M."

"Will do. Thanks."

We hang up, and I glance at the time and see it's eight o'clock. This is when I usually leave for the office, but I don't think leaving Sienna and Ellie alone is the best idea. So, I pull out my phone and let my assistant know I won't be in until Tuesday and to only call if it's important.

She responds, asking if I'm okay since I never take that much time off, and I let her know I'm dealing with some personal shit and to clear my schedule.

I don't want the girls leaving since Sienna has a bounty on her damn head, but I need to do something to cheer them up, and as long as they're with me and my guards in this hotel, they'll be safe. So I decide to text the spa manager and schedule appointments for Sienna and Ellie for this morning, and then I put a call into my personal shopper, letting her know I need more of everything delivered, including a few cocktail dresses. Once she's confirmed she's on it, I make a reservation at the rooftop restaurant for tonight and invite my parents and Lincoln.

It's probably too soon for the whole meet-the-parents situation, but my mom is great about comforting others, and I know once I tell them what's going on, they'll be more than willing to meet us for dinner. Sienna might not think she has anyone, but she has me, which means she has a lot of people in her corner without even realizing it.

After I speak to my brother and parents, catching them up on everything, I head upstairs to try to cheer up the two women who have me feeling all sorts of shit I've never felt before.

I stop at Ellie's room first and knock since she's not in the shower.

"Come in," she says softly, not sounding at all like her usual sassy self.

When I open the door, I find her sitting on the bed, typing on her laptop. It looks expensive and new, and if I had to guess, it was probably one of the gifts her mom gave her.

"Spa appointment in one hour," I say, stepping inside.

"Thanks," she says, smiling half-heartedly. "I was just emailing my teachers so I can take my finals online."

I glance back to make sure Sienna isn't near before I say, "I know I can't replace everything you lost, but if there's anything in particular that can be replaced, please tell me, and I'll get it for you and your sister. We both know Sienna won't say shit, so I need you to speak up, please."

"Truthfully, we really didn't have all that much. I think it just sucks realizing it's possible to have even less."

"We'll get this sorted," I tell her. "I have an appointment with someone on Monday, but until then, I need you and your sister to lay low to ensure your safety."

The girls spend the morning at the spa—after I have to practically drag Sienna there—and when they return, I have clothes, shoes, undergarments, and toiletries in their respective rooms waiting for them.

"This was so sweet of you," Sienna says, closing the distance between us. "I don't know how I'll ever repay you for your generosity."

"Well, I can think of one way," I say with a smirk. When she rolls her eyes, thinking I'm referring to sex, I add, "Wear that dress without complaint." I jut my chin toward the simple black dress that's hanging on the corner of the mirror.

"Where in the world would I wear that?"

"To dinner with me...and my family."

Her eyes widen. "Micah," she hisses, but I cut her off by pressing my mouth to hers for a quick, chaste kiss. Her lips are soft, and she smells like roses, thanks to the oils the spa uses.

"Okay," she breathes when I end the kiss.

"Thank you."

She shakes her head and scoffs.

"What?" I ask, confused.

"You're thanking me for agreeing to go to dinner with you and your family when I'm the one who should be thanking you for everything you've done for me and my sister. You brought Ellie and me into your home after I was almost attacked and then insisted we stay when our apartment was torched, leaving us homeless. On top of that, you paid for a spa day to cheer us up and bought us a shit ton of clothes and other stuff...Oh, and you even offered to pay for my classes." Tears fill her eyes, and I encircle my arms around her, having a feeling all the pent-up stress is about to boil over.

"This is why I tried to give you an out over and over again," she chokes out. "You wanted to have sex in a private room and look what you got instead." She snorts out a humorless laugh, and I lift her chin, needing her to look at me.

"What I wanted...what I *want* is you. Anyway I can have you. And your *mess of a life* hasn't changed that."

"But don't you see?" she says. "My shitty circumstances took your choice away. What were you going to do? Leave us to die?"

"Everyone has a choice. I could've rented you a hotel room, or hell, I could've given you cash to go to a motel. I could've said fuck that, they're not my problem, and turned my back. I'm choosing to have you and your sister here. I want to get to know you, Hellcat, and before all this shit went down you were on board as well."

"I was," she admits. "It just feels selfish, putting me and you before Ellie's safety, or putting you on the backburner..."

"There are no placeholders," I say, kissing her tear-stained lips. "We're all in this together. You can have it all if you'd just lower those walls you've erected and let me in all the way. I know what's happening between us is fast, but I can't deny what I feel...what I *know* you feel too."

I sear my gaze into hers, willing her to accept that there's something between us that's worth exploring. To stop holding me at a distance and to let me stand by her side. To stop trying to go through this life alone when we can go through it together.

"I do," she breathes. "I do feel it, and it scares the shit out of me." She releases a harsh breath, her eyes fluttering closed and then open. "Okay, I'll let you in. But we need to take things slow."

"Slow," I agree, mentally fist bumping the air because she's actually giving in and giving us a chance. "We can take things as slow as you want."

# Fifteen

## SIENNA

"Oh, look at you," Donna gushes. "You're even more beautiful than Micah described." Micah and Lincoln's mom pulls me into a warm embrace, and I can't help returning it. Lenora has never been motherly, but when my grandmother was alive, this is how she'd hug me whenever she came to visit.

Donna is a beautiful woman with dark brown eyes and shoulder-length brown hair that has honey-colored highlights mixed in. She's clearly had some work done like most wealthy women, but it's tasteful and makes her look a good decade younger than her age.

"And you must be Ellie," Donna says, pulling back and taking my sister into her arms. "I've heard all about you," she adds with a twinkle in her eye, telling me either

Micah or Lincoln has filled her in on my sassy teenage sister.

"It's nice to meet you," Ellie says politely. She's dressed in a floral, knee-length dress that makes her look sweet and innocent—which is exactly the look we were going for—it's bad enough I'm a stripper at the club their sons own. (And yes, I'm well aware it sounds ridiculous that they would judge me for working at the establishment their children own, but double standards are a thing for a reason.)

"It's lovely to meet you," Micah's dad, Michael, says, leaning over and giving both me and Ellie a chaste kiss to our cheeks. When he smiles gently at me, he reminds me of Micah, especially when a single dimple pops out, identical to his son's. His face is a bit scruffier with grey hairs speckled throughout, but I have no doubt this is what Micah will look like when he's older.

"Sorry I'm late," Lincoln says, strolling in. "The favorite has arrived. We can eat now."

Donna laughs and gives him a hug, then we all find our seats. Since Micah doesn't want to risk me going out in public, we're eating dinner in a private room at The Lounge, one of the restaurants in the hotel.

I sit in between Ellie and Micah, and Donna and Michael sit on the other side with Lincoln sitting across from Ellie. I say a prayer that she doesn't spend the meal drooling over him, but to be on the safe side, I lean slightly forward to make eye contact with Ellie, who just rolls her eyes, knowing exactly what I'm silently trying to convey without having to say a word.

"So, Sienna," Donna says, "I heard you're a dancer."

I still in my spot. Apparently, we're going to lay all the cards out on the table now without any sort of small talk.

But before I can open my mouth to confirm what she already knows—that I'm a stripper at Wanderlust—she adds, "I drag my husband to see the ballet everywhere we travel, but I would have to say Milan and London are my favorites."

"Sienna's an amazing dancer," Ellie jumps in. "She was accepted to New York University, Julliard, Dominican University, all with a full scholarship," she gushes. "And on top of that, she was invited to join several dance companies, including the American Dance Company."

"That's amazing," Donna says. "My body could never move like that." Her eyes comically widen and she giggles. "But I love watching the ballet."

"I'm going to New York University," Ellie says. "I haven't gotten in yet, but I will."

"That's a great goal," Donna says with a smile. "And will you dance for a company?"

"No, I don't want a career as a professional dancer— that was our mom's dream. When she got pregnant, she lost both her dream and her job. Sienna's dad was injured...same thing, no job. Our dream is to open our own dance studio one day. Right, Sienna?"

Ellie glances my way and I nod, refusing to let the tears that are burning behind my lids fall. I'm happy that my sister has goals and that she loves me enough to want to open a studio together, but she's too young to understand that it would take years to get the money needed to open a studio. My goal is to get Ellie to college. And once she's a little older, she'll be able to understand how loans and business actually work.

"It'll happen," Micah leans over and says, his hand squeezing the top of my pantyhose-covered thigh. I'm wearing a cute lilac, off-the-shoulder mini dress that lands a few inches above my knees when I'm standing, but once I sat down it rode up several inches.

"What?" I murmur, distracted by the way his thumb is now massaging circles into my flesh.

"Opening your own dance studio. One day it'll happen."

I swallow thickly, realizing that while I thought I was doing a decent job of hiding my pain, Micah could see right through me. I'm not used to anyone paying such close attention to my words and actions, reading my thoughts and feelings.

The rest of the meal goes smoothly. We flit from one topic to the next, and not once does either of Micah's parents say or imply a single negative thing about Ellie or me. By the time we're finishing up coffee and dessert and Lincoln is saying he needs to head to the club—and how he's looking forward to the manager returning from his honeymoon so he can have his social life back—Donna is making Ellie and me promise we'll get together soon for lunch.

"It's weird being home on a Friday night," I say to

Micah once we're back at his place. Ellie has already excused herself to her room, probably anxious to gossip with her friends on the phone. "I'm so used to working I don't even know what to do with myself."

Micah chuckles. "What would you be doing if you didn't have to work and you weren't stuck here?"

I think for a moment, then laugh. "I don't know. I've been working pretty much every weekend since I turned fifteen." Whether it was at the diner or the strip club, both of those places brought in the most money on the weekends, so the tips were really good. "And if I'm not working, I'm studying or taking care of Ellie." I start school on Monday, but with everything going on, I switched my in-school classes to online, which works out for the best since I really didn't want to leave Ellie alone.

"Pretend," Micah says, leaning against the island and tugging on the front of my dress so I'm rubber banded into him. "Close your eyes." I do as he says. "It's Friday night and you can do whatever you want. Where are you and what are you doing?"

An image pops into my head, and I share it with Micah as I visualize it. "I'm out with my friends, drinking." Mind you, I've lost touch with the majority of my friends, most of whom have been living it up while I've been working two jobs, going to school, and caring for my teenage sister. "We've gotten dressed up, complete with full-on makeup, and we're downtown club hopping, dancing... just for fun. We're drinking and laughing and having a good time." I open my eyes to find Micah looking at me with a soft smile splayed across his face.

"Well, we can't leave here, so the club is out, but..." He walks over to a cabinet and pulls out a bottle of liquor and then presses something on the wall. Music instantly starts playing, the sound of Ed Sheeran singing about having conversations with strangers filling the space. "We're dressed up, we have music and alcohol..." He scoops the arm that's not holding the bottle around my waist and pulls me into him. "And if it means I get to touch you, I'm down for dancing."

"You're crazy," I say, trying to sound serious, only the giggle that escapes past my lips tells him otherwise.

He releases me and grabs two shot glasses, then he takes my hand in his and guides us outside by the pool—the music continuing to play even out here.

Setting the glasses down, he opens the bottle and pours us each a double shot and hands me one.

"Should we toast?" I half joke.

"Would you toast at the club?" he asks.

I nod. "To good liquor, good music, and—"

"Great fucking company," Micah finishes for me.

We throw our shots back and then he pours us another...and then another. After my insides are nice and warm, he pulls me into his arms and I go willingly, snaking my arms around his neck. The song playing is upbeat, similar to what you'd hear at any club, and I let myself go, rubbing my body against Micah's like I would if we were actually there and out on the dance floor having fun.

It should feel awkward since it's only the two of us and

we're not actually at a club, but it doesn't. With the busy city below us, and the twinkling stars above, it simply feels nice. It feels good to let loose and have a moment where nothing else exists—not the strip club or my mom or the bounty on my head. I'm just a twenty-four-year-old woman having a good time with a guy I'm attracted to.

When I twirl around, giving him my back, his hands glide up my sides as I back up and grind my ass against his groin. I can't help but notice he's hard...very hard.

I reach out and grab the bottle from the outdoor kitchen island, pour us each a messy shot, then down mine before handing him his. He throws it back, then sets it down.

Gripping the curve of my hip, he turns me back around and pushes me against the wall. My fingers trail up his muscular torso and pecks, while he pushes my legs apart, his knee finding my center.

Our eyes meet, our gazes clash, and then our mouths collide. This kiss isn't gentle like the last time. It's filled with passion and lust and want. Our tongues stroke and swirl around one another. His hand palms the side of my face, deepening the kiss. I suck on his tongue, getting drunk off his taste, as his hands glide down my body until he's palming the globes of my ass.

With our mouths connected, he lifts me into his arms, my legs circling around his waist, and walks us over to the island, setting me down. We continue to kiss, taste, devour each other, but it's not enough. I want...no, I *need* more.

I push myself forward and grind my center against the bulge in his pants, creating the best kind of friction. I've kissed guys before, but I've never gone any further than that. Micah backs up slightly, and for a second, I assume he doesn't want to take things any further, but then he spreads my thighs and slides his fingers under my dress and over my pantyhose. He rubs his finger along my center, and when he touches my clit—even through the material of my pantyhose and panties—it feels so good, I let out a loud moan that he swallows down with a plundering kiss.

"You want me to make you feel good?" he murmurs against my lips.

"Yes," I breathe.

"You sure?" he asks, pulling back slightly. I wonder why he's asking, until he says, "We've been drinking, Hellcat. I don't want to do anything you'll regret once you're sober." And just like that, my heart swells in my chest that he cares enough to ask, to make sure.

"I'm sure," I tell him, nowhere near drunk enough to regret any decision I make. "Please make me feel good."

"You got it," he says, then his mouth is back on mine—tasting, licking, devouring. His fingers press into me, but the material he encounters halts his access. And before I can lift so he can remove them, he rips a hole into my pantyhose, shoves my panties to the side, and pushes his fingers into me. I'm so wet, they slide right in.

"Fuck, you're so tight," he mutters. "One day, after

we're married, I'm going to fuck this tight cunt, baby, stretch it out and mold it to the size of my cock. But until then, I'll be gentle."

His words should probably scare me. I mean the guy's talking about marriage...*marriage!* But my brain is too caught up on the part about him fucking me, and my body is lost to the way he's curling his fingers inside of me and rubbing my vaginal walls. I've used small dildos and vibrators to get off plenty of times, but none of them have ever made me feel like this.

His thumb pushes against my clit, and it's my undoing. My walls clench around his fingers, my legs shake, and when his mouth crashes down on mine, swallowing my moans, stars—bright and colorful—explode behind my lids as I come harder than I've ever come in my life.

He doesn't stop coaxing every ounce of pleasure from my body until I gently push him back, my sex sensitive, my body satiated.

When I open my eyes, I find him smiling softly at me.

"What?" I murmur, still trying to catch my breath.

"You look so beautiful when you come." He leans forward and presses his lips to mine, and I sigh into him, not wanting the moment to end.

Without thought, I reach between us and squeeze his hard length, making it clear what I want. He groans into my mouth and I—

"Oh, shit! My bad."

Ellie's voice has Micah pulling back and spinning around. I wonder why he's standing in front of me until

I realize my dress is up around my waist. Shit! I pull it down quickly and close my legs, pushing him forward slightly.

"Sorry about that," Ellie says with a knowing smirk.

Oh. My. God. How could I forget that Micah and I weren't alone? I wasn't lying when I said I wasn't drunk enough to regret any decisions I made tonight, but I obviously drank enough to forget that my fifteen-year-old sister was here.

"I was just going to ask if you guys wanted to watch a movie with me, but please"—she grins like a Cheshire cat, and I want to die—"carry on."

"A movie sounds great," I say, my voice squeaking at the end.

"Yeah," Micah agrees. "Let me just…" He clears his throat. "I just need to take a quick shower and then I'll meet you guys in the theater room."

He takes off inside, and I feel bad that he's totally going to have to rub one out since I got him all worked up and then left him hanging. I'm torn between following after Micah, staying to talk to Ellie about what she just walked in on, and running to my room to hide.

"Poor guy," Ellie says. "He looked like he was in pain."

"Ellie!" I hiss.

"What? I'm fifteen not five. I know what a guy looks like when he's been cockblocked. Maybe you should… I don't know… go help him out."

"Eliza Bardot! Not another word."

"Fine, fine." She raises her hands. "But for what it's

worth, I'm happy for you."

Her comment catches me off guard. "Happy for me?"

"Yeah," she says with a smile. "Micah is a good guy. I thought for sure you'd push him away, but I'm glad you came to your senses and are giving him a chance. You deserve to be happy."

My throat clogs with emotion and tears burn behind my lids. "Thank you." I jump off the counter and walk over to her, wrapping my arms around her for a hug. "You know you'll always come first, though, right?" I need her to know that regardless of me seeing where things go with Micah, she'll always be my priority. She might be cool with us dating, but I still need her to know, she'll always come first.

"Well, duh," she says, laughing lightly. "But in three years I'm leaving for college, so it makes me happy to know you won't be alone. I mean, I won't be far, only in the city." She shrugs. "But I'll be living in a dorm and won't see you every day."

Oh, this child...when the hell did she grow up?

"C'mon, sweet girl, let's go watch that movie."

"Or you can join Micah in the shower and help him out."

Oh, this girl...I'm going to kill her. Or..."I think it's time we have the talk."

"What talk?" she asks, pulling back and eyeing me suspiciously.

"The sex talk."

"Sigh, I'll never get tired of watching this movie," Ellie says, when the credits for Twilight start to rise to the top of the screen.

When she picked the movie and Micah agreed to watch it— despite me trying to convince him otherwise—I figured we were in for a boring two hours. But little did I know that watching a movie with Micah would be anything but boring.

He plopped onto the couch, dropping a blanket over us, and spent the entire movie feeling on me. Touching me just enough to turn me on but steering clear of the parts that would send me soaring. Halfway through the movie, I was so turned on I had to excuse myself to use the bathroom because I was so freaking wet. And when I returned, the sexy quirk of his lips told me he knew exactly what he was doing to me.

I wanted to get him back, to rub on him to the point where he'd be just as turned on and uncomfortable as he'd made me, but I fought the urge to do so. I knew I couldn't finish what I started, and I'd already left him hanging once today thanks to Ellie interrupting us.

"What's on the agenda for tomorrow?" Ellie asks, as we head out of the theater and toward the stairs. It's late and I'm beyond exhausted. How has it only been twenty-four hours since our lives imploded? In that short span of time, I was nearly attacked, we found Phil dead in our apartment, and after taking temporary refuge in Micah's penthouse, we learned that our home and car had been torched, leaving us with nothing. To top things off, there's a million-dollar bounty on my head!

"Nothing," I tell her. "We have to lay low."

"We can still do stuff," she says with a pout. "What about a pool day? We could order some floats for the pool and buy stuff to make fruity drinks and get pool snacks. It would be fun!" She glances at Micah, hopeful, and he chuckles.

"Sounds good. Make a list and I'll have everything on it delivered tomorrow morning."

I mock glare at him, and he shrugs. "It's okay to say no to her, you know," I tell him.

"No it's not," Ellie disagrees, stopping in front of her door. "Okay, well, it's been fun, but I'm just gonna go to bed now with my earbuds in my ears…They're noise canceling, so I can't hear anything." She shoots us an exaggerated wink and I groan. "So, if you guys wanted to…I don't know…pick up where you left off, you won't be interrupted."

Micah chuckles and looks at me with a smirk. "That's not happening," I say to him, reaching up and giving him a kiss on his cheek. "Good night." I glance at Ellie. "Both of you."

"Sorry, man," she says to Micah as she opens her door. "I tried."

# Sixteen

## MICAH

"I think you're starting to burn. I could put some sunscreen on you if you want." I run my finger down Sienna's arm, and she slowly turns her face toward me, popping one eye open to glare at me. We've spent the day at the pool, just as Ellie wanted, complete with fruity drinks—virgin for Ellie, alcoholic for Sienna, and scotch for me—and plenty of food to snack on. I can't remember the last time I've lounged anywhere all day, let alone by the pool, but I can see the appeal. Despite my phone blowing up, I've fielded the majority of the calls to my assistant or replied that I would be back in the office Tuesday. It's nice to just…relax.

"Something tells me you're only using that as an excuse to rub on me." She rolls to her side, and I do the same. We're lying in the double lounger while Ellie floats around in an oversized donut, listening to her music that's blasting in her earbuds.

"That's definitely part of it," I admit, reaching out and grabbing the globe of her ass so I can tug her closer to me.

"I was thinking about you last night," she murmurs, dragging the tip of her pink-polished nail down my shirtless chest. The entire day has been the best and worst form of torture. From the tiny—and I mean fucking tiny—string bikini she's sporting, to the way she's been not-so-innocently touching me all day. Playfully feeding me during lunch, hanging onto me while we lounge in the pool, and snuggling up into my side while we took a nap on the lounge chairs earlier this afternoon.

"What were you thinking about?" I ask, nipping at her finger when she drags it up to my face and runs it along the seam of my lips.

"I feel bad that I got off and you were left...unsatisfied." She glances up at me through her lashes and my stomach knots at how much I want this woman. I've only known Sienna for a short time, but she's quickly begun to mean so much to me. Before her, settling down wasn't on my radar, but now, I can't stop thinking about what it would be like to have her as my wife, to bear my children, to live with me here. I love sharing my home with her and Ellie. It's only been a couple of days, but I already dread the thought of them moving out once everything is resolved.

"Watching and hearing you as you came all over my fingers was plenty satisfying," I tell her honestly. Sure, I look forward to the day when I can bury my cock into her tight cunt and be with her completely, but until then, I'll take her anyway I can have her. I love that she's a virgin… that she's waiting for someone worthy of both her heart and body before giving that part of herself away.

But I imagine much of her trepidation stems from her mom's indiscriminate behavior as it pertains to men, having witnessed firsthand the ensuing fallout when you give of yourself too freely. I hate how it's negatively affected her, but despite her circumstances, she's proven herself to be so damn strong, and she's raising her sister to be the same way. I have no doubt they could take the world by storm if given the chance. And my hope—*my goal*—is to be there every step of the way, cheering them on as they do it.

"Still," she says softly, so her sister can't overhear. "Maybe tonight, once Ellie's asleep, I can sneak into your room so we can finish what we started."

"I'm sunburned and hungry," Ellie yells, making Sienna and I separate. "I'm going to take a shower. Feel free to carry on."

Sienna rolls her eyes. "Actually, I think I'm kind of hungry too. After I shower, we'll figure out what we're going to do for dinner."

"DAMN, SMELLS GOOD." AFTER TAKING A SHOWER AND then spending some time in my office to handle a few time-sensitive matters, I came out looking for the girls and found the table set up with food from one of the hotel restaurants. Candles were lit and music was playing in the background, creating a romantic ambiance.

"Oh, hell yes, I'm starved," Sienna moans, plopping into a seat that has a covered plate of food in front of it. She lifts the lid. "This smells delicious." She leans in and inhales deeply. "What is this?"

I sit across from her and lift the cover of my plate. "Crab and lobster stuffed shrimp. It's from Shells, one of the restaurants in the hotel."

Sienna takes a bite and moans, and even though it's in response to the food, my dick still takes notice since it sounds a whole lot like the sound she made when I got her off last night by the pool.

While we eat, we make casual conversation about school, work, Ellie's dance, and how nice my parents are. I've lived here for the past four years, yet it's the first time I've ever had dinner at this table with a woman. It's nice... natural. But then again, everything regarding Sienna feels genuine, not forced. Having her here just feels *right*. Anytime I imagined a woman moving in, I'd freak out, picturing them taking over the place, their shit being everywhere, and being forced to pay attention to them when I needed to focus on business. But with Sienna, I find myself wanting that. I was only working in my office for less than an hour when I stopped what I was doing to go in search of her.

When we're both stuffed, she leans back and sighs.

"That was freaking good. Thank you. Keep it up and you just might convince me that you're husband material after all." She winks playfully and I chuckle. But then, something hits me...

"Wait, I didn't order this food."

She glances around. "You didn't do this? The food, the candles... the music?"

"No..."

We stare at each other for several seconds before we both say "Ellie" at the same time.

"That girl." Sienna shakes her head.

"Hey, you can't be too mad. The food was good, the ambience was on point, and I got the chance to enjoy a nice meal with you."

"I know, but she shouldn't be sticking her nose where it doesn't belong." She gets up and walks toward the stairs, and I follow after. "Ellie! You can come out now."

When it remains quiet, aside from the music, Sienna's features morph into concern. "Eliza!" Nothing.

She glances back at me and then ascends the stairs, two at a time. She swings open Ellie's door and finds the room empty. While she checks the bathroom, I'm already pulling my phone out and clicking on my security system app.

Fuck. She opened the door twice. Not good. I click on the camera and rewind and sure enough, she's accepting the food brought up by the restaurant and then heads out a few minutes later.

Not good. Not fucking good at all.

"Oh my God," Sienna cries, glancing at my phone. "She left? How did I just enjoy an entire meal without realizing my sister was gone? This is exactly why I told you I can't date. She has to be my priority. What if someone takes her?"

As I'm dialing security, the alarm sounds, indicating my front door has been opened. A second later, Ellie's voice rings out. "You better be careful. The last time I snuck up on them they were—

"Yo, Bro," Lincoln yells, cutting Ellie off. Sienna and I both rush to the top of the stairs and find Lincoln and Ellie in the doorway. "Missing something?" he asks, pushing Ellie inside the foyer.

"Oh, thank God!" Sienna flies down the stairs and pulls her sister into a hug. "Where were you?" Before Ellie can answer, she turns toward Lincoln and asks, "Where did you find her?"

"She convinced Bruno to let her into my place," Lincoln says dryly. "I was in the shower getting ready to go to the club. Came out and she was sitting on my couch."

"Ellie!" Sienna hisses.

"What?" Ellie scoffs. "It's not like I was naked or anything. I was just trying to give you two some quiet time to make up for walking in on you guys last night."

Lincoln chuckles. "I gotta run."

"Thank you," Sienna says. "I'm so sorry. This won't happen again."

"It's all good," Lincoln says with a small grin. He

reaches out and ruffles Ellie's hair playfully, which has her glaring his way. "Try to stay out of trouble, kid."

"I'm not a kid," Ellie yells as he closes the door behind him.

"Yes, you are," Sienna says with a glare. "And now you're a grounded kid. Phone." She extends her hand and Ellie gasps.

"Seriously?"

"Seriously," Sienna says in a stern voice, reminding me of my mom when she would punish us.

Ellie rolls her eyes but drops it into her sister's palm. "Try to do something nice and end up grounded. So ridiculous," she mumbles, as she stomps up the stairs. A few seconds later, her door clicks shut, and it's just Sienna and me, alone again.

"I'm sorry," she says with a sigh. "I'll try to keep her under control while we're here."

"Hey." I snake my arm around her waist and pull her into me. "I think your sister is pretty fucking awesome. I mean, she's the reason I finally got to take you out on a date. She's clearly team Micah." I shrug, and Sienna snorts out a laugh. "Besides, with Ellie in her room for the night, I get to have you all to myself." I press my lips to hers, loving that I can do that and she won't push me away.

"Nice try," she says dryly. "But my dear sister never ate dinner. Which means, she'll be coming out at some point, bored and complaining that she's starved, and I'll be damned if she catches me in a compromising position *again.*"

# Seventeen

## MICAH

"Micah."

My lids snap open, and I sit up quickly, instinctually reaching for the gun I keep in my bedside table. But when my eyes adjust, I find Sienna standing in the doorway. She's wearing a tiny pink silk tank top and even tinier matching shorts, the light from somewhere outside of my room making her glow like a goddamn angel.

"What's wrong?" I ask, trying and failing to ignore the way her pebbled nipples are poking through the thin material of her top.

"Nothing," she says, her voice cracking. "I was just…" She sucks her bottom lip into her mouth, and I'm momentarily distracted. Between being half-asleep and her looking like a walking wet dream, it takes me a second to focus. But once I do, I get the impression she's nervous about something.

"Come here." I nod toward my bed for her to join me. Clearly she needs to talk to me, otherwise, she wouldn't be coming into my room at—I tap the screen on my phone—two in the morning.

She closes the door behind her, and the room goes dark with only the lights from the city peeking in through the slats. "What's going on?" I ask, once she's seated on the edge of my bed. "Is Ellie okay?"

"Yeah, yeah. Everything's fine. Ellie's asleep."

"Okay, then—"

My words get stuck in my throat when she reaches out and palms my cock. It's soft since I was asleep, but with her squeezing it, it wakes up instantly.

"I was hoping we could pick up where we left off," she says softly, releasing me and crawling onto the bed. My legs are already spread, and she settles between them. "I've never done this before. Well, I did once… kind of… to my high school boyfriend. He shoved my head down and then I threw up in my mouth. I broke up with him right after."

Not exactly the visual I want in my head, but I like that she's honest with me. That she feels she can talk to me about the hard shit.

"You don't have to do this," I tell her, needing her to know that she always has a choice. I've accepted we're going at her pace, and I'm okay with that because I believe the wait will be worth the reward. *And the reward is Sienna being mine forever.*

"I know," she says, "but I want to. Until you, I never trusted someone enough to be intimate with them, but you've proven to be trustworthy. The few guys I've dated never put me first, but when we were out by the pool, your only focus was on my pleasure, and now I want to focus on yours."

She reaches for the waistband of my sweats and pulls them down along with my boxer briefs. Then she looks at my cock, assessing it. It's at half-mast and laying against my stomach. I shift myself upward so I can watch her easier. She follows my movements, her tongue peeking out and running along the seam of her lips like she's hungry for me. She glances up at me momentarily, her blue eyes hooded with lust, and then drops her eyes back down as she wraps her fingers around my shaft. At her touch, it starts to swell, and when she dips her head and licks the tip, it grows even bigger and harder.

She licks me several times like it's a fucking lollipop and then opens her mouth wide, taking me all the way in until her nose is nestled in the neatly trimmed pubes that surround my cock.

I know she wants to give me pleasure, but I can't help it when I reach out and tweak one of her nipples through the thin material of her tank. They're there and hard and begging to be touched. Sienna groans around my hard shaft causing my hips to buck slightly in response.

"Shit, sorry," I murmur, not wanting her to think I'm just like that self-absorbed pubescent boy she dated all those years ago.

She sucks harder in response, taking my sac between her delicate fingers and massaging it, clearly knowing what she's doing.

I lift her by her ponytail and her mouth pops off my dick. "Where did you learn to suck cock?" I ask, because if she's fucking with me and is actually experienced, we're going to have a damn problem. I've seen women pull that bullshit, thinking it's cute and sexy and will turn a guy on, but I didn't take Sienna for someone who would play those kinds of games.

"I...I've listened to the women at Wanderlust talk... and...I've watched some porn." She sucks her bottom lip into her mouth, then releases it. "Does it feel good, what I'm doing?"

"So damn good," I tell her. Then, because her swollen lips are like a damn beacon, I pull her up my body and kiss her hard, needing to taste her, not giving a shit that her mouth was just wrapped around my dick.

"I wasn't done yet," she murmurs against my mouth. She backs up and lifts my shirt over my head, then presses her warm, soft lips to my collarbone. She works her way back down, trailing fiery kisses all over my flesh, paying special attention to the happy trail that leads to my dick.

When she's back to where she started, she goes to town on my cock, sucking and licking and massaging my ballsac, never letting up. It's not long before I'm warning her that I'm about to come, but she only takes me deeper, sucks harder, causing me to swear to fucking Christ as I come down her throat harder than I've ever come in my life. It takes everything in me not to beg this woman to marry me right here, right now. Because after experiencing her mouth around my cock, I can't even imagine what it will feel like when I get to fuck her tight little cunt.

"WHILE I'M GONE, I NEED YOU BOTH TO STAY HERE." I glance at Ellie. "If you leave, I can't protect you."

I have an early meeting with Eleazar, and I have no idea how it's going to go, but what I do know is that he's not touching a hair on Sienna or Ellie's head. I don't care what it fucking takes, I'll make sure to protect them.

"I'm scared," Sienna admits, and I pull her into my arms, rubbing her back and neck comfortingly. After Sienna gave me a mind-blowing orgasm, I made her come twice before we fell asleep. It was the third time I've fallen asleep and woken up with a woman in my bed. The first two times I was a bit younger, and I freaked out both times. But as I watched Sienna snuggled into my side, her head resting in the crook of my arm, there was no freaking out because I knew I wanted this   wanted her— for the rest of my life. And I'll do everything in my power to keep both her and her sister safe.

"I have two guys standing outside, and I'm going to set the alarm when—"

"Not for us," Sienna says. "For you."

I stop my movements and stare at her, momentarily

taken aback. In the life we live, I'm used to the danger, to the risk that comes with doing the type of business we do...work with the type of people we work with. Aside from my mom, I've never let another woman get close enough to worry about me.

"I'm going to be just fine," I assure her. "I'm going to talk to the guy who's put the bounty on your head and clear everything up." I kiss the corner of her mouth. "Don't worry. Go swimming, lay out by the pool with your sister, watch a movie. I'll be back soon."

Twenty minutes later, I'm standing in what was once Eduardo's office, shaking hands with his son, Eleazar. "What can I do for you?" he asks, offering me a drink.

Not wanting to offend him, I nod and thank him for the drink purely out of respect. "I'm here to speak to you about a personal matter."

He raises a single brow, gesturing for me to continue. Growing up, Eleazar and I went to the same private school, hung out with the same circle of people. We were friends. But just after graduation, his brother was killed, and Eleazar left unexpectedly to take over his part of the family business in Mexico. Soon after, he met his wife and never returned...until now.

"It's been brought to my attention that you have a bounty on Sienna Bardot's head."

Eleazar takes a sip of his drink and sits, setting the glass down and clasping his hands together in front of him. "Her whore of a mother killed my father, stole his money and drugs."

"I've heard, but she shouldn't be held responsible for her mother's actions."

"Blood for blood," he says simply.

"So, it's only Sienna you're after?"

He chuckles. "If you're asking if I've put a bounty on the child's head, no. Children are off limits, even for monsters such as myself." He smirks, and I sigh in relief.

I take a sip of my drink and set it down, then lean forward, locking eyes with Eleazar. "Your father died owing me a debt, and I'm here to collect."

## EIGHTEEN YEARS AGO

"I gotta go. If I'm not home by dinner, my mom's gonna kill me." I jump on my bike and take off down the street toward our house. As I'm crossing the street, I notice two men grabbing a woman, her body flailing in an effort to get away. When I look closer, I see it's not just any woman. It's Marta Gutierrez, the wife of Eduardo Gutierrez, one of the most dangerous crime bosses in Tesoro. Because he does business with my dad, we've had dinner with them a few times, and I'm also friends with Eleazar, their son.

I don't know what possesses me to do it, but instead of minding my own business like my dad taught me to do, I follow the car that leads to a dark alley where they drag Marta Gutierrez out. She's kicking and screaming, so one of the guys slaps her across the face. "Shut the fuck up, bitch. Save the screaming for when I'm fucking your ass."

I should probably call my dad, ask him what I should do, but something tells me this woman won't be alive long enough to save if I don't act soon.

I watch as one of the guys turns around to make a phone call. Then I make my move. With the baseball bat I was still carrying after playing ball at the park with my friends, I come up behind the guy and hit him across the head with it. He falls to the ground, and I quickly grab his gun, aim it at his head, and pull the trigger. Then I aim for the other guy and do the same. My dad taught us how to shoot a gun at a very young age, so I have no problem taking out both guys. Assuming it's over, I'm about to lower the gun when the door they were dragging Marta toward swings open and a guy steps outside to see what's going on. Before he can wield his weapon, I fire the gun, hitting him directly between the eyes.

"C'mon, let's go," I say to Marta, pulling her into the car. I grab the keys from the dead guy, and we take off to her house.

When we arrive, she insists I come in. When she tells Mr. Gutierrez what happened—that had I not shown up when I did, they would've raped and killed her—he shakes my hand and says, "I owe you, son. One debt to be repaid any time, no questions asked."

"You saved my *mom's* life. And you think it's equivalent to saving that bitch's life?" Eleazar spits. I ignore him calling Sienna a bitch since it wouldn't do anyone any good to start a war over name calling.

"You seem to have taken a special interest in this girl. Who is she to you?" he asks. "Your wife? Your lover? Your daughter?"

When I shake my head, he shrugs as if that's all he needs to know. "That deal was done with my father, not me. And maybe I would consider honoring it if she was someone of any real significance, but she's *no one*. She's not worthy of being spared." He shakes his head. "I'm sorry, Micah, but no deal. She and her mother are dead."

Because I'm not on a suicide mission, I stand and shake his hand, thanking him for his time. I head out knowing exactly what I need to do, certain that Sienna isn't going to be happy about it at all.

Before I go home, I stop by my parents' place to talk to my dad. He's been the man I've looked up to my entire life, and I trust his opinion. I already know what I'm planning to do, but I still want to hear what he thinks.

"Son, nice of you to stop by," Dad says. "Business or pleasure?"

"A bit of both," I say with a light laugh.

"Can you bring us some fresh pastries and coffee, please?" Dad asks Adeline, the woman who's been running the house for the past thirty years. She cooks, cleans, and when Lincoln and I were younger, she was like a nanny to us, making sure we were taken care of when Mom and

Dad were busy.

"Of course," she says with a smile.

He gestures for me to have a seat on the couch in his office, and we make light conversation until after the food and drinks have arrived and we're left alone.

"I'm going to ask Sienna to marry me."

Dad chokes on his coffee. "Don't you think it's a little soon for that? I know you care for her but—"

"I'm in love with her," I admit. "And if I don't marry her, Gutierrez is going to kill her. I can't let that happen."

"That's a lot of info in one sentence. I think you're going to need to start from the beginning."

I explain how quickly I've come to care about Sienna and how I know she's the one. I can feel it in my heart and soul. When we kiss and touch, the way I crave her all the time. I tell him all about the life she and Ellie have had to endure. And then I go on to explain what her mom has done and how it's fallen down into Sienna's lap.

"And you believe by marrying her it will stop Eleazar from killing her?"

"I believe it's my only shot. He practically told me as much. If I go to him with a marriage certificate, I think he'll agree to call off the bounty. His father owed me a debt, and while Eleazar won't be happy about it, I trust he'll call it even."

"And what about Sienna's mother?"

"I don't give a fuck about that woman. She made her choices and fuck her for running and leaving her daughters to deal with the fallout. From what Sienna and her sister have said, she's done nothing but hurt them their entire lives. It ends now."

Dad nods in understanding. "You know you always have your mother's and my support."

After talking with my dad, I call my mom into his office and tell her what needs to be done. She hates that Sienna is going to be forced to do something she doesn't want, but she understands that it's our only shot at saving her life.

"I would love to help plan the wedding," Mom offers.

"It'll have to be quick. I can't chance someone getting to her before we're married and Eleazar *hopefully* agrees to call off the bounty. I'm thinking this weekend...maybe Friday?"

"We can make it happen."

"And what if Eleazar doesn't agree?" Dad asks the question I've been thinking about since the solution came to me.

"Then I'll find another way," I tell him. *Even if it means I have to end his life.* Any enemy of Sienna's is an enemy of mine, and I won't stop until she's safe.

# Eighteen

## SIENNA

"No. No. No. No. This is *not* how it's supposed to go." I back away from Micah as tears fill my lids.

"How what is supposed to go?" he asks gently, looking at me like I'm a rabid animal ready to attack. When he got home, I could tell something was wrong. His hair was a mess like he'd been running his fingers through it repeatedly, and the look on his face was as if someone had died. When his eyes met mine, I could see the sympathy and sorrow in his gaze. I thought he was going to tell me I needed to pay back the money or run. What I didn't expect was that he was going to tell me that the only solution is to get married.

"Falling in love," I choke out, answering his question. "I was supposed to wait. I have goals. Get my sister and me out of this hellhole and get her off to college before that happens."

"Falling in love?" he asks, trying to follow along with my hysteria.

"Yes! I'm not supposed to make the same mistakes my mom made," I cry out. "I'm supposed to meet a man who *chooses* to be with me, who *chooses* to love me and marry me." My sobs increase and the tears blur my vision. "He'll wear a sharp black tux, and I'll wear a beautiful white dress, and when he says, 'I do' it'll be because he loves me and wants me and *chooses* to spend forever with me… not because it's the only way to save my life."

Micah steps toward me carefully and I shake my head, not wanting him near me. "You said you wouldn't force me. You said you wanted it to be my choice! You lied."

"I *am* choosing you," he argues, bridging the gap between us. He palms the sides of my face and wipes the tears that are sliding down my cheeks. "I love you, Sienna. I've fallen so fucking hard for you. This isn't how I wanted to say the words. It's not how I wanted this all to go. But I swear to you… this is me, *choosing you*." He kisses my lips softly, and for some reason. it only makes me cry harder. "I'm choosing to save you, Hellcat. Please, let me save you."

"No." I shake my head. "No. Choosing to save me isn't choosing me. We're supposed to date and then get engaged and then get married. Because we want to, not because we need to."

Unable to be in this room with him a moment longer,

yet knowing I can't leave, I do the only thing I can do and run upstairs to my room, slamming the door behind me.

I've only barely fallen onto my bed when the door opens behind me. "Sienna, it's me," Ellie says, her voice unnaturally soft. She climbs onto the bed with me and guides my head into her lap. For several minutes, she strokes my hair, attempting to calm me. And it works... until she speaks.

"I don't want you to die." Her words are said with such raw emotion that goose bumps spread across my flesh. "I've never had a dad, and you're as close to a mom as I've ever had. If you die, I'll have no one. So, if marrying Micah will keep you alive, I really think you should consider it. I know that makes me sound selfish but..."

Her voice trails off, not needing to finish her sentence, and I lay with my head in her lap thinking about what she's said. What she needs. And I know deep down that I don't have a choice. And that right there is the whole crux of the problem.

All I've ever wanted in my life is to have a choice, to *be* someone's choice. And by marrying Micah—despite having feelings for him, despite being attracted to him—both of our choices are being taken away from us.

He can say he's choosing me but he's doing so under duress. He's not choosing to spend the rest of his life with me, to stand at the altar and vow to love me forever. He's simply *choosing* not to let me die. My heart deflates at the thought.

The truth is, I've enjoyed spending time with Micah, even thought maybe there was a chance something between us was developing. The circumstances weren't ideal recently, but our first date was real, filled with only pure intentions. Micah claimed to want to get to know me on more than just a sexual level, and for the first time, the possibility of finding love left me feeling hopeful. But now everything feels tainted. I'll always wonder if Micah marrying me is out of obligation or if he's truly making the decision because he wants to be with me.

But at the end of the day, the only thing that matters is keeping Ellie safe. And in order to do that, I have to be alive. Bottom line...There never really was a choice at all. I have to marry Micah.

"How long?"

Micah glances up from his laptop and quirks a brow.

"How long do we need to stay married?" I clarify, walking further into his office.

"For a while," he says. "At least until you're off Gutierrez's radar or his men find your mom."

"Okay, I'll do it. I'll marry you."

He juts his chin, silently beckoning me to come closer, but I'm too raw at the moment to be near him, so I shake my head. "I'm not feeling well. I think I'm just gonna go to bed early. Can we discuss the specifics tomorrow?"

He frowns, and I can tell he wants to say something—

but really, what is there to say? After a few seconds of him staring at me, warring with how to handle this situation, he simply nods and says, "I'll see what Ellie wants for dinner and order something extra in case you're hungry later."

I thank Micah and head up to my room, feeling like shit because he doesn't hesitate to take care of me even though I'm upset and sounding ungrateful. I cuddle into the soft blankets and go to sleep, cursing my mother to hell for tainting everything good in my life.

"Why am I putting this on?" I ask, as I eye the cream-colored, floral print dress that's set out before me. It's a knee-length wrap dress that will look absolutely stunning paired with the champagne Christian Louboutin heels that accompany it.

"Because I said so," Ellie smarts. "And once you're done, I'm going to curl your hair and do your make up, so you don't look like your puppy was run over by a truck." Her eyes suddenly light up. "Oh! Do you think you could convince Micah to get us a puppy?" For a moment, she looks so young and innocent, reminding me of a normal teenager who has zero cares in the world. "What kind would you want? A big one or a small one? Do hotels allow dogs?" She shakes her head. "Doesn't matter. Micah owns the place. He makes the rules. I'd want a small one, all cute and cuddly that I could put in my purse and carry around."

"Does Micah look like the kind of guy who likes puppies?" I ask, unsure why I'm even discussing this with her. My sister has a way of absorbing you into a conversation before you even realize what is happening.

"That man would give you anything, including a puppy," she deadpans. "Now, up! Get that dress on. We need to get going."

I sigh, not having the energy to argue with her. I have no idea what she's up to, but at this point, it doesn't even matter. For all I know, this is my wedding dress and I'm about to get married.

Of course, the dress and shoes fit perfectly, and once Ellie's done playing fairy Godmother, I look like a princess, ready for the ball.

When we get downstairs, I find Micah standing in the living room, staring down at his phone. Ellie clears her throat and he looks up, his gaze landing on me. His eyes immediately heat with molten lust, warming my insides from his look alone.

"You look perfect," he says, pocketing his phone and sauntering toward the stairs. He's dressed in an all-black suit, but his tie is burgundy, the same color as the flowers on my dress. His hair is neatly styled, and his face is sporting the perfect amount of stubble. He's beautiful. That's the only way to describe him. Sure, he's masculine, has that dangerous vibe going on, sporting arms adorned with intricate tattoos, but he's also really fucking beautiful.

I meet him at the bottom of the stairs, and he leans

in and gently kisses the corner of my mouth. He smells intoxicating—the perfect mix of fresh and masculine—and it takes everything in me not to beg him to let me inhale his scent for a few more seconds.

Tucking my arm into the crook of his, he guides us to the front door when I realize we're leaving without Ellie. "Is she okay being here alone?" I look back at her. "And what about dinner?"

Ellie rolls her eyes. "I'll be just fine here. And I won't leave. I only went to Lincoln's because he lives on the same floor, and I knew I'd be safe there. Plus, I have exams I need to study for and take since it's my last week of school. If I get hungry, I'll order room service. So go, have fun. Stop worrying so much."

It doesn't surprise me when we end up at a restaurant in the hotel since Micah won't chance me leaving the property. We enter through the back and end up in a private room. Unlike the last time we ate here with his parents, the table is only set for two, and there are gorgeous roses in the center with candles glowing on each side. Soft music plays in the background just loud enough to create the vibe without it being overbearing.

Like the gentleman he is, Micah pulls out my chair before taking the seat adjacent to me. Once our drinks have been delivered and we've placed our food orders, Micah shifts toward me, his eyes meeting mine. "I was going to wait until the end of the meal to do this, but the tension between us has me wanting to talk to you now."

I know what he means. We went from us flirting and

kissing and making out, to me hiding in my room and crying at the thought of marrying him.

"What is it you'd like to talk about?" I ask, sounding more formal than intended.

Micah reaches out and takes my hand in his and then brings it up to his lips, giving it a gentle kiss that acts as a key starting the engine to my heart. A simple kiss shouldn't cause such a disturbance in my body, yet it does.

"The moment I saw you on that stage at Wanderlust, I knew I had to have you in every way possible. I know that sounds crazy and a tad bit stalkerish," he says with a chuckle, "but it's the truth. I've only known you for a short time, but I'm attracted to everything about you. The way you're passionate for dance, how hard of a worker you are. Your determination to come up in a world that's hell-bent on keeping you down. The unconditional love you have for your sister and the way you selflessly put her first every day."

He squeezes my hand, and I choke up at the way he sees me. Nobody has ever *really* seen me before... not like that, not until Micah.

"I love how determined you are, which is not to be confused with stubbornness. It's simply that you have goals and dreams and expectations that you are hell-bent on achieving. You want so much out of life and you're willing to fight for it. You could've easily slept with the members of Wanderlust and made a shit ton of money, and nobody would've faulted or judged you for it, but you refuse to go against the bar you've set for yourself."

"I don't want to be like her," I murmur.

Micah smiles and palms the side of my face. "Hellcat, I don't know your mom, but from what I do know, you couldn't be like her if you tried." He presses a soft kiss to my lips, and I sigh into him. I might not be happy with the situation, but I can't ignore the way I feel when I'm around him. The way his touch lights up my body and his words spark such emotion in my heart.

He reaches into the pocket of his jacket and pulls out a black velvet box. My pulse quickens, knowing what that is.

"In the short amount of time I've gotten to know you, I've fallen hard," he says, his gaze searing into me. "I've fallen in love with you, Sienna."

My breath hitches at his words and tears pool in my lids. "I... I—"

"Shh," he says calmly. "I know, you're not there yet. And the situation doesn't help. You've had so many choices taken from you and I hate that, but I need you to understand that while we're getting married sooner than planned..."

"It was never planned," I choke out.

Micah chuckles. "Trust me, Hellcat, marrying you is part of every single one of my plans." Tears track down my cheeks and Micah gently wipes them away. "This is my choice," he says. "Nobody is forcing me to do anything. I'm choosing you. And if you agree to marry me, I'll keep choosing you every day for the rest of our lives if you let me."

"But you said you wanted me to choose you, too," I remind him. During our first date at his penthouse, he told me that this was a sentiment we both shared.

"I know," he says, his voice turning solemn, "and my hope is that one day you will. But right now, your safety comes first. In order for you to fall in love with me, you need to be alive, and us getting married seems to be the only way to ensure you stay that way.

He pops open the box, exposing a beautiful diamond ring. "I want to give you the world, Sienna. Starting with me in a black tux and you in a white dress. And I promise that when I say, 'I do,' it's because I love you and want you and desire nothing more than to spend forever showing you just how much."

A sob escapes past my lips at his admission, at the fact that he's always listening, absorbing, taking in what I say. I hate that I'm being forced into this, that even if one day I do fall in love with Micah—which, at this point, he's making it damn near impossible not to—it will always feel marred. Still, I can't deny that Micah cares about me, that his feelings for me are genuine. He's made those feelings and his intentions clear from the first time we met and he's never, not once, faltered from them.

The scrape of Micah's chair being pushed back catches my attention. And then he's down on one knee, looking up at me with the ring between his fingers and hope in his eyes. "Sienna Bardot, will you do me the honor of becoming my wife?"

My first instinct should be to say no, to tell him I need

to think about this, ask more questions, consider if there are any other options, but my heart takes over before my head can respond, and I blurt out, "Yes, I'll marry you."

As Micah slides the ring onto my finger, I think about how I always pictured this moment. Although I'm not in love with Micah, I can't deny how much I've come to care about him in such a short amount of time. Nor do I doubt the love I feel radiating off of him. Despite this marriage being forced upon me, I know that Micah is a good man, and he'll make a good husband. He's made it a point to put me first from the beginning, and every day he shows me how much he cares. I might not be doing things the way I imagined, but he's right, I'm not following in my mom's footsteps. If anything, I'm stepping out of her shadow and moving toward a better future, leaving her destructive path far behind us for good.

Once the ring is on my finger, he pulls me onto my feet and into his arms. "I know this isn't how you envisioned your engagement," he says, knowing exactly what I'm thinking, yet again. "But if you give us a real chance, I think you could be happy."

"It's not that," I say with a choked sob. "I was happy getting to know you. Going on dates with you. I just…" Fresh tears fill my eyes as I try to explain what I'm feeling. "I just wanted to do things the right way. For once, I wanted some control over my life. To not suffer from the bad choices thrust upon me by our mom. Even now, she has managed to tarnish and sully everything, and I just wanted one thing to feel pure and clean and right."

Micah nods in understanding. "I know, and I'm sorry, but I'll do everything I can to make sure you never regret this."

# Nineteen

## SIENNA

"You look stunning," Donna coos. "Like a queen. I'm so honored to have you as my daughter-in-law." She pulls me into her arms carefully, mindful not to ruin my hair and makeup, and murmurs, "I've always wanted a daughter," and my emotions get the better of me.

Today is my wedding day. It's been three days since Micah proposed. When we returned home from dinner, we were greeted by his family and my sister. They congratulated us on our engagement, and I felt bad, thinking that everyone is under the impression this is real, until Micah told me they're all aware of what's going on. I was shocked that they were welcoming me with open arms, knowing what they know, but it also warmed my heart because it's clear that Micah's family is close, and

I'm thankful to have them in my corner.

The next few days were spent with Micah working, Ellie taking her finals—she's officially done with her ninth-grade year—and Donna helping me with the wedding arrangements. Since I couldn't leave the hotel, everything and everyone came to me. And in only a few short days, all of the wedding plans were set.

"And you," she says to Ellie, who's donning a beautiful maid-of-honor dress. "This will make you family as well." She hugs Ellie. "If you need anything, I'm always here."

Since the wedding needs to be kept private to ensure that the asshole who's after me doesn't find out, only Micah's family and Ellie are attending the wedding. I told Micah we didn't need to dress up or have a formal ceremony. All we needed was a marriage certificate to show that guy Eleazar as proof of our nuptials. Then, hopefully, he'll stop coming after me as a favor to Micah.

But Micah insisted on having as much of a traditional wedding as possible, complete with the black tux and white dress.

"Thank you," I say to Donna. Having people in our corner isn't something Ellie and I are used to. Micah's mom didn't have to embrace us, but she has, so it really means a lot to me.

Donna scoffs. "No need to thank me. I swore my son would die a bachelor until he met you. Seeing him in love makes me so happy. That's all a parent wants, for their children to fall in love and be happy."

Ellie and I glance at each other, and I know she's

thinking what I'm thinking: our mother couldn't care less if we ever find love or happiness.

When I step into the space where the ceremony is being held, Micah is talking to his brother who's standing beside him as his best man. But the moment he sees me, it's as if everyone else disappears. Micah's full attention goes to me, and as I walk toward him, I see only him. He's beyond handsome in his tux, with his hair freshly cut, and his face cleanly shaven.

But what has my attention is the way this man looks at me. When Micah asked me to marry him, he confessed that he's fallen in love with me. I wanted to tell him it's too soon, that he doesn't know what he's talking about, but as I watch him watching me, the look in his eyes can't be misconstrued as anything other than love.

Our vows are standard repeat after me, and once we both say them, the officiant pronounces us husband and wife. Then Micah kisses me. And it's in that moment—when his soft yet strong lips meld with mine—that I realize how much I've missed him this past week. I was starting to get used to his touches and kisses, but he stopped it all to give me the space I needed in order to come to terms with what was about to happen. Yet before this marriage idea was thrust upon us, we were slowly getting to know each other, and I was beginning to fall. I don't know where our future lies as husband and wife, but what I do know is that I want to continue moving forward with Micah to see where things go from here.

After the service has concluded, we move to a private

room where champagne and dinner is served. I've just finished eating when Micah stands and extends his hand. "May I have this dance, wife?"

It's only then that I realize a song has started to play and Micah is waiting for my response. I take his proffered hand, silently accepting his request for our first dance as a married couple. This wonderful man has thought of everything, determined to give me the most memorable wedding possible, despite the circumstances.

With my hand in his, he guides me to an open area and encircles his arms around my waist. As we dance, with my arms around his neck, I take in the lyrics and wonder if Micah picked out this song himself or if he had someone else choose it for him.

But then his lips brush against my ear and he whispers the words, clearly knowing the song, and warmth spreads through my body. As he continues to relay the words about climbing mountains and swimming oceans just to be with me, I lay my head against his chest wondering what I've done to deserve a man like Micah Alexander.

"When I heard this song, I knew it was the one," he says, answering my earlier question. "You're my reason, Sienna." He taps my chin and raises it to look at him. "I've spent years focusing on work, helping to take Alexander Enterprises to the next level. I thought my life was complete until you and your sister appeared, and I realized just how lonely I really was. How regimented my life had become. I love you and marrying you today will always be one of the best decisions of my life."

Without waiting for me to say anything back, he kisses me with such passion it feels as though I'm syphoning every ounce of love from his body into mine. The kiss ends too soon, and when we separate, he must see the want in my eyes because he chuckles. "It's good to know you want me almost as much as I want you."

Once the song is over, Micah shocks me by suddenly announcing that it's time for us to go. When I glance at Ellie, Donna smiles knowingly. "Don't worry. She'll be fine. I'm staying with her tonight." She winks playfully. "Enjoy your wedding night."

Oh, shit. My wedding night.

I've been so preoccupied with the actual wedding and the reality of getting married, I didn't even consider there would be a wedding night.

We thank everyone for being here, and I tell Ellie to behave. Then Micah guides us up to a room that isn't his penthouse. The suite is similar to the room Ellie and I had stayed in, but it's even more luxurious.

Micah takes the champagne that's being chilled in a bucket and pops it open, pouring us each a glass and then handing me a flute. "To finding love," he says. I nod in understanding, knowing that he's referring to himself and hoping one day I'll find it too.

After taking a few sips, he sets his glass down and I do the same, my nerves suddenly electric. I'm assuming this is the part where we consummate our marriage, where I finally have sex for the first time.

My mind races to think about the specifics: What am

I wearing under this dress? Did I shave everywhere? Shit! I'm not on birth control. Did he bring condoms with him?

A million questions and thoughts are flying through my head when Micah takes the side of my face in his strong hand. "Breathe, Sienna. I'm not going to force you to do anything you're not ready for."

"What? What do you mean?"

"The fear is practically radiating off of you at the thought of having sex with me. Don't worry, that's not why I brought you here." He hands me a manila envelope, and I take it in shock.

*That's not why he brought me here? He's not planning to have sex with me?* I don't understand.

"What's this?" I ask in confusion, my head spinning.

"I guess it's kind of a wedding present." He scrubs the side of his face, looking nervous. Why is he nervous?

I open the envelope and pull the papers out, skimming the text. Initially, I assume it's a prenup, which would make sense since Micah is wealthy. I, on the other hand, bring nothing to this marriage but issues. He has every right to protect himself.

But then I see the words: **Decree of Divorce**

"Are these divorce papers?" I choke out. I flip to the end and see Micah's signature. "Did you marry me and file for divorce on the same day?"

"I'm not divorcing you," he says softly. "These papers were drawn up for *you*. My hope is that you'll fall in love with me and never use them. But you said you feel forced, that the choice to marry has been taken from you. Yes, we married out of necessity in order to save your life, but I don't ever want you to feel trapped in our marriage. I told you before that I want you to choose me the way I'm choosing you."

"You chose to *save me*," I mutter.

"I've said it before and I'll continue to say it," he replies, setting the papers down and pulling us onto the couch and me into his lap. "I chose to marry you because I'm in love with you, and I see an entire future with you. Sure, the circumstances sped up the timeline." He smirks. "But I told you at Wanderlust, I want it all with you. The love, the marriage… Hell, if you're willing, someday I'd like nothing more than to have you pregnant with my babies." He sucks his bottom lip into his mouth and glances down at my belly, heat filling his gaze.

And suddenly, I can picture it: going to bed and waking up together, creating a family together. The dinners, birthdays, holidays. Everything I've ever wanted but refused to believe I could have is now at my fingertips.

"But I'm getting a little ahead of myself," he adds, looking back up at me. "I want this marriage to work, and if you give us a real chance, I'll show you just how good it can be. I can only hope that one day you'll be telling me that you love me, too. But I want you to know that with me, you *always* have a choice. So…" He nods toward the papers sitting on the table. "I had divorce papers drawn up. Once you're safe, you can file them at any time. My signature is already on them."

Most women would be deeply offended if their husbands gave them divorce papers on their wedding night, but I understand exactly why Micah did it, and the gesture has me falling harder for him.

"Thank you," I say, wrapping my arms around his neck.

"You're thanking me for divorce papers?" he half-jokes.

"I'm thanking you for making me feel a little less trapped."

I lean in and kiss the corner of his mouth first, then the other corner. When I glide my lips to meet his, my insides tighten with need, and I tell myself I can do this. I can have sex with my husband. I might not love him yet, but I hope with time, I will. And if anyone has a chance of winning my heart, it's definitely Micah.

But sex is suddenly off the table when he breaks the kiss and lifts me off his lap, setting me onto my feet.

"What are you doing?" I ask, confused as to why he would stop our kiss.

"As much as I love kissing you, having you in my lap wearing that sexy wedding dress is absolute torture." He chuckles lightly. "Especially since we won't be having sex tonight."

"Wait, what? We're not having sex?"

"Oh, we're going to have sex," he says with a smirk. "But no, it won't be tonight. When we finally do, it's going to be because you choose to, not because you were forced into a marriage meant to save your life.

"I don't understand," I say in shock. "If you didn't plan to have sex with me, why did you get us this room?"

"You said you wouldn't be having sex until you were in love and married. I can't help the marriage part, but I can help the love part. Starting tonight, I'm going to do everything in my power to get you to fall in love with me, but the sex won't happen until you say so. As for the room…" He shrugs. "Just because we aren't having sex doesn't mean we can't enjoy our wedding night together." He pulls me toward him, and I go willingly. "I packed us bathing suits. What do you say we take that champagne outside and enjoy the hot tub?" He waggles his brows, and I swear I fall again.

Hell, at this rate, if I keep falling like I am, I'm going to hit the ground in no time. And I'll have to hope that Micah is there to catch me.

"The hot tub sounds good."

"Your clothes are in the luggage placed in the master bedroom along with mine, but if you want to sleep separately, that's fine. The suite has three bedrooms."

Of course it is. Because he's the most understanding and patient man I've ever met. "What do you want?" I ask. When he raises a brow, I clarify. "I wasn't sure if you would want me in the same room as you, in your bed, knowing we aren't having sex."

"Being with you is more than sex. Sleeping next to you, holding you, kissing you. I want you any way I can have you, and when you're ready, I'll be here." He takes my hand and guides us into the room. "Turn around."

I do as he says, and he carefully undoes each button along my back until the dress is parting ways down the middle. I consider taking it to the bathroom to change, but since he is my husband and we've been intimate, I figure *what the hell*, and I let the dress fall to the floor, leaving me in only my lacy white bra and panty set. They're nothing special since I didn't even consider buying a bridal set, but you wouldn't know that by the way Micah is staring at me in the mirror with heat in his gaze.

"Sorry, should I go change in the—"

"No," he says, spinning me around. "I can handle seeing my wife like this. Is it torture? Yes. But it's the best kind. Because one day, this…" He drags the tip of his finger down the center of my breasts and torso, stopping just below my belly button. "*You* will be all mine, in every fucking way."

I swallow thickly as liquid heat flows through my body, ending at the center between my legs. I've never wanted a man the way I want Micah, never allowed myself to want anyone like I do him. For a split second, I consider throwing my rules out the window and begging him to fuck me, to show me what it's like to be with someone in the most intimate way, but I take a deep breath and push the thought away. I refuse to be like my mom. When I have sex, we'll both be in love. But until then, there's nothing wrong with being with him in other ways, right?

As if he can read my thoughts, Micah grins knowingly. "Go change, and I'll meet you outside."

After changing into my bikini, I head out to the hot

tub and find Micah already there in board shorts, sans shirt. His muscular chest and torso are on display, and I imagine licking my way down each hard ridge.

He drops into the bubbling water, the bottom half of his body disappearing, and he extends his hand for me to join him. I take it, allowing him to lift and set me on his lap so I'm straddling his thighs. The water is warm, and it feels good, relaxing my muscles.

"Did you have a good day?" he asks after a few minutes of silence, a hint of uncertainty in his tone.

"The wedding was beautiful. Thank you for doing everything you could to make it as perfect as possible." I wrap my arms around his neck, and his shoulders visibly sag in relief.

"I would do anything for you," he murmurs. "You're my wife in every sense of the word, and from this day forward, you come first. Always."

The way he says it, so matter of fact, sends goose bumps across my flesh. I've never come first to anyone, not until Micah. I don't know how to respond to his confession, so I lean down and kiss him, trying to convey without words how much that means to me. Knowing I have someone I can trust in my corner. It's something most people take for granted. Something I've never had. It's always been me against the world, standing front and center, protecting Ellie.

Micah reaches around and gently fists the back of my head, deepening the kiss, and I moan into his mouth, wanting more. He tastes sweet like the champagne, and I suck on his tongue as I grind down on the bulge between his legs, hitting the sweet spot between my own.

It doesn't take long before the best kind of pleasure is ripping through my body and pulsing in my veins. Micah holds me tight, kissing me hard, as I ride out my orgasm.

"It's addicting," I admit softly, making him chuckle.

"It's why the world revolves around sex. We connect through it, fight for it, fight over it. Hell, some of the greatest wars were because of beautiful women." He smirks.

"If it feels this good without having actual sex, I can't even begin to imagine how it will feel when I actually do," I say absentmindedly, as I run my hand down Micah's torso to where he's still hard. "Lift up."

It takes him a second to understand what I'm saying, but once he does, he lifts his body onto the edge of the hot tub so he's no longer sitting in the water, and I'm situated between his legs. If my husband can't get laid on our wedding night, the least I can do is get him off with my mouth. The last time I gave him a blowjob, he enjoyed it so much, he thought I'd lied about my inexperience.

Getting onto my knees, I pull the waistband of his shorts down and watch as his cock springs to attention, the swollen head begging for me to put my mouth on it. I thought giving head would be gross. My mom used to bitch about it all the time, but with Micah, I enjoyed it. Not only does he taste good, but knowing that I'm the reason for his pleasure is such an aphrodisiac.

I use my mouth and hand to work him over—tasting,

licking, sucking—until he's moaning my name and coming down my throat. And then he's pulling me into his lap, kissing me, devouring me. He carries me back inside to the bathroom where he gives me another orgasm on the counter, this time with his mouth.

Once we're both rinsed and dried off separately—since I'm not ready for that kind of intimacy yet—he takes me to bed, refusing to let us get dressed. He pulls me into his arms, our warm, naked bodies entwined, and then he kisses me softly as he runs his fingers through my hair. Soon after, my body becomes limp, and my eyes flutter closed.

"I love you, Hellcat," he murmurs, as I slowly drift off to sleep, feeling things I never thought I'd feel—safe and cherished and loved.

# Twenty

## MICAH

"You on your way to see Gutierrez?" Lincoln asks over Bluetooth.

"Yeah. Figured it'd be best to get it over with. He's either going to accept it or we're going to end up in a war."

When I woke up this morning with Sienna's body wrapped around mine for the third morning in a row, I knew I needed to get this shit handled. Until we know where we stand, we're at an impasse. She and Ellie can't leave the hotel, and as much as I love having Sienna all to myself, she deserves to live her life. And my hope is that once things calm down and she doesn't feel like her back is against the wall, she'll give us a real chance, one that isn't overshadowed by all the bullshit.

"Fuck," Lincoln breathes. "I know you care about this woman but going to war with Eleazar would mean—"

"I don't give a shit what it would mean," I bark, cutting him off. I meant it when I told Sienna she comes first. I'll do everything in my power to ensure she's safe and out of harm's way, even if that means going up against the dirtiest underground crime boss. The Alexanders might be cleaner, have more legit businesses, but we're also wealthier and have more clout in this town. I'm trying to handle the situation without a bloodbath. But if that's what it takes…

"All right, all right." He sighs. "Let me know how it goes. You know I got your back no matter what."

"Thanks."

We hang up just as I pull up to the guard gate at Gutierrez's home. It's risky coming here without clearing it with Eleazar first, but if I attempt to arrange another meeting, he'd definitely know something is up.

After getting my info, the guard lets me know Eleazar is home and will see me. I walk through his house and into his office, and without so much as a hello, I slap the marriage certificate on his desk.

He reads over it, shakes his head, and chuckles. "This girl must really mean something to you," he says, his accent heavy. There are several beats of silence as Eleazar contemplates his decision. "Fine, we're even. I won't touch her, but the mom is dead."

"I don't give a fuck about that bitch. So the bounty…?"

"I'll have it removed today. Just to be on the safe

side, I would have your new bride wait a few days before she ventures out… Just in case someone doesn't get the message." He smirks, and I ball my fists, holding myself back from punching him in his face since that wouldn't end well. Besides, I've already gotten him to agree. Sienna is free.

I extend my hand and Eleazar shakes it, but before he releases my hand, he says, "Just remember that I'm doing this favor because she's your wife. If that ever changes, I can't help what happens."

Without responding, I grab our marriage certificate off Eleazar's desk and walk out the door. His threat doesn't matter because if I have it my way, Sienna will be my wife for the rest of our lives. I just need to get her on board.

On the way home, I stop to pick up coffee and breakfast for Ellie and Sienna, along with a dozen roses for my new bride. I've never been the romantic type, but she makes me want to do all kinds of things I hadn't wanted to do before.

"For me?" she asks, when I hand them to her. The smile that spreads across her face as she sticks her nose into the bouquct to sniff them has me wanting to buy her every goddamn flower on the planet. "What are they for?" she asks, hugging them to her chest.

"We're celebrating." I wrap my hand around the back of her nape and pull her face to me. "You're free, Hellcat. The bounty is being lifted as we speak."

"What?" she breathes. "Seriously?"

"Yep."

Sienna drops the roses onto the table and jumps into my arms, her legs encircling my waist. She peppers kisses all over my face and then crushes her mouth against mine. "Thank you," she murmurs. "I don't know what I would've done without you."

"You don't ever have to find out," I say, kissing her back.

"Does that mean we can leave this penthouse now?" Ellie asks, her question making me tense up. I didn't consider that they'd want to leave once they were safe. I assumed they would continue living here. Give me a chance to get Sienna to fall in love with me and choose to stay with me. If they're not living here, it will be harder, but it won't stop me from trying to make my wife love me in return.

"You need to give it a few days so word can spread but then, yeah," I choke out. "You guys are free to leave. I know money is tight right now since you haven't been able to work, but I can pay for whatever place you find."

"Wait, what?" Ellie says. "We're leaving? Like moving out?" She glances at Sienna in confusion, who looks at me.

"Isn't that what you just asked?" I say, confused myself.

"No," Ellie scoffs. "I just want to leave this building. I missed my dance competition last weekend, but I'd like to go to the studio and see how everyone did." She looks at Sienna. "We're not moving out, are we? I like it here."

I stay quiet, not wanting to sway Sienna either way. She was already forced into marriage. She doesn't need me trying to force her to live here as well.

"Do we have to stay here?" Sienna asks. "In order for it to look real?"

I could try to tell her that it's safer to live here because it looks more legit. But in our world, a lot of couples don't live together. Hell, Eduardo Gutierrez had several mistresses while he was married, and his wife lived in a completely separate home than he did for years.

"No, you can live anywhere you want. We just need to remain married."

She nods and nibbles on the corner of her lips for several seconds before she finally speaks. "I'd like to stay living here if you're okay with that... On one condition."

"Anything," I blurt out, shocked that she's willing to stay. That has to mean something, right? That she's wanting to try, that she wants more than a fake marriage of convenience?

"I want to continue to work..."

Okay, so she wants to be independent. That doesn't surprise me. This is definitely something I can—

"...at Wanderlust."

Fuck. I should've seen this coming.

"I like my job there. I enjoy dancing plus I make good money. I want to make sure that if something happens between us I'll be able to take care of myself and Ellie."

As my wife, everything that's mine is hers, but I refrain from telling her this because I know it isn't just about the money. It's about her not wanting to depend on me by earning her own way. Unfortunately, anywhere else she works won't pay her what she makes at Wanderlust. It's going to damn near kill me to watch her get on that fucking stage and take her clothes off for other men, but I won't force her to quit. I met her at the club and there's no shame in what she does there.

"Friday," I say. "You can go back to work then." I glance at Ellie. "And you can go back to the dance studio. By that time, the word should be out. But I want you driving something safe," I say to Sienna. "I have a shit ton of cars. You can drive one of them. Ellie already has an updated phone, so I'm getting you one as well, and I'm putting both of you on my plan."

"Okay," Sienna agrees. "I can live with all that."

After Ellie runs up the stairs to let her friends know she'll see them in a few days, I tug Sienna close to me. "One more thing," I murmur. "Until you tell me otherwise, you're mine. Other guys can look, they can dream, hell, they can even fantasize." I lick the seam of her lips and she shudders in response. "But nobody is touching you but me."

# Twenty-One

## MICAH

"I can't believe you're letting your wife work here," Lincoln snickers. It's Friday night and, as agreed upon, Sienna is back to work, which means, I'm here to watch her. The past few days have been good. She and Ellie have been hanging out, and Sienna started her online classes, so she let me get her a laptop. When I get home from work, we eat and hang out, and instead of sleeping in her own room, she's been continuing to sleep in mine without me having to ask. Her clothes are still in her room, but every night when Ellie excuses herself to go to bed, Sienna crawls into my bed. We spend hours talking and kissing, which leads to getting each other off, before she wraps herself around me and falls asleep in my arms.

"She needs to feel in control." I shrug. "If she needs

to dance naked for a room full of men to do that, who am I to say no. Besides, she agreed not to give any private dances."

Lincoln whistles, shaking his head. "You're a stronger man than I am. I would've yanked her ass off that stage and—"

His words are cut off by a knock on the door, followed by Marina, our house mom, entering through the partial opening with Ellie trailing closely behind.

"Mr. Alexander," Marina says curtly. "We have a bit of a problem. It seems Miss Bardot has taken it upon herself to work here. Security caught her delivering drinks and asking the members if they needed anything."

At her statement, I turn around to look at Ellie, who doesn't look the least bit apologetic or embarrassed.

"What the hell do you mean, if they needed anything?" I bark. "You're fifteen years old. There's nothing you got that they should want."

"Not like that." Ellie huffs.

"You can go," Lincoln says to Marina. "We'll handle it from here. Thanks."

"Wait, where's Sienna?" I watched her on stage earlier, so she's not due to go back on for a few more hours.

"She's performing for a private party," Marina says, before making her exit.

"Explain," I say to Ellie, once it's just the three of us.

"I need a job," she says simply. "So... I offered to deliver drinks so the ladies can focus on giving lap dances, and in exchange, I would get a cut of their tips." She shrugs like it's no big deal, and I have to give it to her, it'd be a solid plan if Lincoln weren't hell-bent on making sure this club is run correctly—and that includes not having an underage girl serving alcohol.

"Don't fifteen-year-olds get jobs at the grocery store bagging?" Lincoln asks.

"Did you bag groceries when you were fifteen?" Ellie sasses.

"Well, no," he says, looking slightly perplexed by the teenager. "But that's different. We were learning to run the family business."

"Well, my sister works here, *and* she's married to him..." She points at me. "So technically, this is the family business."

I cough to cover my laughter, and Lincoln glares my way, silently telling me to handle this. I should let this continue just to fuck with him, but I don't, since I need to get back out to the main area soon to watch my wife dance.

"What do you need money for?" I ask Ellie.

"Dance camp. It needs to be paid this week, and since Sienna wasn't able to work because our mom's a bitch who likes to fuck her over every chance she gets, there's no way I can ask her for the money. I figured if I could deliver drinks or something, I could earn enough cash to go."

"Is Sienna okay with you going to dance camp?"

"Of course. Dance is my life," she says matter-of-factly. "This camp is for the elite and it's my first time being invited. They've offered me a partial scholarship, and if I could just do something around here, I would be able to come up with the rest." She glances at Lincoln. "I'll do whatever you need."

"Send me the info and I'll pay for it." I expect her to be excited, so I'm confused when she looks uneasy. "What?"

"It's just...Sienna told me to stop taking things from you because if it doesn't work out it'll be more she has to pay back."

Fuck. Looks like I have more work to do than I thought.

"It is going to work out, and if it doesn't, you guys don't owe me shit. I promise. Send me the info and I'll pay for it. When does it start?"

"I leave next week."

"It's not here?"

"Nope! It's in New York City! It's going to be amazing!!"

"You paid for her dance camp?"

Sienna and I are in a private room where she's grinding her ass against my groin while I glide my hands up and down the sides of her thighs. The music is pumping, though I couldn't tell you what's playing. My only focus is on my sexy wife who somehow looks even more beautiful when she's frowning. She had several private parties this evening, so when I saw an opening in her schedule following her second dance, I booked her for the rest of the night. And then I told the hostess I want to book her every night she's on the schedule. She wants to dance on stage? Fine. But the private shows will only be for me.

"This just happened like twenty minutes ago." I chuckle. "How the hell did you already find out?" When Ellie sent the link over to me, I saw I was able to pay online, so I did.

"I got a confirmation email," she says, encircling her arms around my neck.

"Your sister deserves to go to camp. She's a good kid and wants to spend her summer dancing. She was trying to earn her own money by working the floor here."

Sienna's eyes widen, clearly having not known that little fact.

"I wasn't about to let my sister-in-law miss out on a huge opportunity over money, especially when I have more than I'll ever be able to spend."

Her features soften, and I tighten my grip on her hips. "You're mine, Hellcat, which makes your sister mine to take care of by default. And I'll do whatever I can to ensure you're both taken care of...always."

She presses a soft kiss to the side of my neck, and I sigh into her, inhaling her fresh, floral scent. "Thank you," she murmurs, peppering kisses along my flesh and across my jawline. When she gets to my mouth, she licks across the seam of my lips. "You might not have noticed, but I'm not good at accepting help..." I chuckle at her dry humor. "But I really do appreciate it."

Her mouth descends on mine and her thighs tighten around me. She's dressed in a tiny top and bottoms that leave damn near nothing to the imagination, and I want nothing more than to lay her ass out on the couch and devour her. So I do just that.

I carry her over to the leather couch and lay her on her back, taking a moment to look at her. Her head is propped up against the arm of the couch, and her creamy legs are slightly spread, beckoning me to slide between them. Fuck, what I wouldn't give to rip those tiny excuse for shorts off her body and fuck her into tomorrow.

Patience, I remind myself. In time, she'll trust me enough to let her guard down, and then her heart will be open and ready for the taking. Tonight was definitely a step in the right direction. I was expecting her to freak out and insist on paying me back, but instead, she accepted my help and even thanked me.

Sienna watches with hooded eyes as I climb between her legs and trail fiery kisses along her heated flesh, starting at the juncture of her neck and working my way down, stopping at her top and unlacing it so it opens to expose her perfect perky tits.

Before Sienna, being with a woman was always about getting off. Like most people, I enjoy sex. But I never paid attention to the small details, like the way Sienna's nose has a light smattering of freckles that darken when she's in the sun. Or the beauty mark on the top of her left breast. Or how when she's turned on, goose bumps prickle her skin, and her flesh gets overheated.

I love watching her facial expressions. When she's happy and sad and frustrated. But most of all, I love watching the way she looks at me when she wants me.

"Micah," she groans. "What are you doing?"

"Looking at you," I say honestly. "I can't believe you're mine."

Her cheeks tint pink, and I love that no matter how badass she comes across, when I say something sweet, she gets shy with me, momentarily letting down her wall.

I kiss her beauty mark and then suckle each of her nipples. She squirms, clearly turned on and wanting more. I move lower, kissing down her middle and stopping at her navel, swirling my tongue around it. I kiss each of her hip bones and then slide her shorts down her legs, tossing them to the side. Her cunt is trimmed neatly, and when I spread her thighs wider, it's glistening with need.

I lean over and press a kiss to the hood of her pussy, and she groans, her fingers delving into my hair, silently begging me for more. Always wanting more.

I dip lower, separate her pink lips, and lick up her center slowly, inhaling and tasting her essence. Everything about Sienna has become an addiction. Her words, her touch, her mouth, her body, her pussy. I can't get enough.

Lifting her thighs, I lick from bottom to top, and her moans grow louder. When I do it again, my tongue brushing against the sensitive spot between her pussy and ass, she starts to pant, her fingers tightening their hold on my hair.

"You like that, Hellcat?" I murmur. She moans in

response, so I do it again and again. "One day, after I ruin this tight cunt, I'm going to claim your ass."

I look up at her and instead of seeing fear, want is shining in her gorgeous blue eyes. She wants me as much as I want her. She's just determined not to follow in her bitch of a mother's footsteps, so she holds back, not wanting to make the same mistakes. And I can respect that, but soon she's going to see that she and I are not a fucking mistake. And when she does, I'm going to claim and devour every inch of her, leaving nothing untouched, including her heart and soul.

I lick her until she's falling apart at the seams, and then I thrust two fingers in, bringing her to a second orgasm. By the time I'm done, she's come all over my face, my fingers, and the leather couch. Her lids are heavy, and her entire body is languid. She strokes my hair as I pepper small kisses over her flesh, and within minutes, her eyes are closed and she's snoring softly.

I could wake her up since her shift isn't over, but I don't. Instead, I text Marina to let her know Sienna's off the clock for the remainder of her shift and tell her to keep Ellie in the dressing room until we come get her. I gently reposition myself to watch her sleep, and I know without a doubt, I could spend the rest of my life simply watching her.

A couple of hours later, we get home and Ellie goes straight to bed, exhausted. Sienna always showers after work, so I turn the water on to let it heat up. Then I help her out of her clothes since she's practically dead on her feet from the multiple orgasms I gave her earlier.

"In you go," I tell her, guiding her into the bathroom.

"Mmm," she moans when she steps in and the steamy water hits her body. "Join me."

I stop in my place and glance at her, unsure if I'm hearing her wrong. Yeah, we've done shit, but we've yet to do anything as intimate as shower together. Hell, thinking about it, I don't think I've ever showered with a woman.

"You sure?" I ask, just to be certain.

"Uh-huh."

Not wanting her to change her mind, I quickly undress and then step into the shower that's big enough to fit four people easily. She's still standing under the spray, letting the water rain down on her. When she feels my presence, she opens her eyes and drags her gaze down my body.

I'm not hard, but even soft, I know I have nothing to be embarrassed of, so I own that shit and grab the soap, squirting some onto the loofah. I start to wash my body when Sienna steps toward me and takes it out of my hand.

I stand still, watching as she scrubs my arms and chest and torso. By the time she gets to my cock, it's no longer soft. It's hard as a steel beam, and if it could talk, it'd be begging her to touch it. Luckily, she doesn't need to be begged because without me—or my dick—saying a word, she drops to her knees and takes it into her mouth.

I push the wet strands of her hair out of her face so I can watch as she takes me down her throat. It doesn't take long before I'm ready to explode. I know she doesn't mind swallowing, but since we're in the shower and it'll be easy cleanup, I fist the back of her hair and pull her off my cock just in time to come all over her chest. When she stands, I can't help palming her tits and massaging my cum into her flesh. I want to own this woman in every way possible. To mark her and make her mine. Being my wife isn't enough. I want her to love me and crave me the way I do her. I want her to let me in and trust me. I want to give her the entire world. I want to fill her with my seed and knock her up, create a family and a life with her.

As if she can sense my thoughts, she asks, "What's going through your head?"

I pull her into my arms and kiss her lips. "I was just thinking about how much I love you." Despite knowing she won't say the words back, every chance I can, I tell Sienna exactly how I feel about her. I need her to know that my feelings are real, and I'm in this marriage for the long haul. At first she looked a bit uncomfortable, but now she simply smiles softly and kisses me back.

When we're in bed—with Sienna's body splayed out across mine—I run my fingers through her hair, and she sighs deeper into me, feeling safe and content.

"I think it's possible," she murmurs after a few minutes.

"What?" I ask, unsure what she's talking about.

"To fall in love with you. I didn't think it was possible, but now...I think it is."

# Twenty-Two

## SIENNA

"It's so quiet," Micah says, coming out of his office. "How long is she gone for, again?" He leans against the wall and pouts while I continue to type my paper for one of my online classes. "She at least pays attention to me."

I outwardly laugh at how adorable he is when he's not being paid attention to, but inside, my heart swells that the man I'm falling for doesn't just love me and crave my attention, but he also cares about my sister and genuinely enjoys her company.

Before we dropped Ellie off for dance camp, he took her shopping to make sure she had everything she could want or need. He also gave her a credit card so she would have money in case she wants or needs anything else. Then he made her promise to call and text daily. After she left, Micah told me he's having one of his men guard her surreptitiously. Even though Gutierrez has called off the bounty and Ellie was never on his radar, Micah isn't taking any chances. Watching him with her showed me the type of man he is and what a good dad he'll be one day. The thought of having kids always scared the hell out of me, but seeing Micah in pseudo-dad mode has me seeing things in a different light, one filled with possibilities.

The following night, he insisted on driving me to work, and he has been doing so every night since, watching me dance and then booking me the remainder of the evening. We spend the time talking and getting to know each other more—with some delicious orgasms mixed in—and once we're home, we shower together and then fall asleep in each other's arms. He doesn't know it, but he's slowly knocking down my wall brick by brick, and pretty soon that wall—which has done a damn good job of guarding my heart—will be nothing more than rubble on the ground.

"She's only been gone four days," I point out. "And I pay plenty of attention to you."

"Only when I'm making you come," he smarts, smirking like the damn devil he is. "We should go out and do something."

"Like what?" I click save on my document and close my laptop since it's clear I'm not going to get anymore work done right now.

It's Monday morning, but since my classes are online, I spent all day yesterday working on my assignments to stay ahead. Since dance season is over and Grace takes over the summer program, I don't have any classes to teach, either. That leaves my week completely open, aside from Thursday through Saturday nights when I work at Wanderlust.

"I don't know." He sighs. "But it's a beautiful day out and we're wasting it cooped up inside. I'm bored."

I throw my head back with a laugh. "Did Micah Alexander, millionaire, CEO businessman, and king of Tesoro just say he's bored? Don't you have like a gazillion businesses to run?"

"Eh, they practically run themselves. I want to do something fun."

"Okay, so go do something fun."

"With you."

"I'm not fun. I'm the opposite of fun. I'm boring. I work and go to school and raise Ellie."

"Well, Ellie isn't here, and your classes are online, and based on the amount of work you've been doing, I'd bet you're ahead." I open my mouth to argue, but before I can get a word out, he adds, "And you don't have work until Thursday." He walks over and plops down on the couch next to me. "C'mon, let's do something fun. Anything you want." He bats his lashes at me playfully, and I shake my head at his antics.

"Anything?" I joke.

"You name it, and we'll do it. If you could do anything, go anywhere, where would it be? What does fun look like to Sienna Alexander?"

I think for a moment, refusing to acknowledge that he just referred to my last name as his, and then tell him exactly what I would do, knowing there's no way it's going to happen. "I would fly to London and attend the Royal Ballet at the Royal Opera House in Covent Garden."

His jaw drops and he stares at me like I've grown a second head. "That's what you would do? Go watch the fucking ballet? Of all the things to do in this world, you would go watch a boring ass show where people dance to a story that nobody even understands." There's no heat or accusation in his tone, more shock than anything.

"Yep. You asked, and I answered."

He nods slowly, then says, "All right. Let's do it." Standing, he pulls his phone out of his pocket while I'm still trying to register what he just said.

"Wait, what?" I stand as well.

"You want to go to London to see men in tights dance with swans...let's go. Go pack a bag."

"What?" I say again. "We can't just go to London."

"Of course we can," he says, completely nonchalant like we're discussing going to a drive-thru fast-food restaurant and not to another freaking country across the pond.

"Actually, we can't. One, I don't have a passport..." And now that I'm thinking about it... "Or a birth certificate, or social security card. All of our important documents were lost in the fire. And even if I did have all that, I still have to work on Thursday."

Micah glances up from his phone. "Challenge

accepted."

LESSON NUMBER ONE TO REMEMBER: WHEN YOU TELL Micah Alexander something can't be done, he will prove you wrong.

Case in point: we're about to land at Heathrow airport in London, and I have my brand-new passport in hand, ready to show customs. The flight was long, but thanks to Micah's luxurious private plane, we slept through it in a bed—yes, the man's company has a plane with an actual bed that's bigger than the apartment I lived in before it was burned down.

"This is insane," I tell Micah, nervously tapping my foot on the floor as the plane lands, but really, deep down, I'm so freaking excited because holy shit! We're in London! When I was growing up, my dream was to join a traveling dance company, which would've meant dancing here. That's a dream no longer possible, but getting to see a show here is beyond amazing.

"I meant what I said," Micah tells me, leaning over and kissing the shell of my ear. "Whatever it is you want, whatever you need, I'll make it happen."

At his words, a bolt of emotion shoots through my veins and straight to my heart. It's not about him giving me whatever I want. To be honest, there isn't a lot that I want or need—a safe home for Ellie and me, a job that pays the bills, and my mom to drop off the face of the earth. Those are my top priorities. It's that for the first time in my life, I have someone who cares enough to *want* to give me those things. It's as if he thrives on me being happy. I've felt alone for so long, and now, I have someone by my side, who listens and cares.

Since we slept during the flight, we're both wide awake when we arrive, so Micah surprises me by spending the day showing me around London. We visit all the touristy attractions like the London Eye, Big Ben, and the London Bridge. He's obviously seen it all already, but rather than appearing bored, he seems to enjoy watching me gush over all the sights. He takes pictures of me, and with me, and joins in my excitement and happiness.

And when I mention how I would've tried to get Harry Potter tour tickets had I known we were coming here, he assures me that we'll come back, but next time with Ellie, since she loves Harry potter just as much as I do.

I had assumed it would be a quick turn-around trip to see the ballet, but Micah said the show we're seeing isn't until Wednesday, so we spend the next two days sightseeing and having a blast. The food is divine, the city is magical, and my husband is so much fun to be around. He might be a serious businessman to everyone else, but with me, he's funny, playful, attentive, and affectionate.

Tonight, we're attending the ballet, and it's also our last night here. Since I have to work tomorrow evening, we're heading back home first thing in the morning.

When I step out of the room in the gorgeous floral

print, tiered, silk gown by Marchesa that Micah surprised me with, I feel like a princess in a fairy tale, once again. Growing up the way I did, I'd come to believe that fairy tales are nothing more than fantastical stories giving false hope to people just like me. But now I'm starting to believe that fairy tales can come true. That it's possible for me to find my very own Prince Charming, to fall in love and live happily ever after.

The thought both scares and excites me.

"Jesus," Micah says when he sees me. "You look stunning, Hellcat."

He's dressed in a sharp suit that somehow is even sexier than the usual suits he wears, his hair is gelled in that messy look only men can get away with, and his face is sporting some sexy five-day stubble that burned the inside of my thighs last night when he ate me for dessert and made me come several times.

He steps toward me and kisses the corner of my mouth, careful not to ruin my lipstick, and I inhale his fresh, masculine scent. I don't know what it is about the cologne he wears, but every time I smell it, I instantly relax, like just the scent of him alone calms me.

"For you." He reveals a black box and opens it, exposing an exquisite chain in white gold or maybe platinum. Hanging from the chain is a simple, yet elegant, ballet slipper.

When I glance up at him in question, he smiles softly. "You once told me it was your dream to dance but that life got in the way. This is to remind you of your dream.

It may not be for a traveling ballet company, but one day you will dance again the way you were meant to.

He removes the necklace from the box and gestures for me to turn around. As I turn, I lift my hair, and Micah clasps the chain around my neck. When the charm falls onto my chest, I glance down at it, my emotions getting the best of me.

"Thank you," I choke out, turning back around to look at him. "Thank you for everything you've done for me and for Ellie." I sniffle loudly, trying and failing to hold it together, and he gently swipes a tear from my cheek. "But also… thank you for loving me even when I tried to push you away."

"You never have to thank me for that," he says. "Loving you is the easiest thing I've ever done."

Once I've gotten a handle on my emotions and have touched up my makeup, Micah takes us to an upscale restaurant before we make our way over to the Royal Opera House. Dinner is delicious, and the show is breathtakingly beautiful. I laugh and I cry, and the entire time, Micah holds my hand and listens to me talk about the details of the performance.

When it's over, we head back to the hotel so we can get some sleep before our flight the next day. As I sit on the bed undoing the straps of my heels, I watch Micah shrug his suit jacket off his shoulders and loosen his tie. As I do, I can't help but imagine us both getting completely undressed and then him laying me out on the bed so he can make love to me. But I quickly shake off the thought because as much as I want Micah and have grown to like him, I'm not in love with him.

Sure, my heart beats quicker when he's around.

And yes, butterflies have taken up permanent residence in my belly every time he's near.

And yeah, he's thoughtful and caring and puts me and Ellie before everything else.

And when he smiles at me, it feels like he's looking straight into my soul.

And when we're together, his focus is solely on me, like we're the only two people in the entire world.

And when he's kissing me and touching me, it's as though he knows my body better than I do.

And when we finish and he makes it a point to carry me to the shower to clean me up, I feel cherished and treasured.

And when we go to bed, and I wrap myself around him, he holds me tight, making me feel safer than I've ever felt in my life.

But love? No. It's not love. It can't be.

Micah turns around, his tie hanging loose around his neck, his shirt partly unbuttoned to expose a small spatter of chest hair. He smiles softly at me, and then suddenly it hits me like a train going at full speed with no brakes... Holy shit, it's happened. He warned me it would, but I didn't want to believe it. But he was right. I've fallen in love with him. *I'm in love with Micah Alexander!*

"What?" he asks, as he continues to unbutton his shirt.

When I don't say anything, unsure of what the hell to even say, he walks over and kneels in front of me. "Hellcat, what's wrong?"

As I consider how to word what I need to say, my fingers go to the ballet slipper charm that Micah gave me. Patiently, he waits for me to gather my thoughts.

"When I was a little girl, my dream was to dance. I lived and breathed it, and it was all I wanted. And when I got older and learned it wouldn't be possible, I was so devastated that I stopped dreaming. I stopped living. I went into survival mode. I picked a major that would ensure I could take care of Ellie, I got a job that paid the bills and my schooling. The only future I allowed myself to see was one where Ellie and I were out of that hellhole and away from our mom. These past several years have been rough. I've struggled every day to keep a roof over our heads and food in our bellies. I couldn't afford to dream. Not about my future and definitely not about love…until you."

Micah's eyes shine with hope, and my heart swells in response. "I've fallen in love with you," I tell him. "It wasn't supposed to happen, it wasn't part of the plan, but I did anyway. And as much as I hate that our marriage was forced upon us, I don't regret becoming your wife. I love you, Micah, and I want to be with you…in every way."

Micah's quiet for several seconds, and I worry I've made a mistake, that maybe he changed his mind or that his feelings have changed. It doesn't make sense since he literally told me tonight he loves me, but your brain doesn't always think clearly when it's in freak-out mode.

But then the most beautiful smile spreads across his face, and he flashes me that sexy dimple. The warmth I feel wraps around my frosty heart, heating it up.

"It happened sooner than I thought," he says.

"What?" I choke out.

"I thought it would take at least two, maybe three months for you to get on the same page as me, but it only took…" His eyes rise to the ceiling before returning his gaze to me. "Six weeks. It took six weeks for you to fall in love with me."

"What?" I gasp, mentally doing the math. "That's it?" I shake my head. "No, that can't be right. It's too soon." Nobody falls in love that quickly. That's the shit my mom does, not me.

"Hey, stop," he commands. "There's no timeline on falling in love. And you are not your mother." Oh shit, did I say that out loud?

"I don't need to hear your thoughts to know what you're thinking," he says, creepily responding to another thought I didn't say out loud. "Maybe we didn't do shit in the socially acceptable order, but there's nothing wrong with how we're doing it."

I take a deep breath, knowing he's right. This isn't like my mom or her situation. What Micah and I are building is real. In the middle of the darkness, I met a caring, selfless, amazing man who shined his light on me, refusing to let me stumble alone in the dark any longer. He's everything that is right in this world, and I won't allow my mom to ruin what I feel for him. She's taken enough from me, and I won't let her take him too.

"You're right," I say, palming the side of his face. "It doesn't matter how long it's taken. I know what my heart feels. I love you, and I want to consummate our marriage, but more than that, I want you to make me yours."

# Twenty-Three

## SIENNA

"Are you sure?" he asks. "I need you to be completely certain because there's no going back. Once I'm inside you, I'm never going to want to leave. A lot of things can be undone, but not this."

A giggle at his words escapes past my lips, and he frowns, probably thinking I've lost my mind. "Sorry, but I was picturing you burrowing inside me like an animal hibernating in the winter."

His lips quirk into a boyish grin. "Hellcat, I've tasted that sweet pussy, and I wouldn't mind burrowing in it all winter."

I bark out a laugh as his grin widens. "I was being serious, and you spoiled it!" I pout. "Now the moment is ruined." His smile drops, and I laugh again.

"I can fix the mood," he says, standing and giving me a kiss. "You get undressed and put this on." He walks over to the robe that's hanging on the back of the door and hands it to me. "Give me a few minutes." He kisses me again and then disappears into the bathroom.

Just as I'm securing the knot on the belt of my robe, Micah opens the door wearing a matching robe and gestures for me to join him.

The bathroom lights are dimmed, and a couple of candles have been lit. The large Jacuzzi tub has been filled with water and bubbles, and soft music is playing in the background.

"I was thinking we could take a bath together."

"You want to take a bath?" I repeat like a dumbass.

"Yeah. I love taking baths." He shrugs. "They always relax me."

"You want to take a bath instead of having sex?" I ask, since I've apparently lost my filter.

Micah chuckles. "Of course I want to have sex," he says, grabbing the knot of my robe and tugging me toward him. "But it should happen naturally. I would like to take a bath with you, relax and talk. And if it happens afterward, great. If not, then it will happen eventually."

And just like that, I fall for my husband even harder. Only now, I'm not as scared to fall because I know he'll be there to catch me when I do.

"Okay, then a bath sounds good," I say, unknotting my belt and shrugging out of my robe. I don't miss the way his eyes heat with molten desire as I walk over to the tub with a little extra sway to my hips. He might want to play the gentleman and not jump my bones the second I tell him I'm ready, but that doesn't mean I have to be a lady. I've experienced the way he works his tongue and fingers, and I'm ready to find out if he works his cock just as expertly.

I step into the steaming hot water and sigh at how good it feels and then wait for Micah to join me. He disrobes, and my mouth waters at the sight of him. Hard chest, ripped abs, and a thick, long cock that's standing at attention, practically begging to be inside of me.

He climbs in and sits behind me, and I settle between his muscular thighs. Once we're situated, I lean back and sigh into him, loving the feel of his hard body pressed against mine. We sit in comfortable silence for a few minutes while Micah strokes a finger up and down my arms, and I revel in the calmness.

"What are you thinking about?" he asks, when I absentmindedly reach behind me with one arm to play with his hair. With my arm up, he strokes the curve of my breast and then moves to my nipple, circling the areola. I let out a soft moan and push my chest out slightly, silently telling him not to stop.

"Us," I finally say. "How calm it is when I'm with you. For so long it felt like my life was a rollercoaster, going so fast I couldn't catch my breath, with loops and turns and flips that never allowed me to get comfortable. But since I've moved in with you, I feel calm, and I really like that."

"Good," he says, leaning forward and placing an open-mouthed kiss to the crook of my neck. "That's exactly what I want. You calm and happy." His large hand covers my breast, and he massages it for a moment before he pinches my nipple, making me squirm in my spot.

When he continues to tease me and it's clear he's not going to take things further, I decide to take matters into my own hands. It's like buying a chocolate bar and then placing it on the counter to stare at and not eat. Micah is mine. I love him and I want him, so why the hell am I just staring at him instead of devouring him?

Taking his hand in mine, I bring it down and spread my thighs so his fingers can easily brush against my clit. I tilt my head slightly as he suckles on my heated flesh. He works me up higher and higher until I'm coming all over his fingers. My legs shake, the water sloshes over the sides, and my body loosens, sated and happy.

Once I've come down from my orgasm, I twist around in my spot, maneuvering myself so I'm still between Micah's thighs. Then I reach over and release the plug for the water, so it goes down enough that his cock is on display.

"What are you doing?" he asks curiously.

"Checking things out."

I get onto my knees and slide downward, wrapping my fingers around his shaft and sucking the mushroom head into my mouth. I lick and suck his dick until I know he's good and hard and ready. Then I stop, glancing up at him.

When I raise myself up, using the side of the tub to

steady myself, Micah gives me a confused look. But before he can ask or figure out what I'm doing, I grab ahold of his shaft, lift up, and then guide myself onto him.

"Whoa," he says, catching on as my pussy sucks in the head of his cock. "I was thinking we'd do it in a bed… or…" More of me wraps around his shaft, stretching me little by little, and it must be too much for him because he doesn't finish whatever he was about to say. Instead, his hands grip the curves of my hips, and he looks me in the eyes. "Is this what you want? For me to fuck your virgin cunt right here in this tub?"

"Yes," I moan, loving his dirty words.

"Go ahead," he murmurs, leaning forward so our mouths are so close I can feel his sweet, warm breath. "Sit on my cock."

I do as he says, slowly lowering myself. The farther down I go, the more my walls stretch to accommodate him. When I'm almost all the way down, it begins to burn and sting. I wince, feeling the pain I knew to expect when having sex for the very first time.

"That's it, wife," Micah says, his hazel eyes locked with mine. "Keep going. All the way down. Give me that fucking cherry."

His filthy words cause me to clench around him, and he groans in response. "Fuck, Hellcat, you're so goddamn tight. You're going to choke the hell out of my cock."

With a deep breath, I lower myself the rest of the way down, crying out as Micah's cock tears through my virginity. When I'm completely stuffed full of him, he fuses his mouth to mine and takes over. Holding the curves of my hips, he slowly makes love to me from the bottom. With every languid thrust, the pain slowly morphs into pleasure. Then, something tightens inside of me. It's unlike anything I've ever felt. A building of some sort.

"That's it," Micah says. "I can feel you, baby, you're about to come. Don't fight it." He swivels my hips in just the right way, and like a rubber band being stretched too far, I snap. My entire body detonates, my eyes close, and stars flash behind my lids when I come harder than I've ever come in my life.

My head lulls forward onto Micah's shoulder as I sink farther down onto his shaft, unable to hold myself up any longer. My legs are shaking and feel like Jell-O. My heart is racing behind my rib cage.

We sit like this for I don't know how long—me trying to catch my breath, while Micah runs the tips of his fingers up and down my back in a loving way—until the water turns cold and the chill in the air causes goose bumps to prick my skin.

With my legs less shaky, I lift my head and attempt to stand. As I slide off Micah's semi-hard shaft, the pain from earlier comes back slightly, and when our bodies separate, he glances down between us, his entire body going rigid.

"What?" I ask. The little bit of water that's left is tinted pink, but that's to be expected since I just lost my virginity. I read that not all women bleed, but some do, and the amount of blood can vary.

When he doesn't say anything, I start to freak out. "Micah, what's wrong?"

"Sienna." Chills run up my spine at the way he says my name. "I need to ask you something, and I need you to stay calm. Okay?"

"Stay calm?" I hiss. "You can't tell a woman to stay calm and expect her to stay calm. What's wrong?"

"Before I ask, I need you to know that whatever your answer is, we'll deal with it together."

"Micah!" I screech. "Just fucking—"

"Are you on birth control?"

"What?" I shake my head, confused by the direction of the conversation. "Why would I be on birth control? I'm not even having sex." He quirks a brow and looks back down between us.

"You know what I mean. I wasn't having sex… up until a few minutes ago. So there was no reason for me to be on—" And then like a wrecking ball, it hits me. "Oh my God, Micah…"

"Baby, stay calm."

"Stay calm?" I stand and scramble out of the tub, and Micah follows. "Stay calm?" I grab my robe from earlier and wrap it around me. "How the fuck am I supposed to stay calm? We just had sex without protection… and I'm not on birth control."

"Sienna."

"Oh my God. I'm pregnant." My hand goes to my belly, and deep down, I know I'm acting like a crazy person, but right now, I'm not thinking clearly. "I'm pregnant." I look at Micah. "What are we going to do?" I cry. "I did this. You wanted to wait, but no, I had to take control, and now look what I did! I knocked myself up."

Micah snorts out a laugh, earning himself a glare. "What do I do?"

"You have two options," he says, way too calmly for a man who's about to become a dad. "One, we get you the morning-after pill."

"Here? In London? Is that even possible? And won't it be in British?"

He laughs again but quickly schools his features. "British is just an accent," he says. "I think you're having a panic attack. Let's take a shower, get cleaned up, and then we can talk. Okay?"

We go through the motions of showering and getting ready for bed, and the entire time my head is spinning. Once we're settled in for the night and Micah is holding me, I start to finally calm down and think more clearly.

"I'm sorry," I murmur into his chest. "I wasn't thinking."

"Stop," he says softly. I feel his lips press a kiss to the crown of my head, and instantly, my body relaxes. "If you don't want to take the next day pill here, we can get it once we arrive home. But if that's not something you want to put into your body, that's okay, too."

"I could be pregnant," I mutter.

"You could, and if you are, we'll cross that bridge when we have to." He tucks my wet strands of hair behind my ear and tilts my chin so I can look at him. "*If you're* pregnant, whether you choose to keep the baby or not, I'll be right there by your side. Whatever you decide, I'll support you."

"What if I want to keep the baby?"

"Then we'll turn a room into a nursery. I'd bet you'd be even sexier swollen with my baby in you."

For a moment, I imagine what it would be like, being pregnant... having a baby. But it's so hard to picture it. "I never thought about having kids," I admit.

"No? You don't want any kids?" he asks, zero judgement in his tone.

"It's not that I don't want kids. I just never allowed myself to think about it one way or another. My life was consumed with taking care of Ellie and trying to make ends meet so we wouldn't end up homeless."

"That makes sense."

"What about you?" I ask. "Do you want kids?"

"I wouldn't say no to a little blue-eyed mini you running around. All full of sass and charisma. Or, a little boy who has your freckles."

He runs his finger along the curve of my nose to where my freckles are. Unlike before, I'm able to picture it. The pregnancy, the babies...creating a loving home. I would make sure it's nothing like the home I was raised in. My child would be loved and cherished and protected. But even though I'm in a better place, I'm not ready for that responsibility yet.

"I think I'd like to have kids someday," I admit out loud. "But not yet. Not with Ellie still at risk with my mom out there somewhere. First, I need to graduate so I can apply for guardianship of my sister. It's the only way I can keep her safe from Lenora, who still has Eleazar's men out hunting for her.

"And we should be married for a while first. We don't want to rush into something and regret it. My mom getting pregnant is what drove my parents apart, and when she got pregnant with Ellie, it only made things worse. I don't want that to happen to us.

"This is all too new. We need to spend time together, get to know each other better. We have to plan and make sure it's at the right time." I take a deep breath. "When we get back, I'm going to get on birth control to ensure no accidents happen."

"Whatever you want to do is fine by me," Micah says, wrapping his arms around me tightly. "But just remember, you are not your mom, and we are not your parents. If you end up pregnant, it's not going to tear us apart. That baby will be loved and cherished every day of his or her life."

He strokes my back, and as my eyes close and I drift to sleep, an image pops into my head of a beautiful, hazel-eyed little boy with a dimple identical to Micah's... laughing, smiling, happy.

I want to believe him, but I saw what a surprise pregnancy did to my parents, and I don't want to risk it. Having a baby isn't worth losing the love and happiness I feel right now.

# Twenty-Four

## MICAH



**Good news! I got my period, so I'm going in today to get the shot.**

I CHUCKLE AT HER TEXT AND SEND HER A QUICK ONE BACK:



**Does that mean I get to come in my wife any time I want?**

I hit send and glance back up at the marketing team who is presenting their ideas for the upcoming opening of a new restaurant. I should be focused on what they're saying, but these days, my wife seems to be the only person who can hold my attention.

It's been a week since we returned from our trip, and Sienna has been worried about being pregnant. She didn't want to take the morning-after pill, so we agreed to wait it out. Due to the stress of the situation, we haven't had sex since the one and only time. I've been counting down the days until we would know one way or another, eager to get back inside my wife. One time in her tight little cunt and she's already got me addicted. Which shouldn't surprise me since I'm addicted to everything regarding her.

HELLCAT

**Yeah, once my period is over and the shot has kicked in.**

MICAH

**There are other things we can do in the meantime...**

Did I mention I've really missed being with my wife? A little blood won't stop me.

HELLCAT

**Eww...I'm on my period!**

MICAH

**I'm okay with getting my redwings.**

HELLCAT

**I DON'T WANT TO KNOW WHAT THAT MEANS.**

HELLCAT

**OMG! I looked it up.**

MICAH

**Or, I could claim your ass.**

She doesn't respond right away, and I assume she's going to leave me hanging until my phone indicates an incoming text.

HELLCAT

**Will it hurt?**

Hmm...That wasn't a no. I was only half-joking, but I can definitely work with this.

MICAH

**A little, but I'll make it good, I promise.**

HELLCAT

**That's what my high school boyfriend told me when he was begging to take my virginity.**

I bark out a laugh and everyone's gaze swings over to me. As I quickly scan their features, I realize they're waiting for my feedback. I trust my team, and really, this meeting was more of a formality, so I stand and button my suit jacket, ready to get home to my wife. "Everything looks great. We can go ahead and move forward."

They sigh in relief, and I take off, stopping at the store to pick Sienna up some flowers and chocolates and then swing by the sushi place she loves. It's Tuesday night, which means, I get my wife all to myself since she's not working.

When I walk through the door, she's curled up on the couch watching some girly show she loves. She sits up when she sees me, and when she spots the flowers and huge box of chocolates, a beautiful smile spreads across her face.

"You spoil me," she says, taking and smelling the flowers before setting them down and ripping into the chocolates.

"I love you." I press a kiss to her forehead and then head into the kitchen. "I got us sushi for dinner."

"Mmm, you really do love me." She comes up behind me and wraps her arms around my middle, laying her head against my back. "Thank you."

I turn around and pull her into my arms. "You don't have to thank me for feeding you. How are you feeling? There's Tylenol in the cabinet."

"I'm good. I actually don't have bad periods. No cramps and the bleeding is never too heavy. I'm one of the lucky ones."

"Well, in that case." I waggle my brows playfully and she smacks my chest.

"Sorry, buddy. You will not be getting any wings tonight. But..." She trails off and smirks. "I did look up anal sex and I'd be down for trying that. At least if you come in my ass, I won't risk getting knocked up."

And just like that, I fall even more in love with my wife.

I DON'T END UP CLAIMING HER ASS. AFTER WE EAT DINNER and she devours half the box of chocolates, we cuddle on the couch, watching one of her shows, and Sienna passes out. I turn the television off and then carry her to bed before I head to my office to get some work done.

I'm working on the books when the sound of feet padding across the wood floor sound, followed by my sexy wife entering my office, dressed in only my shirt.

She heads straight for me, sliding into my lap and nuzzling her face into my chest. "I missed you in bed," she rasps. "Are you almost done?" She presses a kiss on my neck and whatever I was working on is done for the night. All these years I never knew what I was missing until I found Sienna. Now, I can't imagine not having her here, in my home, in my bed, in my arms.

"I'm done," I tell her, closing out of what I was working on and then standing with her in my arms. She wraps her legs around my waist and holds on to my neck, while I walk us back to bed.

My brother fucks with me daily, telling me I've gone soft, that he never imagined I'd let a woman control me the way Sienna does, but nothing he says bothers me because I'm okay with it, knowing I get to wake up and go to bed with her in my arms. Spend my life with her.

When I lay her out in the middle of the bed, she grins up at me, not looking the least bit tired. "I was thinking... if you're up for it, we can try out what we talked about earlier."

"And what was that?" I ask, playing stupid as I hover above her, my arms caging her in.

"You know…"

"Mmm." I edge downward and stop at her tiny cotton underwear. "I believe there was talk about wings." I press a kiss on the top of her mound through the material.

"No way." She giggles, trying to pull me up. "I meant you fucking my ass."

"Oh, *that*." I smirk and then kiss her. "You sure you're up for that?" I lift my shirt over her head and pull a nipple between my lips, sucking on it.

"Yes," she breathes.

I swirl my tongue around her areola and then move to the other one, giving it attention as well.

Turned on and in need, Sienna's breathing increases as I suck and lave at her breast and then dip a finger into her underwear. When she tries to stop me, I shake my head and gently slap her hand away. "Let me do what I want," I murmur against her lips. She gives in, her hand instead going to my sweats, pulling them down so she can stroke my cock. I grab the bottle of lube out of my drawer and squirt a little onto my fingers. I use it to massage her clit, and within minutes, she's writhing under me, screaming out her release.

Without waiting for her to come down, I flip her onto her stomach and shove her underwear down her legs.

"Give me that ass, Hellcat," I say, giving her perfect round ass cheeks a playful slap.

She immediately lifts, and I bend over and take a bite out of her cheek, making her shriek in surprise.

"You sure you want my fat cock in here?" I ask, spreading her cheeks and running the tip of my finger along her puckered hole.

"Yes," she moans, wiggling her ass teasingly. She twists her head around slightly and looks back at me. "I trust you."

Her words are like a vise to my heart, wrapping tightly around it and making it hard to breathe. For most people, trust comes easy, but for Sienna, her telling me she trusts me is huge. That wall she was using to keep everyone out—including me—has been lowered, and I'll do everything in my power to make sure she never regrets it.

I grab more lube and squirt it between her cheeks, then push a finger into her tight hole. She moans, telling me it feels good, so I add another digit, working her up, stretching her out. Once she's begging for more, I lather a shit ton of lube on my shaft and then slowly enter her. Inch by inch, I watch as her perfect ass swallows my cock.

When I'm halfway in, I ask how she's doing, and she rasps to keep going, so I do, not stopping until my entire shaft is inside her ass.

"Fuck, baby. You should see how good your ass looks with my cock in it," I say, as I slowly slide back out, exhaling harshly and praying I don't blow my load yet.

"Micah, I love you, but if you don't make this good, I'm never letting you back inside my ass again."

I chuckle and start to move in and out of her. She's too tight, her ass too goddamn sexy, and I know I won't last long. So, I reach around and find her clit, and as I fuck her tight little hole, she starts to meet me thrust for thrust, moaning and begging me to fuck her harder. It's such a fucking turn on the way she loves to take control.

She finds her climax first, and then I allow myself to let go as well, coming deep and hard in her ass. When she drops onto the bed, her legs giving way, my cock slides out of her ass and I'm able to get a quick glimpse of my cum leaking out of her. Fuck, I could spend my life with this woman. Around her, with her, in her. I can't get enough.

"I think I need a shower," she whines, half asleep.

"You definitely need a shower," I say, rolling her over and lifting her into my arms. "Thank you, baby." I kiss her and when I pull back, she gives me an odd look.

"Did you just thank me for butt sex?"

"No." I chuckle. "I thanked you for trusting me."

"So, you're really going to watch every one of her shows?" Lincoln asks, as I watch Sienna perform on stage.

"Yep. It's not like I have anything else going on since my wife insists on spending three nights a week working here."

We've been married for two months, and Sunday we're leaving for the city to celebrate. We'll also be attending Ellie's end-of-dance-camp showcase, which happens to fall on the very last day of our trip. But first...I get to enjoy one uninterrupted week with my wife—no clothing required.

Sienna's performance comes to an end, and I get up to head to the private room where I'll get my nightly dance. She no longer lets me book her for hours at a time, but since she stopped performing private shows for other men, she spends her time either on stage or serving drinks.

The music starts and the lights dim, and then my gorgeous wife appears on the stage. It doesn't matter how many times I watch her dance, it never gets old, and each time I'm just as mesmerized and turned on as the last.

When the show ends, she saunters down to where I'm sitting and straddles my thighs, and I love that I get to touch her whenever the fuck I want.

"I booked our room for the week," I tell her, as she peppers kisses along my jaw. She's no longer performing, but my wife loves to be affectionate. Maybe it's the honeymoon phase, but the past couple months—ever since she got on birth control—I've spent more time in her than not. We've fucked in every damn room, on every surface of our home at least twice. I imagine it'll be a little harder once Ellie is home, but that just means we'll have to get creative.

"I can't wait to see my sister," she says, lifting her head and looking at me. "The summer has flown by. She's had such a good time. Thank you for making sure she could go."

She presses her lips to mine and then her tongue slides

inside my mouth. When I suck on it, she moans, grinding down on me. "Fuck me, Micah," she breathes, and since she doesn't have to tell me twice, I do just that.

Lifting her, I carry her over to the couch and lay her out. After removing her clothes, I trail kisses all over her body and then eat her sweet pussy until she's coming all over my mouth. And then I'm lifting one of her legs over my shoulder and sliding inside her. She grabs my nape and pulls my face to hers, kissing me while I fuck her, both of our bodies pulsing with adrenaline as we chase our pleasure.

Sienna falls first, squeezing the fuck out of my cock and taking me straight over the edge with her.

When we've both caught our breath, she shocks the hell out of me when she says, "I'm going to quit working at Wanderlust."

I pop my head up to look at her. "Really? Was the sex that mind blowing?"

She laughs. "No...I mean, yes. It's always amazing. I just...it's time. Ellie will be returning home soon, and if I work nights, she'll either have to come with me or stay home all alone. Besides, if all goes well, I'll have enough credits to graduate in December."

"With a degree you don't love," I add. We've had a lot of conversations about this, and I've told her she should do what she loves: Dance. But she insists on wanting a job that looks good on paper since she's planning to apply for guardianship of Ellie now that it's been over two months and Lenora is still missing. With her gone, Sienna should have no problem becoming Ellie's guardian. But to be on the safe side, I've insisted she let me hire the best attorney.

"Actually, I was thinking about that too," she says, shocking me for the second time tonight. "I'm going to ask Grace if I can pick up some more classes at Lola's."

"Yeah?"

"Yeah," she says with a smile. "Being a dance teacher pays well, and the judge will see I can provide a stable home, especially since we're married."

"Whatever you want to do is fine with me," I tell her, pulling out. She stays right where she is, knowing the drill. I grab a wet washcloth from the bathroom and come back so I can clean her up. Once she's halfway decent, she pads to the bathroom to finish cleaning up.

"I told Lincoln tonight. I offered to give him two weeks, but he said it's all good, so tonight was my last night."

Bastard. He didn't say a damn word to me. "You have no idea how happy this makes me," I tell her, lifting her into my arms.

"Because you hate me dancing?"

"No." I shake my head. "Because now I get you every damn night, including the weekends. Let's get the fuck out of here," I say, kissing the curve of her neck. "I'm ready to start our vacation early."

# Twenty-Five

## MICAH

"What the hell do you mean they've raised their asking price? I thought the contract was locked in?" I'm standing outside on the terrace of The W, staring down at the bustling city. Unlike in Tesoro, Manhattan is overcrowded and never sleeps. I enjoy coming to the city, but I don't think I could live anywhere but Tesoro. The cars honk and people yell, and at least three people on bikes almost get hit.

"There was some miscommunication and…"

A feminine throat clears from behind me, and I turn around, coming face to face with my gorgeous wife. She's dressed in what appears to be bridal lingerie—an arousing blend of white lace, innocence, and seduction—and tall, very sexy heels. Her hair is down in waves and her lips are glossy. When she said she was going to go to the bathroom to freshen up after we arrived, I thought she meant brush her teeth.

George, my legal department manager, continues to speak, but I couldn't tell you what the hell he's saying because I'm too entranced by the woman in front of me.

"George, I'm going to have to call you back," I say, and then hang up without waiting for him to respond. Pocketing my phone, I stalk back inside.

"Where did you get that?" I ask. When we packed for our trip, I didn't see it, and she rarely goes anywhere other than to work and home. Not that she can't go wherever the hell she pleases, but I'm just wondering how she got it, and where I need to shop to buy her more.

"I ordered it," she says, running her hands down her body. "I was thinking about our wedding night and how it should've went down, and since we're in a hotel room, just the two of us, I thought we could have a do-over." With a seductive sway to her hips, she closes the distance between us, and flashes me a coy smile while her fingers work to unbutton my shirt.

Fuck, this woman.

She slides her hands under the material of my shirt and removes it from my body then presses a soft kiss to my pec before swirling her tongue around my nipple. I stand in place, watching as she kisses her way down my chest and torso, stopping just above my navel.

While glancing up at me through her lashes, she presses an open-mouthed kiss to the bulge in my pants, then backs up slightly. "But first," she says, "I have something to give you."

She reaches into the cup of her bra and pulls out a… "Is that a ring?" I ask in confusion.

"It's a men's wedding band." She stands back and extends her hand so I can get a better look at it. It's all black with tiny black diamonds going around the center of the band. Sienna takes my left hand in hers and slides the band I'm currently wearing off my finger. Since she wasn't thrilled about being forced into marriage, I didn't want to bug her about the details. She was already having a hard enough time planning the wedding with my mom. So, I went to the store and picked up a simple band to wear.

"The day we said I do, I wasn't in a good place, but since then, things have changed," she says. "I love you, and I want to be married to you for real." She places the ring she's holding between her fingers. "I had it engraved." I take it from her and read the words that are inscribed inside: *I'll always choose you.*

"I choose you, Micah. I choose us…forever." She slides the ring onto my finger, and my heart swells in my chest with so much love for this woman, I can't think straight.

"One more thing," she says, walking over to where her luggage is. She pulls out an envelope and brings it back over to me. I immediately recognize it as the divorce papers I gave her on our wedding night. "I don't need or want these." She pulls the papers out and rips them in half, and I have never been as turned on as I am right now. "Now," she says, tossing them to the side. "Make love to me, husband. The way it should've happened on our wedding night."

Fisting the back of her hair, I crush my mouth to hers, tasting and devouring, as I walk us to the bed. When we reach it, I reluctantly stop kissing her so I can lift her onto the mattress.

When she's lying in the center, looking like a goddamn fallen angel, I take a moment to memorize everything about her. And then I make love to my wife, bringing her to orgasm several times before sinking inside her to find our joint release. Not that what we've been doing for the past several weeks isn't making love, but this time, I go slow, worshipping every inch of her just like I would've done on our wedding night.

"Thank you" I murmur once we're both cleaned up and she's lying in my arms, her body draped over mine, "for choosing me the way I choose you."

"Oh my God, you guys are totally in love," Ellie squeals. "I knew it would happen!" She throws her arms around Sienna and then me. "Welcome to the family, big bro. Now that you're really married to my sister, you're stuck with me, too."

Sienna groans, and I chuckle. "I'm okay with that, kid." I ruffle Ellie's hair, and she swats my hand away, rolling her eyes.

"I'm fifteen. That's hardly a kid." She scoffs.

"The show was fabulous, and you did amazing," Sienna says, changing the subject. "I'm so proud of you."

"Yep," I agree. "I didn't even sleep through it." I hand her the flowers Sienna and I picked up and Ellie takes them, thanking me.

"So, I know school starts in a couple of weeks," she says, as we walk to the car. "But there's something I want to talk to you about." She glances between Sienna and me nervously, a trait that Ellie doesn't usually sport.

"Okay," Sienna says, stopping at the car but not getting in.

"So, there's this school of the arts and the headmaster attended the camp and offered me a spot. I could possibly get a partial scholarship, but it would mean you having to drive me to and from school every day because they don't offer transportation. At least until I get my own license."

"What's the name of the school?" Sienna asks.

"Anderson School of the Arts," Ellie says, and Sienna's eyes go wide.

"They offered you a spot?" Sienna breathes. "That's huge."

"I know." Ellie grins, practically bouncing on her toes.

"And expensive," Sienna adds. "Even with a partial scholarship, it would be—"

"Handled," I say. Sienna and Ellie both look at me. "I'm not saying you can go because that's ultimately up to Sienna, but if she decides it's okay, we'll pay for the tuition, and I can arrange for a driver to drop you off and pick you up."

"Seriously?" Ellie shrieks. "Can I go, please?" She fists her hands in a prayer-like manner and begs.

"We'll see," Sienna says sternly, brooking no room for argument. "Micah offering is very generous, but he isn't aware of how expensive the school is. He and I will talk about it later and then let you know what we decide."

"Ugh, is this what it's like having two parents?" Ellie grumbles. "I think Micah should make all the decisions if that's the case."

Sienna chuckles. "Oh yeah? Hey, Micah, Ellie likes this boy and wants to go on a date with—"

"Hell no," I bark, not letting her finish that asinine statement. Dance school, I can handle. Dating, fuck that. "I was fifteen and know exactly how boys act at that age," I say to Ellie. "Focus on dancing."

"I WAS THINKING…"

"Does your head hurt?"

I glare at Sienna, who laughs, thinking she's cute. I mean, she is, but that's beside the point. "I was thinking," I say again. "I could buy you a dance studio, and then you could do what you love."

We're in bed, both of us naked and glistening with sweat. Sienna's eyes are hooded over from the two orgasms I gave her, and my dick couldn't get up if I begged it to. This is how it is every night after Ellie goes to bed. We talk and fuck and then fall asleep spent.

When Sienna doesn't respond, I roll over to get a better look at her and find her staring up at the ceiling with tears in her eyes. "Hey, did I say something wrong?" I ask, pulling her into my side.

"No," she chokes out. "You're perfect. It's just...I love dancing, but sometimes it's hard because my love of it stems from my parents. They were dancers. It's how they met. They fell in love dancing together. But once my dad was injured, and my mom got pregnant with me, everything slowly fell apart. Sometimes, I think I hold on to dancing because I couldn't hold on to my parents."

I squeeze her hip, so she knows I'm listening, encouraging her to continue. "I want to hate my mom," she says softly. "After everything she's put us through, she deserves for me to hate her. But I can't because I can still remember the woman she used to be. I was young, but I can still remember her happy...before her broken heart destroyed her."

She lifts up on her elbows, looking at me, and I edge higher so we're more comfortable. "Ellie once said that maybe if our mom would've met a man like you, her heart wouldn't have broken the way it did. I didn't get it at the time, but now I do because every day, you put me together. If you broke my heart the way my dad—"

"It's never happening," I tell her. "I can't predict the future, but I know I will *never* break you."

She nods, but I can see a bit of hesitation in her features. I get it because heartbreak is all she's ever known, but over time, she'll see I mean it.

"I used to wish for her to disappear or die," she says, after a few minutes of silence. "But now that I know what it's like to be in love and can imagine what it would feel like to have my heart broken, I wish she'd get help. It's probably too late, but...yeah, I hope one day she gets the help she needs."

I wrap my arms tightly around her and kiss her soft lips. "And that's why I love you, Hellcat. Because despite the fact that that woman has hurt you, you still wish her well. You have a huge fucking heart, and out of all the men you could choose to give your heart to, I'm so grateful that you chose to give your heart to me." I kiss the tip of her nose and then her forehead. "And I promise, I will do whatever it takes to protect it."

"Thank you," she murmurs, laying her head back down on my shoulder. "I'll think about the dance studio. I appreciate the offer, but I'm not sure if dancing is in my future. Right now, my only goals are to graduate and get guardianship of Ellie."

Speaking of which..."You know you could apply now, right?"

She pops her head up. "What do you mean? I haven't graduated yet."

"You're married to me. What's mine is yours. And your mom has been gone for months. No judge is going to deny you guardianship of Ellie. As a matter of fact, it's probably a good idea for you to apply now before the state finds out her mom has gone AWOL. You've already been raising her for years. At this point, it's just about making it legal."

"I don't even know where to begin…"

"If you knew you could get approved, would you want to pursue it?"

"Hell yes," she says. "Knowing Ellie is safe and can't be taken away from me would mean everything to me."

"Then I'll make sure it happens."

# Twenty-Six

## SIENNA

"By next week, I need the name of the professional you'll be shadowing. Thirty hours is required." The professor nods, indicating we've been dismissed, and I quickly jot down what I need to do in my planner, so I don't forget.

"I'd be okay with you shadowing me," a masculine voice says, making me practically fall out of my seat. When I spin around, I find Micah standing there, dressed to the nines in his CEO bad boy suit and grinning at me. With the threat gone, thanks to Micah, I'm back to being able to take classes on campus instead of online.

"What are you doing here?" I ask, jumping out of my seat and wrapping my arms around him.

"I thought I would surprise my wife by taking her to

lunch. Your classes are done for the day, right?"

"Yeah." I peck his lips, loving that he knows my schedule. "Let me just grab my stuff." I shove my laptop and planner into my bag, and then with my hand laced in Micah's, we head out.

"I meant what I said," he affirms, as we walk. "If you need someone to shadow, I'd love to help you." He pulls me into his side and his voice lowers. "I could even give you some hands-on experience."

I snort out a laugh at his adorable banter but stop when I imagine him shoving his papers to the side so he can lay me out across his desk and fuck me seven ways to Sunday.

"You're thinking about it, aren't you?" he asks, his lips quirking into a devilish smirk. "Me bending you over my desk and fucking you."

"Actually, I was imagining you laying me out on the top of the desk but bending me over it would work, too." I waggle my brows at him, and he barks out a laugh.

"Do you want to eat on campus or meet somewhere?" I ask since we came in separate vehicles.

"I already had someone grab your car so you can ride with me."

"Damn, am I that much of a sure thing?" I joke.

"No, but I think I'm wearing on you."

"Yeah, you are," I agree as he opens the door for me so I can get in.

"This impromptu lunch date actually has another purpose," he says, once we're sitting in a Greek restaurant we love, devouring our gyros. "We have a meeting afterward with Oliver Stein, a family law attorney who's good friends with my dad. I explained our situation, and he believes it should be an open-and-shut case. He needs some information from you, though, before he can file."

It doesn't go over my head that he says *our* situation. It shouldn't be that big of a deal, it's only a simple three-letter word, but when you've been going at life on your own for as long as I have, the use of that word coming out of his mouth is like a direct link to my heart.

Reaching across the table, I throw my arms around Micah and lay a big, fat kiss on his cheek. "Have I told you today how much I love you?"

"This morning, right after I made you come in the shower," he says, with a smirk. "But you can tell me as often as you like."

The meeting with the attorney goes smoothly. He assures me that applying for guardianship of Ellie will be simple, especially since I'm her only living relative aside from our mom, who has been missing for months. Once he has the papers drawn up and I come back in to sign them, he'll file them immediately.

"My assistant texted that she needs me to approve something. Apparently there was a mix-up and it's time sensitive. Do you mind if I run to my office really quick?" Micah asks on our drive home.

"Is this your way of turning that sex on the desk fantasy into the real thing?"

"No," he says with a laugh. "But we can definitely

make it happen if you want."

Alexander Enterprises is a ten-story corporate building located downtown. With their name etched in large, mirror letters at the top for all to see, the building screams luxurious without being over the top. I've seen the building a million times over the years, but I never thought twice about it. Now, that name is also mine.

As Micah strides through security and into reception, speaking to people with authority and demanding answers regarding whatever got messed up, I can't help comparing this man—who is sure of his place in the world and doesn't take no for an answer—to the man I've grown to love. This side of Micah I'm witnessing right now is the same man I first met at the club, the one who was cocky enough to believe he could snap his fingers and I'd do whatever he wanted. But when that didn't work, he showed me another side of himself—the vulnerable side that told me he was looking for more than just sex. It's weird seeing him like this, but I also love that he saves all his softness for me.

Taking my hand in his, Micah guides us into his office so he can sign the papers, and while he does so, I take an opportunity to explore his workspace. It's as lavish as the rest of the building. Clean and modern with expensive looking furniture and a view most would die for. Yet, there's nothing personal, no photographs, nothing that denotes that this is even his office, a place where he spends most of his day working. And now that I think about it, his home is exactly the same way.

But when I step around his desk, my heart swells at the sight of the two photographs placed right next to his laptop. One is of the two of us from our trip to London. There was a photographer outside the theater offering to take pictures of the guests. He handed Micah a card afterward and he must've ordered this one and had it printed. The other is a photo taken at our wedding with the two of us in the center, surrounded by his parents, brother, and Ellie.

"What?" he asks when I've been standing here pensive for a few minutes.

"Your home doesn't have any personal touches. No pictures or knickknacks. Nothing that screams you. Neither does your office."

Micah turns his chair and grips the curve of my hip, dragging me over to him so I'm situated between his legs and leaning against the desk. "First of all, it's not my home, it's *our* home. And I've honestly never thought about it. When it was built, I hired an interior decorator to handle it all. Before you and Ellie came to live with me, I rarely spent any time there. It wasn't until you two moved in that it even felt like a home."

Once again, his words wrap around my heart like a warm comfy blanket on a chilly night. "I like the sound of that," I admit. "A home. I always tried to provide as much stability for Ellie as I could, but we never had a home… until now."

"I'm glad you both feel safe and comfortable there," he says. "If you want to add pictures or decorate, that's fine with me. If Ellie wants to paint her room and make it more girly or whatever, I'm completely okay with that. It's your home as much as it's mine."

"Thank you," I say, leaning forward to kiss him. "Now, how about we lock that door and test out this desk. Add our own personal touches?"

"Sounds like a fucking plan."

"So, remember a few weeks ago when you *jokingly* said I couldn't date," Ellie says to Micah. It's Friday night and she's dressed, ready to go out.

"No," Micah deadpans, making me laugh. We're lounging on the couch with my feet in his lap as I watch One Tree Hill and he does some work from his phone. "I remember saying hell no, you can't date, and nothing about it was spoken jokingly."

"Micah." Ellie groans. "There's this guy at school. He's in a few of my classes, and he's asked me out for a *study* date."

I already knew about this since my sister texted me the second it happened, and of course, I told her she could go as long as I meet him first. The problem is, he's on his way over to pick her up—he's sixteen and drives—and there's no way he's getting past Micah's security without him knowing about it, which means, she needs him to approve the kid to come up.

"No," he repeats, deadly serious, which only makes

me laugh harder, and in turn, has him glaring at me.

"Babe," I say, rubbing his arm. "Ellie is going out tonight, and he's already on his way to pick her up." Just as I finish my sentence, there's a knock on the door.

"He's here," Ellie whisper-yells. "Please, please be cool," she begs Micah, whose jaw ticks. "Remember, it's a *study* date, so not a real date."

"Does it have the word date in it?" Micah volleys. "Then it's a real damn date."

Ignoring Micah, she rushes over to the door and swings it open, but standing on the other side is Lincoln, Micah's brother, not Ellie's date. "Oh, it's you," she says, sighing in disappointment. Me, on the hand...I mentally rejoice because her hanging out with someone else might mean she's finally moving past her crush on Lincoln.

Only I've apparently thought this too soon because as he walks in, the look in her eyes tells me she's definitely still sporting that crush.

"What's up?" Lincoln asks.

"Ellie is about to go on a study date," I say, ignoring the way Ellie is glaring daggers my way.

"Really?" Lincoln says. "Aren't you only fifteen? Should she even be allowed to date?" His second question is aimed at Micah and me.

"Of course I can date," Ellie hisses as the security system chimes. "But it's not a *date* date. It's a study date. We're going to get coffee and work on a project for school."

She rushes over and answers it. "There's a Jameson Reynolds here," security states. "Says he's here to pick up

Eliza."

"Tell him to go the fuck away," Micah yells, making Lincoln laugh.

"Ignore him," Ellie says. "Please let him up."

Lincoln grabs Micah and him beers from the fridge and then drops into a seat just as Ellie glances my way, silently begging me to save her. Even if this is not technically a real date, it's still a first for Ellie, who deserves to finally act and feel like a normal teenager. I pat Micah's leg and say, "Please behave. This is important to her," and then glare Lincoln's way so he knows I'm talking to him as well.

"Fine," they both mutter, sounding more like children than grown men.

Jameson is a tall and lanky brown-haired, blue-eyed cutie. He's polite when he introduces himself and mentions that he's going to the school of arts that Ellie attends for music.

"He has the best voice," Ellie gushes, making Jameson blush.

"And where are you going?" Micah asks, even though Ellie already told us.

"To Coffee Grind to work on a project," Jameson says. "Then, maybe to hang out with some friends after."

"What kind of car do you drive?" Lincoln asks.

"A GTR."

"That's a pretty badass car," Micah adds. "How fast have you gone in it?"

I hold my breath, realizing it's a trap, but luckily, Jameson doesn't fall for it. "I don't speed," he says, his voice cracking.

The guys take turns interrogating poor Jameson, and as embarrassing as it is for Ellie, I love that we have people in our life who care. For too long it has just been us against the world. But now, we have family.

When it seems the kid has passed whatever test they've given him, Micah sighs and says, "You can wait for her outside." Jameson wishes us a good night and walks out the door.

"What was that for?" Ellie hisses.

"You have your phone on you?" Micah asks, standing and walking over to her.

Ellie nods.

"And money?"

Another nod.

He pulls a credit card out of his wallet and hands it to her. "This is in case of an emergency."

She takes it from him and mutters, "Thank you."

"If you need anything, I mean anything at all, you call us," he says to her. "He might seem cool and have a decent car, but he's still a teenage boy. Don't let him talk you into doing anything you don't want to do."

Ellie's eyes well up, and I worry Micah's pushed her too far. But then she throws her arms around him and hugs him tightly.

Micah pats her head, and a lump of emotion fills my throat. "Behave," he says to her. "And remember, if you're ever in a situation and need us to pick you up, we're here. You won't be in trouble. We'd rather you call us and be safe than have something bad happen because you're afraid to tell us."

"Thank you," she says, pulling away and wiping her tears. "I've always wondered what it would feel like to have a dad." She glances at me. "I guess it's not so bad." With those words, she's out the door, leaving us all speechless.

My phone goes off a few minutes later, and I grab it, worried it's her already, but it's Micah's mom, Donna.

**DONNA**

**Micah never lets us celebrate his birthday. Any chance you can convince him to let us celebrate this year? (And yes, I'm trying to get you to use the wife card. LOL)**

I laugh at her text and then it hits me... "When is your birthday?"

"What?" Micah asks at the same time Lincoln barks out a laugh.

"How are we married, and we don't know when each other's birthdays are?"

"Speak for yourself." Micah scoffs. "Yours is April 3rd."

"Of course you know when it is...You're like a professional stalker!"

Lincoln laughs again and I glare at him. "And on that note," he says, standing. "I'm out of here."

"Did you come by for a reason?" Micah asks him.

"I wanted to talk about the restaurant's grand opening, but we can talk later." He glances at me and grins. "His birthday is next Saturday. Let me know where the party is."

"Your birthday is next week, and you didn't tell me?" I pout.

"It's not a big deal." He shrugs. "I'll be thirty-three. I'm practically an old man. That's hardly anything to celebrate."

"But you're such a sexy old man," I joke, snaking my arms around his neck. "Can we throw a party?" I ask, batting my lashes.

"You already know I can't say no to you," he groans, capturing my bottom lip between his teeth and tugging playfully. "I say we take advantage of the fact that we have the house to ourselves. I'm thinking kitchen island. I don't think I've fucked you on it yet."

"I don't know," I say, keeping my voice serious. "Are you sure an old man such as yourself can handle fucking me on the kitchen island?"

"Oh, I'll show you what this old man is capable of," he growls. Picking me up and carrying me over to the island, he proceeds to show me *exactly* what he's capable of—twice!

# Twenty-Seven

## MICAH

"Happy Birthday, baby. Make a wish and blow out the candles," Sienna says, grinning from ear to ear.

"I already have everything I could ever want," I tell her, not giving a shit that the fifty people gathered to celebrate my birthday can hear me sounding like a damn sap.

Everyone sighs and Sienna scrunches her nose in embarrassment. "Just blow out the damn candles," she says, playfully nudging my shoulder.

"Or, I can do it," Ellie cuts in. "I could always use an extra wish." She smirks like the teenage brat she is, and Sienna rolls her eyes.

"Go for it," I tell her.

Ellie doesn't waste any time closing her eyes and

then blowing out my candles. Everyone claps and then the caterer appears to cut and serve the cake. The party is being held in a private room at the hotel. There's an open bar, a four-course dinner, cake, and a dance floor where I've spent the majority of the evening dancing with Sienna.

"Here, have a bite," Sienna says, forking a piece and putting it up to my mouth. "Good?" she asks once I've chewed and swallowed.

"It's my favorite." Chocolate with whipped cream and strawberries.

She takes a bite and moans. "So good. Too bad we didn't get to have cake at our wedding. I saw in a movie once that the bride and groom are supposed to feed each other." She forks another bite and feeds it to me. "She starts off giving him a bite and then ends up smashing it in his face." She giggles and I pull her into my arms.

"You even think about smashing that cake in my face, and I'll take the rest of it home, cover you in it, and eat it off your body."

"Is that supposed to be a threat?" She laughs. "You can eat food off me any time you want." With another piece on her fork, she teasingly brings it up to her lips, making a show out of slowly sliding it into her mouth. She moans, sounding a lot like when I make her come, causing my dick to swell in my pants.

"I think it's time to go," I rasp. "Someone promised me a birthday blowjob, and I'm ready to collect."

It was how she convinced me to go along with this

birthday party bullshit. *"If you're a good birthday boy and let us throw you a party, afterward, I'll give you the birthday BJ of your life."* And how the fuck could I say no to that?

Sienna cackles and shakes her head, but I see the glint in her eye. She's ready to go as much as I am. "Okay, fine," she concedes. "You've done good. We can start saying our goodbyes so we can go upstairs and I can give you your birthday gifts."

It takes way too fucking long to get away, but once we're back at our place, the wait is well worth it when Sienna walks out of the bathroom wearing some sexy lingerie I've never seen her in. Ellie asked if she could spend the night at a friend's house after the party, so we have the place all to ourselves.

She clicks the wireless remote to the sound system that connects to our devices via Bluetooth and some chick starts to sing about some guy being obsessed with her. I chuckle, knowing this was intentional. My wife loves to poke fun at the way we started—my obsession for her. And she isn't wrong. If anything, that obsession has only increased over time.

With a sway to her hips that she knows turns me on, she saunters toward me, pushing me back onto the edge of the bed once she's reached me.

She wastes no time stripping me down to nothing before she goes to town on my cock, giving me the best damn blowjob of my life. Before long, I'm shooting my cum down her perfect, slim throat, gripping her to me as she swallows. Once she's drained me of every last drop, she sits back and licks her lips, flashing me a shy but satisfied grin. Quickly, I turn the tables, and Sienna is taken by surprise when I splay her out on the bed and feast on her until she's screaming out in pleasure.

When we've both come multiple times and she can barely keep her eyes open, we rinse off and climb into bed. Just as she does every night, she drapes herself across my body like the best kind of blanket and nuzzles her face into my neck.

"Did you have a good birthday?" she asks, her voice raspy with sleep.

I run my fingers through her hair, knowing it will put her to sleep quickly and murmur, "The fucking best." Dipping down slightly, I kiss the crown of her head, inhaling her floral scent that I'm addicted to.

I don't know when we fall asleep, but at some point, something wakes me up. I glance around and find Sienna still curled up into my side. And then my phone lights up.

I grab it and see a text from Oscar:

OSCAR

**Was dealing with a shipment and heard Sienna's mom was spotted. Grabbed her before she was brought to Gutierrez. Figured I'd let you decide what to do with your mother-in-law. I've got her at the warehouse. And FYI: she's a crazy fucking bitch, so good luck with that.**

The text was sent a couple minutes ago, and I also have a missed call. This must be what woke me up. I text back that I'll meet him at the warehouse and then carefully remove Sienna from my side. She groans softly but stays asleep.

As I get dressed, I think about what I want to happen regarding her mom. I should call Gutierrez and tell him I have her. Feed her ass to the wolves. But as I pocket my phone and keys, Sienna's words come back to me: *"I hope one day she gets the help she needs."*

Fuck, Lincoln is right. I really have turned soft.

"I DON'T NEED REHAB!" LENORA HISSES. "WHAT I NEED IS for my daughter to tell me why the fuck my home was burned to the ground."

When I told her I would take her to Sienna, I lied, but she went along with it, thinking she was being taken to her daughter. Until she saw the sign for the drug rehab facility.

"You don't have a fucking house because you screwed with Gutierrez," I bark, at my wit's end with this drug-addled woman. "You killed and you stole and then they came after you, and when they couldn't get to you, they went after Sienna. They killed your druggy pimp and were going to kill your daughter." This has Lenora stopping in her place and finally paying attention.

"They burned your place down, and I moved your daughters in with me to keep them safe. Gutierrez is still after you, and he won't stop until you're dead. So, you have two choices here...You can either go to rehab, get clean, and I can help you disappear, or I can drop you off at his doorstep. Which one will it be?"

"Wait," she says, her brow furrowed. "How is he after me if he's dead?"

"Not him, his son," I explain. "Eleazar Gutierrez came back from Mexico to extract revenge on his father's killer."

"Eleazar...it can't be." She glances up at me. "Eleazar Sanchez?"

Almost nobody refers to him with his mother's maiden name. I only know it because we were close at one time. Whenever he didn't want someone to know the family he was linked to, he would use his mother's last name. "Eleazar Sanchez Gutierrez," I correct.

"Okay, I'll go to rehab," she says, scrambling out of the car. I have no idea why she's suddenly changed her mind, but I don't give a shit. She's going to rehab—that's all that matters.

"Where were you?" Sienna asks when I walk through the door a couple of hours later. "Everything okay?"

"Yeah." I kiss the top of her head and consider telling her the truth, but I don't want to get her hopes up. The woman in admitting told me that Lenora can check herself out at any time, and unfortunately most do. "I had some business to deal with. What do you want to do today?"

"I was thinking a picnic. Ellie is spending the day at her friend's. We can go by the deli on the corner and pack a lunch and take it to the park."

"That sounds like the perfect way to spend our day."

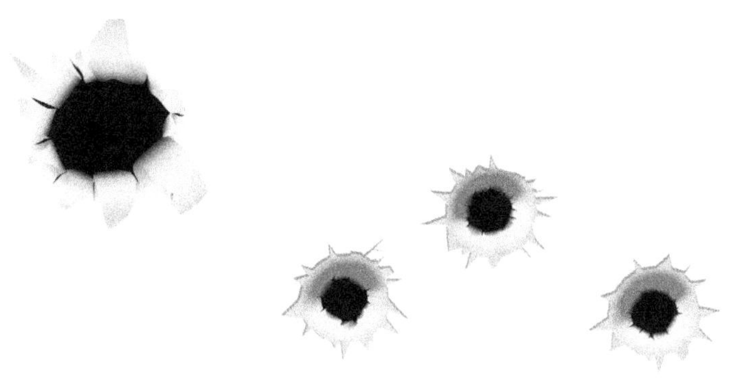

# Twenty-Eight

## ELEAZAR GUTIERREZ

"Boss, there's a woman here to see you. She fits the description of the woman who killed your father."

I drop my fork onto my plate and glance at my wife, who quirks a brow. Could it be that easy? Could the woman who killed my father be handing herself over on a silver platter? If she thinks she can convince me to spare her life, just as I did for her daughter, she couldn't be more wrong.

"Bring her around back to the holding cell," I say, not wanting her to taint this home more than it already is, thanks to her. This is where she stole and killed my father, and I won't allow her back in here again.

"After this, can we please go?" my wife whines. "I've already missed two appointments." We've been trying for years to have children, but we haven't been blessed yet. She's suffered four miscarriages, and now she can't seem to get pregnant at all. The only doctor she trusts is back home in Mexico.

"Yes, you can start packing," I tell her as I stand. "We'll leave this afternoon."

I've already gotten a handle on the business. The only thing keeping me here was the hope of finding this bitch so I could end her life the way she ended my father's. Now that she's resurfaced, once I put a bullet in her head, my business in this town will be concluded.

"Why have you come back here?" I ask the strung-out whore when I enter the holding cell. The question is born out of curiosity more than anything else. Her brown hair is greasy, and her clothes are tattered. The report said she's in her early forties, but this woman looks like she's at least a decade older.

"You don't remember me, do you?" she asks, smiling like she's in on a secret I know nothing about.

"I know you're the bitch who drugged, stole from, and killed my father." Reminding myself what she did has my temperature rising. I pull my gun out from its holder and aim it at her head, ready to blow her brains out. I considered torturing her, but now I just want her gone.

She shakes her head and grins wider—crazy bitch. "Sixteen years ago at Gloria's. Your eighteenth birthday."

It takes a second, but once I wrack my brain, I vaguely recall the night she's talking about. "What about it?" I ask, removing the safety, ready to end the whore's life.

"You won't kill me," she says smugly.
"And why the fuck not?"
"Because I have something you want…"

# Twenty-Nine

## SIENNA

"I can't believe she's dead," I say, as we stare at the urn that holds Lenora's ashes.

"It was inevitable," Ellie murmurs. "Maybe now she can finally be at peace."

"When did you get so wise?" I ask, wrapping my arm around her. When the police department notified Micah that our mom was found dead—a single gunshot to her heart—they said they didn't have any suspects, but I didn't expect they would. Not after Micah confessed he tried to save her by bringing her to rehab, only for her to run once he left.

I don't know what was going through her head, but whatever it was, it cost Lenora her life. Micah asked if we wanted to hold a service for our mom, but Ellie and

I decided against it. We have her ashes in the urn and knowing she's finally at peace is enough for us. We should probably be sadder than what we are, but it's been a long time coming, and I think we were both waiting for the day it finally happened. She made her choices, Micah tried to get her help, and her ending was completely her own undoing.

"I've learned it from you," Ellie says, leaning into me.

"At least now with her being declared dead, we should be able to get guardianship of you quicker," I say, trying to spin what's happened into a positive.

Ellie glances up at me and nods. "I agree. Once I know no one can take me from you, I'll feel a lot better."

"How about some lunch?" Micah asks. "You've been holed up in here for a few days now. Let me take you both out to eat."

"Sounds good," Ellie and I say at the same time. She took a couple of days off from school and will be going back on Monday. She didn't feel it was necessary, but I'm concerned that our emotional detachment over Lenora's death is only temporary, and once the numbness wears off, she might break down and need some time to work through her feelings.

"Sienna Alexander," a gentleman says when we step outside the building. Because it's a beautiful day out, Micah suggested we walk to the restaurant to get some fresh air.

"That's me."

"You've been served." He thrusts an envelope at me

and then adds, "Please sign here."

I scribble my signature on the line and then he nods and takes off.

I glance at Micah, confused, and then open the envelope. When I pull the papers out, I skim the words over and over again. "No," I gasp. "This can't be true."

"What is it?" Micah asks, as I stumble toward him, needing his comfort. This can't be happening. It doesn't make sense.

"Paternity test for Ellie?" Micah says, reading the papers.

"For me?" Ellie asks. "Who?"

"Eleazar Gutierrez," Micah answers.

"The man who wanted Sienna dead?" Ellie shakes her head. "I don't understand."

"According to these papers, he has reason to believe that you're his daughter. He's seeking a paternity test and full custody of you."

"What?" she shrieks. "Can he even do that?"

"He's claiming to be your only living parent."

"Oh, God." I pull Ellie into my arms while still being held by Micah. "We're not going to let him do this." I glance up at Micah. "Right? I can't lose my sister to a fucking crime boss. He's dangerous. Look what he's already done. He tried to have me killed, and we both know he's the one responsible for murdering our mom. Who the hell knows what else he's capable of?"

"We'll figure it out," he says, but the worry in his eyes has me on edge. Micah is rich and powerful, and his name alone holds a lot of weight in this town, but if there's one man who could give him a run for his money, it's Eleazer Gutierrez. And then it hits me…

"Eleazar…" I back up and look at Ellie. "Eliza." Her eyes go wide. "That bitch knew the name of your sperm donor this entire time and never told us." I asked her so many times over the years and she refused to tell me, swearing he wasn't worth remembering. She was a damn liar.

"We can't stay here," I blurt out. "We have to run. Get as far away from him as possible."

"Sienna," Micah says, reaching for me. "Running isn't the answer."

"Why? Because it would mean leaving you?" I hiss, averting his touch. "I told you I didn't have room in my life for anyone but Ellie, but you didn't listen, and now," I choke out. "We have to go. We can't stay here. I can't risk him taking her."

Micah grabs me and pulls me into his arms, refusing to let me go. "I promise we'll do whatever it takes to keep him away from Ellie, but he already knows about her, and even with my money and resources, she's on his radar. He won't stop looking until he finds her."

His words have my blood turning cold. This can't be happening. I thought with our mom dead, we would finally have a chance at a safe, normal life, but I should've known it wouldn't be that easy. Everywhere we turn, there's always someone trying to bring us down.

"Sienna," Ellie says softly. "Please don't push Micah

away. He loves you, and no matter what happens, you deserve to be loved."

"Hey," Micah says to Ellie. "Your sister isn't the only one who deserves love. You do, too. And as much of a pain in the ass as you are at times, this place wouldn't be the same without you." He pulls Ellie into a side hug and kisses her temple. "I love you, kiddo."

"I love you, too," Ellie chokes out. "And I love my school and my life and my friends. For the first time, I'm safe and happy and we have a home. I don't want to leave. I don't want to run." She glances at Micah. "Set up a meeting with Eleazar. I want to speak to him."

"What? No way," I snap. "No, the man is dangerous!"

"And he's my bio dad," she says. "He's not going to hurt me. If he wanted to do that, he could've come after me, but instead, he filed for custody. Please," she says to Micah, "I want to speak to him."

Micah nods. "I'll make it happen."

# Thirty

## MICAH

"We had a deal." I drop the papers onto Eleazar's desk, and he leans back, casually lacing his fingers behind his head.

"And I honored it," he says. "Is your wife's heart still beating?"

"What will it take for you to leave Ellie alone?"

"Did you know that Arielle and I have been trying to have a baby for the past six years?" he says, ignoring my question. "Rounds of IVF, four miscarriages…The doctors aren't sure if we'll ever have a baby of our own."

"That sucks," I deadpan. "But in case you aren't aware, Ellie isn't a fucking baby."

"No, but she's my blood." He leans in toward me. "I need an heir. Would've preferred a boy, but she'll do. I can always marry her off..."

"She's not fucking cattle!" I bark. "You can't barter with her life."

He shrugs. "Everyone serves a purpose. You'd do better to go along with this. I won't keep her sister from her. She'll have to move to Mexico with me, but she can visit."

As I stare at him for several seconds, knowing he's dead fucking serious and nothing I say or do is going to sway him any other way, it hits me like a freight train at max speed—there's only one way to protect Sienna and Ellie.

"You're leaving."

"What?" Sienna gasps.

"No!" Ellie cries.

"You don't have a choice. Eleazar is not going to stop until he has you. And he doesn't just want custody. He wants to own you."

"Let me talk to him," Ellie begs, while Sienna stands frozen in her place, tears welling in her eyes because she understands the implications of what I'm saying: This is the end for us.

"It's not happening, El. There is no talking to him. You guys have to run now. I have the money and resources to make you disappear, but it has to be before Eleazar realizes what's happening."

"Micah," Sienna sobs, but she doesn't argue because I promised to protect them, and she knows that's exactly what I'm doing.

"Go pack a bag. Make sure you have all the essentials since you won't be able to stop for anything."

"No!" Ellie barks. "I'm not running."

I step up to her and put a hand on her shoulder. "Yes, you will run. Your sister has fought tooth and nail to keep you safe, and I'll be damned if all of that's for nothing. You are her entire world, and the only way to protect you from Eleazar's clutches is by running."

"What about you?" Ellie asks softly. "Will you come with us?"

I glance toward Sienna, whose tears track down her cheeks even harder. "No, I have to stay here. I have my parents and brother. I need to keep an eye on things, keep my ear to the ground for what Eleazar is planning."

Ellie's eyes flit between her sister and me. "But what about Sienna?"

"I love your sister with all of my being. That will never change." I lock eyes with Sienna, needing her to not only hear the words but feel them. "But sometimes you have to love someone enough to let them go."

"Oh, fuck that!" Ellie hisses. "That's so cliché. When you love someone, you fight. You don't let them go."

"You do when you're saving their life," Sienna says, her voice broken. "I couldn't live without you, El. And I don't ever want to find out."

"So, let me talk to him. I can make this right. I'm his

daughter, which has to mean something."

"Yeah, it means he feels he has control over you and your future, and the only way to keep you from being caught under his thumb is for you to get as far away from him as possible," I tell her. "Now, please go pack a bag. I have arrangements to make. We'll plan for you guys to leave tonight."

I'm on the phone, working with a friend of mine who's a retired Marshall and has dealt with his fair share of witness protection cases, when Sienna walks in and goes straight to me, settling in my lap.

"Rodriquez, someone just walked in. Look into what we talked about, and I'll call you back soon."

I hang up just as Sienna situates herself so that her thighs spread across mine, straddling me. "Are you all packed?" I ask, trying to remain strong for my wife.

"Yeah," she breathes, nuzzling her face into my neck. I feel her breathe me in, and I get choked up, knowing she's trying to memorize my scent because this is the last time she'll see me, smell me, feel me.

"I love you, Hellcat," I tell her, inhaling her floral scent. "Never forget that."

"I know," she chokes out. "You've showed me every day that we've been together, but never more so than today."

Slowly, she lifts up to look at me, and the sight of her splotchy, tear-stained face has me wanting to run away with her. But I can't do that. If I want to keep Sienna and Ellie safe, I need to stay behind to keep an eye on Eleazar.

When he finds out they're gone, he's going to flip his shit. Hell, there's a chance he's going to come after me, but that's another reason why I have to stay. I can't risk him going after my brother or parents.

"I will love you forever," I tell her, framing her face. "We won't be able to talk, but just know that I will always be thinking about you. You are my beginning and my end. You are my life. And I'm so lucky to have had this time with you."

Sienna's sobs deepen, and I hate that my words are hurting her. So, I kiss her instead, hoping to convey everything I feel. The moment our mouths fuse, we attack each other with frenzy, both of us knowing this will be the last time we're together like this. It feels like only yesterday when I made love to my wife for the very first time, yet it feels like we've known each other forever. When I'm with Sienna, time seems to stand still.

But as I lay her out on my desk and remove her clothes, it feels like time is suddenly moving too quickly. The clock is ticking. Our time is limited.

Once we're both naked, I start with her mouth and move to her jaw, then to her neck and collarbone, kissing and memorizing every inch of her, trying to get in a lifetime's worth of touches. When I get to her pussy, I stick my nose between her pink folds, inhaling her essence, wondering how the fuck I'm supposed to live without her.

I lick and devour her, bringing her close to the precipice and then pulling her back, not wanting the moment to end. When she begs for release, I give in and take her over the edge.

And then I'm inside her, right where I belong, where I wish I could spend the rest of my life. With one hand digging into the curve of her hip and the other holding her face, I make love to my wife, hoping months, hell, years from now, she'll look back and remember how much I loved her.

As we both find our release, she chokes out my name, and I crush my mouth to hers, needing us to be connected in every way possible. How ironic is it that I waited over thirty years to find the woman I want to spend my life with, and now I have to let her go after only a few short months.

"Micah, I can't do this," Sienna cries. When I separate our bodies and pull her into my arms, I don't give a shit that my cum is dripping out of her and likely all over my clothes.

"You can," I murmur into her ear. "You can for Ellie. She comes first. Maybe one day..." I trail off, stopping myself, not wanting to give either of us false hope.

"Thank you for loving me," she says softly, kissing my neck. "For not giving up on me and tearing down my walls. Before you, I didn't know what it felt like to be in love, but you showed me more love in these past few months than I've felt in my entire life."

"Loving you is as easy as breathing," I tell her, not for the first time.

We stay like this for several minutes, and then, because we don't want the moment to end, I put my shirt on her and carry her to our bathroom where we shower together. We stand under the water until it turns cold and then for a little while after that.

When we can't delay the inevitable any longer, I tell her I'm going to touch base with my contact, and she tells me she's going to check on Ellie.

I'm on the phone when Sienna tears into my office, horror etched in her features. "She's gone," she stammers. "Ellie's gone."

# Thirty-One

## SIENNA

IT'S BEEN OVER THREE DAYS SINCE ELLIE WALKED OUT THE door. During which time I've gone from hating myself for being too consumed by Micah to notice her leaving, to being pissed at my sister because she's not a damn baby and knows better, to hating myself for being pissed at her because being pissed at her won't bring her home.

Micah and his team of men were able to confirm she went to see Eleazar. The cameras showed her leaving the penthouse, going down the elevator, and stepping outside the building, and Micah's contact at the PD was able to get her on camera getting into a taxi that dropped her off at Eleazar's front gate.

Micah has reached out to Eleazar, but he's not responding, and his guard on duty said he's not accepting any visitors. He had her phone tracked, but it was a dead end, so it's probably been destroyed. Eleazar might be a piece of shit, but his family didn't get to where they are by being dumb.

"Here, try to swallow a bit of ginger ale," Donna says, rubbing my back. I'm currently situated with my body wrapped around the porcelain bowl wondering how I'm still throwing up when there's no way there's anything left in my body.

"Thank you," I tell her, sitting back against the cool tile wall. "The stress of Ellie missing is really getting to me."

Donna purses her lips, and I can see it in her features that she's about to say something I'm not going to like. "Do you think it's possible that your sickness isn't due to stress?"

"Like what?" I ask, sipping the warm drink.

"Like, maybe...you're pregnant."

Without even having to think about it, I say, "No, I'm on birth control. Maybe I have a flu bug or something, though."

She nods but doesn't look convinced. She's been with me the past three days, holding my hair back, patting my neck with cool washcloths, all while Micah works around the clock to find Ellie.

"Okay, well, I brought this." She pulls a pregnancy test out of her purse and sets it on the counter.

"I'm not—"

"I know," she says, "but just in case, it's here if you

want to take it." She pulls me into her arms and hugs me tightly. "Micah is going to get Ellie back. I just know it. There's nothing that boy wants that he doesn't get when he's motivated." I chuckle at that, knowing what she's saying to be true.

"I'm going to the store to pick up some things and then I'll be back later with dinner. Do you need anything?"

"No, thank you."

"Okay, rest. I know it's easier said than done, but your sister needs you healthy."

After she leaves, I stare at the test on the counter, wondering if there's any truth to what she said. I think back to the last time I got my period. It was a few months ago, before I got on birth control, but my periods have never been regular, so I didn't think anything of it.

Is it possible? I guess there's only one way to find out.

## PREGNANT

THE BOLD CAPITAL LETTERS FILL THE SCREEN ON NOT ONE, not two, but three tests. I'm pregnant. I did everything I was supposed to do and still ended up pregnant.

I stare at myself in the mirror, my hand going to my still flat belly. There's a baby in there. I can't see it or feel it. But it's in there. A baby that Micah and I created. A baby who will need love and attention, who will need to be nurtured and cared for. There's so much that can go wrong. A million ways we can mess up this baby's life.

*You are nothing like your mother.*

I repeat the words, trying to stop myself from getting in my own head, but what I need is for Micah to hold me, to tell me everything will be okay. He's my safe place. My strength. He'll know what to do, what to say. He'll make it better.

This is literally the worst timing, but that seems to be the theme of my life.

I call his phone, but it goes straight to voicemail. So I call again—voicemail. I'm about to send him a text when my phone lights up with an incoming call from unknown.

"Hello."

"Sienna." Only my name is spoken, but the way it's said sends chills racing up my spine.

"Who's this?"

"I have your sister. If you want her back in one piece, I suggest you come get her. This is her only chance at escaping."

"Who are you?"

"You won't get another chance to save her. She'll be waiting for you at Tesoro Park. Come alone so you don't draw attention."

The line goes dead, and I race toward Micah's office where he keeps his car keys, grabbing the ones I use when I need to drive somewhere. As I run out the door, his security tries to stop me, but I demand they move, desperate to get to my sister. I don't know who that was on the phone, but it doesn't matter. My sister needs me.

As I drive to Tesoro Park, I try calling Micah once more, and this time he answers. "I'm going to get Ellie," I cry out, the second I hear his voice.

"What do you mean you're going to get Ellie? Sienna, where are you?"

"I'm going to get her," I repeat. "Some woman is helping her escape. I have to pick her up from Tesoro Park."

"Sienna, baby. I need you to calm down. You can't go alone. Give me a few minutes and we'll figure this out. I have guys working on—"

"I can't," I say, cutting him off. "She's going to be waiting for me. The woman said it's her only chance. I have to go get her now."

"Fuck," he curses. "I don't like this, Hellcat."

"I have to," I choke out. "She needs me."

"Okay, I'm tracking you now. As soon as you have her, you need to drive toward the edge of town. I'm going to stay on the phone with you and start heading that way, and then we'll figure out what to do next."

"Okay, thank you," I tell him, as I arrive at my destination and pull into the empty parking lot. There's a playground nearby, but nobody is there. I spot an SUV at the end of the road and drive toward it, my heart pounding in my chest.

"Sienna, do you see her?" Micah asks.

"Not yet, but there's an SUV."

"I don't like this," he murmurs.

The door to the SUV opens and a woman gets out. I

don't recognize her, but with her jet-black hair and pale skin, she looks to be Hispanic.

"I think the woman who called me is walking over. I'm going to get out and talk to her. I don't see Ellie anywhere."

"Stay on the phone with me!" Micah barks, as I open my door.

I'm not paying attention to my surroundings, too focused on the woman, so I don't realize what's happening until it's too late. Someone comes up from behind me and snatches my phone out of my hand, sending it flying, while my hands are pulled together and tied.

"What are you doing?" I yell at the woman, who stands there in her tight black dress and stilettos, her blood red lips curled in an evil smirk. "Where's my sister?"

"Don't worry, dear, you're going to see her soon," she says, with a thick accent.

"You said you were helping her escape!"

"I lied," she says, nonchalantly.

I'm dragged down the street to the SUV, where another man opens the trunk and shoves me in. I kick and scream, but it's useless.

What feels like forever later, I'm lifted out and forced into what looks like some sort of basement.

"Sienna!" Ellie shrieks, flinging herself at me just as the door slams shut. "I'm so sorry," she cries, and goes about untying my hands. "I never should've went to see him. I'm so sorry." Tears stream down her cheeks. "I'm so sorry. I'm so—"

"Shh, it's okay," I tell her, wrapping my arms around her shaking body. "It's okay. Who is she?" I ask, rubbing my hands up and down her arms, trying to calm her.

"Eleazer's wife," she cries, burrowing herself into me as she apologizes over and over for going to him when she should've listened to us and stayed.

"It's okay," I murmur. "Micah knows something is wrong. He'll get us out of here."

I move to let go of Ellie so I can check the place out, but she clings to me, refusing to let go. I hold her tight, repeating to her that everything is going to be okay.

When she's finally calmed down, I gently break away and survey the empty, dingy room, trying to open the only window that's shining light in. Of course it doesn't budge, and neither do the doors.

When a weird smell wafts in the air, my stomach roils, and I have no choice but to run to the corner to throw up. Since I haven't eaten anything, it's a mixture of acid and liquid.

"Are you okay?" Ellie whispers. When I glance at her, I notice her bloodshot eyes and the dark circles underneath. Her hair's greasy, and the tank top she's wearing is dirty and ripped. She looks like she's been to hell and back.

"Yeah, something smells rancid."

"Like death," she agrees, her vacant gaze glancing around the room.

"Hey, El, did anyone—"

Before I can finish my question, I'm retching again. This goes on for several minutes until my body finally gives me a moment to take a breather.

"What's wrong?" Ellie asks, when I become too lightheaded to remain standing and situate myself on the nasty basement floor.

"I'm pregnant." I close my eyes and lay my head against the rough wall. "I only just found out."

"What?" Ellie gasps. "No… No. No. No." She shakes her head, fresh tears sliding down her face. "I did this. This is all my fault. I went to go see him and now—"

"Hey, stop it. You couldn't have known. But don't worry, Micah will find us and get us out of here."

"No, you don't get it. She's going to kill us," Ellie mutters. "She—"

"Well, aren't you observant?" The woman from earlier says, as she walks into the room, followed by the guy who helped throw me into the trunk. "You are nothing but a stupid *bastarda* born from a whore." She steps into our space and reaches for Ellie, fisting her hair. "You don't deserve anything, and I'm going to ensure you never get a dime."

I don't know who this woman is, but her words and actions have me jumping up to protect my sister. "Don't you dare speak to my sister like that," I say, getting in her face and forcing her to release Ellie.

"Back up," the guard says, stepping into my personal space. "Or I'll have to teach you some manners, the same way I taught your—"

"Leave her alone!" Ellie shrieks. "Don't you touch her!"

"Looks like you haven't learned your lesson," the man says.

"I've had enough!" the woman barks. "Sit down and shut up!" The woman shoves me back, and I stumble, tripping over my own feet and falling to the floor. When my back hits the harsh ground, the wind is knocked from my lungs.

Just as I'm glancing up, I see a foot coming toward my stomach. I curl into myself like a shrimp, attempting to protect my baby, but before she makes contact, a loud gunshot rings out.

I pop my head up and see Ellie holding a gun and the woman on the floor, blood pooling around her body.

"What the fuck did you do?" the guard barks. He snatches the gun from a shocked Ellie and points it at her.

"Enough!" a loud voice rings out, forcing our attention toward the man who's walked in brandishing his own weapon. "Give me that gun." The guard nods once and hands it over.

The men speak in Spanish for several seconds, and I have no clue what they're saying, but whatever it is, it can't be good because the man who just walked in glares at Ellie.

"First, your whore of a mother kills my father. Now my daughter, my own flesh and blood, kills my wife. I should shoot you dead. But since I still need you, I've come up with a much better option..."

He moves the gun a foot to the right and aims it at me.

"Wait, please," Ellie screams. "It's not her fault. I did this. I killed Arielle. She kidnapped me from the room you put me in and…" As Ellie rambles on, begging him not to kill me, I stare down the barrel of the gun, my life flashing before me. But it's not my past I see. It's the future I'll never have. My belly swelling with a baby, Micah doting on me, putting together a nursery. The baby's first ultrasound, her first cries, first steps, first words. Picnics at the park. Watching Ellie graduate. Making love to my husband.

My fingers splay out across my belly, and my eyes close, wanting the last things I see and think about to be happy. A second gunshot rings out, and as I accept my fate, I pray that death finds me quickly.

# Thirty-Two

## MICAH

While my wife was calling me, *needing me*, I had no idea that a tower was down for maintenance, and my phone was getting zero signal. Then, when it rang, and Sienna was freaking out, I could barely understand a goddamn word of what she was saying. But when she screamed, I heard and felt that shit in my fucking soul.

The second the line went quiet, I knew she was no longer with her phone, and I pulled up the tracker I have on her—which is a tiny chip in the ballet slipper charm I gave her. I never thought I'd need to use it, but better to be safe than sorry.

I was already with Lincoln and our team of men figuring out how to locate Ellie, so when I knew Sienna had been taken, we suited up and took off after her. It didn't take long to track her to the Gutierrez's warehouse. Since they weren't expecting us, we had the element of surprise on our side and were able to easily take them out.

Finding Sienna and Ellie was easy because all we had to do was follow the raised voices. But when we got there, we realized that shit had already hit the fan. Eleazar's wife was on the floor bleeding out, while Eleazar was pointing a gun at my wife and Ellie was begging him not to kill her. Without thought, I put several bullets in him, and Lincoln took out his guard. My wife was in danger, and I meant what I said. She comes first, always.

With Eleazar and his wife dead, I had my men clean up while Lincoln and I got Sienna and Ellie out. Both were trembling and crying, obviously traumatized by what they had witnessed. I don't know who killed Arielle, but even when it's deserved, taking someone's life is never easy.

Now we're back at the penthouse. Sienna is curled up in my lap, and Ellie is still holding onto Lincoln. Both of them are still shaking and crying softly, and if I could kill the assholes who did this to them all over again, I would.

"Hey, Linc," I say, "Someone should probably go to the warehouse." Because there's nobody left in the Gutierrez family, there won't be anyone to retaliate, but we need to double check that all our tracks are covered to safeguard us against the cops.

He nods and starts to sit up, but Ellie latches on tighter, whimpering. "Please don't leave me," she murmurs.

"I'll go," Rex offers. "Bruno has already spoken to the

cops, so everything has been handled."

"Thank you," I tell him. "Keep me updated."

"I need to go to the bathroom," Sienna murmurs, sniffling back her tears.

When Sienna is gone, Ellie turns to look at me, and all I can see is devastation and fear in her eyes. I'm confused as to why she's still fearful since the threat has been removed. Then, in a trembling voice, she asks, "Am I...Am I going to go to jail?"

It takes me a second to wrap my head around her question before it hits me..."You're the one who shot Arielle?"

"She went after Sienna," she chokes out. "Was going to kick her...I couldn't let her hurt the baby."

"Micah," Sienna breathes.

I turn my attention toward where my wife is slumped over, her arms wrapped around her waist, her face way too damn pale.

"Hellcat, what's wrong?" I ask, going over to her.

Tears fill her lids and then spill over. "I'm bleeding."

*What?* "Where?" I drag my eyes down her body, trying to find where she's hurt, but I don't see any blood. "Where are you hurt?" I ask, getting worried. She seemed okay when I carried her to the car. Shaken up, yeah, but not injured.

"The baby," she murmurs, and Ellie's words that I didn't have time to absorb, immediately click.

Sienna's pregnant, and Arielle was going to kick her in the stomach, so Ellie shot her.

Fuck.

"You're pregnant?" I ask softly, palming her cheek and wiping the falling tears.

She nods. "I found out today. I tried to call you," she says, fresh tears sliding down her face, and my heart cracks. She needed me and I wasn't fucking there. Dammit.

"I went to pee and there was blood. I...I don't know what to do." She looks up at me, silently begging for me to make this right, but I have no idea how. So, I do the only thing I can think of. I call my mom, who advises me to take Sienna to the hospital, which is exactly what I do.

I offer for Lincoln to stay with Ellie, but she insists she wants to be there with her sister, and I get it. They've both been through a traumatic ordeal, and now her sister might be losing her baby that she only just found out about.

"I'll drive," Lincoln offers, so I can sit in the back with my wife. I hold her the entire way, praying that everything's okay.

Fortunately for us, it's a slow night at the hospital, so Sienna is seen right away. Since only one person can go back with her, Lincoln stays with Ellie in the waiting room. The nurse asks Sienna a bunch of questions and then attaches a band with a barcode and all of her pertinent info to her wrist. We're taken to a private room where she's given a gown to put on while we wait for her to be seen.

Once she's dressed, she sits up on the bed and her eyes meet mine. "I didn't want to get pregnant," she says quietly, liquid emotion filling her lids. "But now..." she chokes out, shaking her head, and I cut across the room to pull her into my arms. I hold her tight while she silently cries into my chest for several minutes before she speaks again. "I want our baby," she admits. "When I thought I was going to die, I saw it...our baby, our family. I could never really picture it before, but in that moment, it was all so clear. I felt so much happiness. Then, just as quickly, it was gone."

I want to tell her everything is going to be okay, but since I don't know if that's true, I tell her the only truth I do know. "I love you, Sienna, and no matter what happens, we'll get through it together." She nods into my chest and snuggles closer.

"Good afternoon," the doctor says. "I'm Dr. Peterson. Are you Sienna?"

"I am," she says, sitting up and wiping her eyes.

"Can you tell me what's going on?"

She explains to the doctor that she's been sick, but she had passed it off as stress since she's on birth control. When my mom suggested that she might be pregnant, she took three separate tests, all of which came out positive. But then later, she found blood on the tissue when she went to pee.

"All right, I'm going to have the nurse take your blood to run some tests. How far along do you think you are?"

"I don't know," she admits. "I haven't gotten my period in a while, and they're always so irregular."

"Based on the urine sample you gave when you arrived,

there is a high enough level of hCG to indicate you're pregnant. The spotting you noticed can mean several things, so rather than make assumptions, I'm going to run some blood tests and put in for an ultrasound."

After a nurse comes by and takes several tubes of blood, a woman comes in to take Sienna to the ultrasound. "You don't have to get up. I'll wheel your bed there," she says, with a soft smile. I notice the name on her tag reads Madeline.

"Can he come with me?" Sienna asks nervously, as if there's even the smallest chance that I would let her out of my sight. We have no idea what we're going to see, and there's no way I'm leaving her alone with a stranger, even if Madeline does seem friendly enough.

"Of course," she says.

When we arrive, the room is dark, and the tech explains she's setting up the equipment. Since Sienna's not sure how far along she is, she tells us she's going to do a transvaginal ultrasound. I stay by Sienna's side, holding her hand and massaging circles with my thumb, trying to reassure her that I'm here and that everything's going to be okay, one way or another.

The tech is quiet for several seconds, moving the instrument around inside of her and clicking buttons on the screen. My heart drops, thinking there must be something wrong. I can't tell what's on the screen, but it's grey and grainy and it doesn't look like there's a baby in there. Then again, I'm not sure what it is I should be seeing this early in the pregnancy.

A few moments later, a loud *whoosh, whoosh, whoosh* fills the quiet room, and Sienna gasps. "Is that my baby's heartbeat?"

"Yep, it sure is. And it's strong, too. Based on the measurements, you're roughly five weeks."

Holy shit, Sienna is five weeks pregnant. Despite her being on birth control, it seems fate had other plans.

Sienna squeezes my hand and glances up at me, her eyes glassy with emotion. "We're having a baby," she murmurs softly.

"Yeah, we are," I agree, leaning over and kissing her forehead.

The tech walks us through the ultrasound, while taking pictures for the doctor. She can't give us any information as to why Sienna was bleeding, but she says once the doctor has a look at the photos, he can tell us more.

After the ultrasound is finished, Sienna is wheeled back to the room, and we're told that the doctor will be in soon to go over all the results.

We wait in silence, unsure what to say. We saw our baby, heard the heartbeat, but that doesn't change the fact that Sienna was bleeding.

A little while later, the doctor returns and informs us that we have no need for concern. Everything looks good, including the bloodwork. "As for the bleeding, it's common in the beginning of a pregnancy due to implantation." He goes on to explain in more detail what the ultrasound showed, and once he's done, he says, "I'm going to discharge you and recommend a few days of bed rest and then a follow-up with your OB-GYN."

When he walks out, Sienna glances down at her flat stomach. "I can't believe there's a baby in there." I snort at how adorable she is. "Only your sperm would be so potent that even birth control can't stop them." She mock glares, and I bark out a laugh.

"You know you love my super sperm," I joke, waggling my eyes.

"This baby is going to be loved," Sienna says after a moment of silence.

"Damn right," I agree, already thinking of everything my wife is going to need during the next nine months. Then, after the baby comes...Fuck, there's so much to do and buy. "Let's get you home and into bed. Are you hungry? Thirsty? We should probably order more pillows so you're comfortable. And we need to find an OB-GYN. How are you feeling? I know the doctor said—"

"Micah," Sienna says with a laugh. "Breathe."

I don't know why she's laughing. I was being serious. "You better use the ride home to mentally prepare yourself, Hellcat," I warn her. She might be Miss Independent, but she's now pregnant with my baby, and that changes everything.

"For what?" she asks, obviously confused.

"The next nine months. You're carrying our baby. And it's my job to make sure you're taken care of and comfortable. You thought I was crazy when we first met... You haven't seen anything yet."

"Are you sure?" Ellie asks, her nose scrunched up in confusion.

"Yes, ma'am. Mr. Gutierrez put a rush on the paternity test and had me come over as soon as the results confirmed that you are his biological child. He asked me to amend his will to where if something should happen to him, you and his wife would split everything fifty-fifty. But because they both passed away, the entire estate goes to you as his only living relative. Since you aren't eighteen yet, I'll remain the executor of the estate until your eighteenth birthday."

It's been a week since Eleazar and his wife were pronounced dead—burned in an electrical fire at his warehouse. A couple of days afterward, Norman Eisenburg requested a meeting with Ellie. He's the Gutierrez family's attorney, and when he told me that he needed to meet with Ellie for the reading of the will, I damn near choked on my coffee.

"I don't want it," she says softly, her voice cracking with emotion. She's been like this ever since we rescued her and Sienna from the warehouse. Quiet, withdrawn. I told Sienna I thought her sister needed to see someone. She killed a person, and that's not an easy thing to live with, but Ellie refused, saying she just needs time.

Mr. Eisenburg looks at her like she's crazy, but before he can get a word in, I put my hand on Ellie's shoulder. "Right now, your emotions are all over the place. Before you make any rash decisions, why don't you sit on it for a little while? Regardless of how you feel about Eleazar Gutierrez, you are his blood, which means everything he left to you is rightfully yours."

"It's blood money," she mutters. "He was a criminal. Everyone who worked for him were disgusting criminals."

"Miss, if I may say something," the gentleman says gently. "The estate and assets are estimated at two hundred million dollars. If you don't want to partake in the *family business*"—he raises his brows to make it clear he's referring to the illegal aspects of it all—"you can simply sell off and walk away from the parts you don't want. But the rest of the money and investments are all clean."

Ellie swallows thickly. "Two hundred million?"

Mr. Eisenburg nods slowly.

"So, could I sell everything and keep the money?"

"Absolutely, you can," I tell her. "Mr. Eisenburg has to approve it all, but I don't think that will be a problem. And I can help you every step of the way."

She lets out a sigh. "Okay, then that's what I want to do. But anything of his that came from dirty money, I want to donate."

"You got it."

"Umm, Mr. Eisenburg, how soon can I purchase something? Like something kind of expensive?"

He quirks a brow. "It will depend on the amount, of course, but the papers will be processed with the courts later today, and by the end of the week, you will have access to everything."

When we're back in my car and heading home, Ellie says, "Can you stop somewhere for me, please?"

"Sure, where?"

"Lola's Dance Studio."

# Thirty-Three

## SIENNA

"You what?" I exclaim from bed. The doctor recommended a few days of bed rest, but Micah insisted I stay put for a week. Surprisingly, I didn't argue. I think between the traumatic events with Eleazar and learning I'm pregnant, then fearing I'd lost the baby, I needed some time to rest.

For the first few days, Ellie stayed home as well, but then she returned to school, saying she didn't want to fall behind.

"My sperm donor left everything to me," Ellie says, tears filling her eyes. She's been extremely emotional since everything happened. Micah suggested I take her to see someone, but she begged me not to, saying she just needs time.

I glance from Ellie to Micah in shock. "Is she for real?"

"Yep, she was left the entire Gutierrez estate," he confirms with a shrug.

"Wait, does that mean she's like some mob princess?" I shriek, starting to freak out. "Oh my God, is she in the mob?"

"No," Micah says with a laugh, which has me glaring his way. "The guy was corrupt, but like any smart businessman, he also had plenty of legal assets. His estate will be broken down and dismantled. Any dirty money will get donated at Ellie's request, and the legal money will go into a trust account that she'll have full access to once she turns eighteen. Until then, anything she chooses to purchase has to go through the executor of the estate, Norman Eisenburg, who seems like a decent guy."

"And I've already decided on the first thing I'm going to purchase with my money," Ellie adds, raw emotion laced in every word. "Lola's Dance Studio. Grace said she's thinking about selling it, and I want to buy it for you. You love to dance, and your dream was always to do just that."

"Oh, El," I rasp. "But not just for me, right? You've always said you're going to go to school locally and live at home. We could run it together."

Ellie smiles sadly, and not for the first time, it feels like something is off, but I can't figure out what, and she's not talking. "Yeah, maybe," she says noncommittally. "But for now, I just want this to be yours. You've given me so much, and I want to give this to you." She lays a hand gently on my belly. "And who knows? Maybe this little boy or girl will love dance as much as we do."

I choke up, my hormones getting the better of me. "Thank you." I wrap her into my arms and hug her tightly. "I love you, El."

"I love you, too," she says, standing. "I have a bunch of homework I need to get caught up on, so I'm going to go do that."

Once we're alone, Micah takes up the spot where Ellie was just sitting. "How are you feeling?"

"Emotional," I joke, making us both laugh. "I just can't believe how much our life has changed in such a short amount of time."

"For the good?" Micah confirms.

"Definitely. For so long, I felt like we were forced into a life neither one of us asked for. Until you came along, I was scared of falling in love, but you reminded me every step of the way that the risk is worth the reward."

"And what's the reward?" he asks, even though he knows damn well what it is. He just wants to hear me say it.

"The reward is love."

# Epilogue

## MICAH

"I can't find my pink leo!" Ellie shouts from somewhere in the house.

"Blue leo!" London, our almost two-year-old-daughter, adds.

"I haven't seen either one," Sienna yells from somewhere. "And I can't find London's ballet slippers. If anyone sees them, let me know."

It's official. My once bachelor pad has been overrun by women. And not just women—ballerinas.

I walk upstairs to London's room first and find her flinging her leotards all over the place, making a mess. Leaning against the door, I clear my throat to get her attention, and the second she sees me, her entire face lights up.

"Daddy!" She stops what she's doing and runs straight for me. She giggles as I lift her into my arms and over my head, pulling a move she loves from the dancing movie she watches repeatedly. Then she spreads her arms out wide and juts her legs out like she's a professional. When I bring her back down, she wraps her arms around me and kisses my cheek. "Blue leo?" she asks, her bright blue eyes—identical to her mother's—alight with hope.

"I don't know where it is, sweetheart. How about you put on another one?" Her eyes immediately dim, and I regret my words, knowing that wasn't the right thing to say. Like her mother and aunt, my daughter takes dancing seriously, and that includes wearing the leo she wants.

"Blue one." She pouts, wiggling for me to set her down. She runs back to where she's destroying her drawers, so I head out to find my wife next.

She's in the laundry room, sifting through the clothes, and I take a moment to watch her. Today, she's wearing a tight tank top and black leggings that show off every perfect curve. Her hair is up in a messy knot on the top of her head, and though I can't see her face, I would bet it's makeup free, aside from some of that glossy shit she wears on her lips that always gets all over mine when I kiss her.

When she feels me watching her, her head snaps up. "Hey, you're home," she says with a huff, blowing the unruly strands of hair out of her face.

"I am." I pull her into my arms and give her a kiss that's far too short for my liking, but I'll kiss her longer tonight once we're in bed. "How's my baby mama doing?"

"Feeling like a beached whale," she says with a laugh. As if the baby can hear her, her belly erupts with kicks that I can feel since her front is pressed against mine. We weren't planning to get pregnant so soon after she had London, but once again, fate had other plans. We're excited to welcome this baby into the world soon, and London is excited to be a big sister.

"I told you to take some time off," I say, even though I know she won't listen. She's due in a couple of weeks, but that doesn't stop her from dancing and teaching classes at the studio. She did the same thing when she was pregnant with London—I literally had to pick her up from the studio when her water broke.

"I think this is my last week," she says with a pout. "I spoke to Carmen, and she's agreed to take over my classes. I'm tired, and she can use the hours."

"Has anyone seen my pink leo?" Ellie asks, poking her head inside the laundry room. "I'm going to be late to class."

"Maybe use a different one for today until you can find that one?" I suggest.

Ellie's reaction is the same as London's, so I close my mouth and start searching for a pink and blue leo in the pile of clean laundry, mentally noting to hire someone to come in to organize this place as soon as possible. Three girls in one house is insane, and if my guess is correct, another will soon be added to the mix.

"Mommy, blue leo?" London asks, joining us in the laundry room.

"I'm look—" Sienna's eyes go wide. "Oh, God."

"My blue leo?" London asks, hopeful.

Sienna looks down, and I follow her line of vison.

"Mommy, you go pee pee on the floor," London says. "Gross! Use the toilet!"

"Oh, shit," Ellie hisses. "You're having the baby."

Pink and blue leos forgotten, Ellie scoops London up while I help Sienna to the car. The ride to the hospital is quick, and so is her labor. Within a couple of hours, our newborn is delivered. Just as we had done with London, we chose not to learn the baby's gender ahead of time, so we wait for the doctor to announce it.

"Congratulations, it's a healthy girl."

They clean up the baby a little and then place her on Sienna's chest so she can hold her. She kisses the top of our daughter's head and glances up at me, tears shining in her eyes. "You ready for another girl?" she chokes out, her voice filled with emotion.

Images of the clothes and shoes and hormones that have overtaken my home flash before my eyes, and I can't help but smile. "I wouldn't have it any other way."

## SIENNA

"There's something I need to tell you," Ellie says slowly, and I can already tell by her tone it's not going to be good. I thought that once everything settled down and we were safe and no longer struggling to make ends meet, it would strengthen our relationship, but for some reason, Ellie's shut me out. There's something that's eating away at her, but when I ask, she plasters on a smile and tells me everything is fine.

She still goes to school and dances, but she doesn't hang out with any of her friends or show any interest in dating. And she rarely spends any time at the studio. She says it's because she's busy with school and her senior showcase, but something feels off. I try to chalk it up to her being a hormonal teenager, but deep down, I think there's more to it. I just can't figure out what it is, and Ellie won't speak to me about it.

"Okay, what's up?" I say, taking Brooklyn off my breast. Since London was named after the city where I fell in love with Micah, we thought it was only right to name Brooklyn after the city where we renewed our vows.

"I've received my acceptance letters for college, and I've decided I'm going to California School of the Arts."

"California?" I say, confused. "But...I thought you were going to stay local."

"Mommy!" London yells, running in and jumping on the bed. "I give baby kiss." She leans over and kisses Brooklyn's head.

"We can talk later," Ellie says, but I shake my head.

"No, don't go, please. You always said you wanted to go to New York."

"I know," she says softly, "but I think California is a better fit."

"It's five hours away by plane," I choke out, letting my emotions get the better of me. "We've never been that far away from each other." Tears blur my vision, and I know I'm being unfair. Ellie deserves to go to whatever school she wants, but there seems to be something else driving her decision.

"You leaving me?" London asks, looking at Ellie. Despite Ellie keeping everyone at arm's length, she's a damn good aunt to London. Our daughter worships her and is not going to take it well if she moves across the country.

"Oh, London Bridge," Ellie says, silently begging for me to understand. "I'm going to be back all the time, I promise. And you'll come visit me."

"But I miss you," London murmurs. "I no want you to go."

"We'll see her a lot," I say, forcing a smile on my face.

"I no like it." London pouts, making Ellie do the same.

"London, stop," I say gently. "This is amazing news." I give Ellie a hug. "You've worked hard and deserve this. She'll be okay. We'll all be okay."

## MICAH

### FOUR YEARS LATER

"Good job, ladies. You looked so in sync today."

I watch from the back of the room as my wife praises the students in her class. A couple of the girls ask her questions about an upcoming performance, and she answers them with patience and smiles before telling them to have a good night and that she'll see them next class.

Since she doesn't know I'm here, once everyone is gone, she turns on the music and walks over to the barre to stretch. Inside this studio, she's in her element, and the outside world doesn't exist. I hate that she's unaware of her surroundings, but I know it's because she feels safe. It took a long time for her to feel that way, but she knows that I'll always make certain that she and our kids are secure.

When she lifts her foot onto the barre and bends forward, I step out from behind the wall. Her head lifts and our eyes lock in the mirror.

"What are you doing here?" she asks.

"Kids are spending the night with my parents." My mom and dad are hands-on grandparents. With Lincoln still refusing to settle down, London and Brooklyn are their only grandkids, and therefore, they are extremely spoiled by my parents.

"Hmm." A twinkle alights in her eyes as she bends slightly forward again, her gaze never leaving mine. I step toward her, bridging the gap between us until I'm standing directly behind her. She lowers her leg, then lifts the other, stretching it out. When she has both feet back on the floor, I settle my hands on her hips and pull her back against my front, my fingers stretching across her swollen belly. Six months pregnant. Ever since she told me this will be the last one, I find myself wanting to touch her even more, wanting to memorize the way her gorgeous body grows and changes when she's carrying our babies. Because it's our last child, once again, we've chosen to let the gender be a surprise.

With her hair up in a tight bun, I have perfect access to her slim neck. I lean in and place a soft kiss to her heated flesh, and a shiver visibly runs through her body.

I relish how my wife still reacts to me, even after all these years. My dad once told me that the key to a good marriage is to never stop dating your wife and to never, ever get complacent. If you show her your love every day, she'll gladly give you her heart in return. Our days can be crazy, filled with two rambunctious little girls, our careers, and simply life in general, but we always make sure to find time to be with each other.

"Put your hands on the barre," I command gently. She does as I say, and her pert ass juts out slightly. Reaching around, I pull the front of her sports bra down, exposing her breasts. I tweak and pinch her rosy nipples, and she moans in pleasure, her body squirming in want.

My wife loves to be fucked, and I love to be inside her. She's wearing leggings today without a leo, so it makes it easy to tug both the material and her underwear down her legs, leaving her ass on display.

"Micah, please," she moans, then I give it a good, hard slap, the sound ringing out in the room.

"Patience, Hellcat," I tell her, as I spread her legs and then tease her pussy. She's wet, her juices coating my fingers, so I shove two inside her, causing her moans to get louder, competing with the music that's playing.

She lets go of the barre, wanting to take over, but I give her a stern look. "Hands back on the barre," I say, my demand only making her that much wetter.

I fingerfuck her good and hard until her cunt's tightening around me and she's coming all over my hand. Without giving her a chance to come down, I undo my pants, lift her ass slightly, and plunge into her from behind, mindful not to jostle her too vigorously. After all, she's carrying precious cargo.

"Yes," she cries out, meeting me thrust for thrust. "Right there."

I hit her sweet spot over and over again, and all too soon, she's coming for a second time, this time taking me along with her.

While still inside her, I lean over and kiss the top of her shoulder. "I love you."

She glances at my reflection in the mirror, a small, satiated smile on her lips. "I love you."

We clean up in the bathroom where she changes into her street clothes. As we're heading out, her phone goes off and she glances at it, frowning.

"The kids?" I ask.

"Ellie."

I sigh, knowing this won't be good. Over the past several years, while our marriage has grown stronger, her relationship with her sister has slowly deteriorated. It started the day Ellie saved Sienna and our unborn baby and has only continued to worsen, especially once she moved across the country for school.

She rarely comes home, and it's usually only when Sienna guilt-trips her into it. She tried to give her sister space, but Ellie is more than just a sister to her. Sienna views her as a mother would her daughter, and it breaks her heart that the girl she dedicated herself to care for and protect has completely shut her out.

But not wanting to upset Ellie, Sienna has stopped saying anything. She plasters on a smile and takes whatever her sister is willing to give her.

"What'd she say?"

"She's not coming home." She looks up at me with tears in her eyes. "She's decided to stay in California for the summer after she graduates." A sob rips through her. "I've officially lost my sister."

"It's just the summer, Hellcat. You haven't lost your sister."

"No." She shakes her head, sniffling. "I know Ellie. The summer is just her way of easing us into it. Next, it will be just until the new year, and then, before we know it, she'll be living there for the rest of her life."

**ONE WEEK LATER**

"Do you really think it's wise to go visit Sienna's sister without her?" my dad asks, as I press the button for the elevator in the building where Ellie lives.

"Ellie won't talk to Sienna, and Sienna is too emotional to talk to her. We had hoped that once her sister graduated and moved home, they'd finally have a chance to work things out, since Ellie asked for time, which Sienna reluctantly gave her. Enough is enough. I'm not going to have my wife crying every day. I'm going to get to the bottom of this shit, so we can get our family back together."

The elevator doors open, so I hang up with my dad since I'll likely lose service anyway. I press the number for Ellie's floor, and once the car arrives, I step out, heading straight for her door. I'm lifting my hand to knock, but before my fist touches the surface, the door flies open, and I come face to face with Ellie. The first thing I notice is her shocked expression, her green eyes wide with surprise. Since she wasn't expecting me, I find her reaction understandable.

But then she backs up slightly, her features morphing into something else—fear, maybe?—and that allows me to take all of her in. My gaze skates downward, assessing her, making sure she's okay. It's warm in California, so she's dressed in a tank top and cotton shorts. Nothing unusual there. But as my eyes ascend back to her face, something catches my attention.

A bump. I would recognize it anywhere, since my wife has sported the same one three times now. It's not big, but with her tank being so tight, it really accentuates it. Makes it stand out. My eyes meet hers and she instantly sees that I know.

"Are you pregnant?"

She swallows anxiously as her hand goes to her protruding belly, telling me all I need to know. She's pregnant. And she wasn't planning for us to know.

*Reading is like breathing in, writing is like breathing out.*
*– Pam Allyn*

Nikki Ash resides in South Florida where she is an English teacher by day and a writer by night. When she's not writing, you can find her with a book in her hand. From the Boxcar Children, to Wuthering Heights, to the latest single parent romance, she has lived and breathed every type of book. While reading and writing are her passions, her two children are her entire world. You can probably find them at a Disney park before you would find them at home on the weekends!